Praise for Sierra Dean's
A Bloody Good Secret

"Sierra Dean has added even more dimension to the already grand world that she's created."
~ *Reading the Paranormal*

"I love Ms Dean's world, and the fantastic characters that inhabit it."
~ *Long and Short Reviews*

"*A Bloody Good Secret* has thrills, chills, great action scenes and erotic sex, what more could anyone want?"
~ *Joyfully Reviewed*

"Lots of action and never a dull moment... hot sex and a love triangle that gets pretty complicated. I can't wait to see what happens to Secret next, I'm sure it will be exciting whatever it is."
~ *Fallen Angel Reviews*

"From the name, Secret McQueen, to Secret's job and her intricate relationships we are given an energetic and feisty urban fantasy that engages and holds your attention to the end. A wonderful balance of humor and suspense; it's the characters in here that make this story so superb."
~ *Smexy Books*

Look for these titles by *Sierra Dean*

Now Available:

Secret McQueen Series
Something Secret This Way Comes
The Secret Guide to Dating Monsters
A Bloody Good Secret
Secret Santa
Deep Dark Secret

A Bloody Good Secret

Sierra Dean

SAMHAIN
PUBLISHING

Samhain Publishing, Ltd.
11821 Mason Montgomery Road, 4B
Cincinnati, OH 45249
www.samhainpublishing.com

A Bloody Good Secret
Copyright © 2012 by Sierra Dean
Print ISBN: 978-1-60928-711-5
Digital ISBN: 978-1-60928-531-9

Editing by Sasha Knight
Cover by Kanaxa

First Samhain Publishing, Ltd. electronic publication: September 2011
First Samhain Publishing, Ltd. print publication: August 2012

Dedication

To my editor, Sasha Knight, the Henry Higgins to my Eliza Doolittle. You've made me a better writer, and without you Secret and her world would be buried in a drawer somewhere. Thank you for giving life to this series and helping make my dreams come true.

To Nathalie Gray, who makes my covers works of art and made Secret real.

And to my mother, Jo-Anne, who never complained when I spent all my waking hours reading and writing stories as a child. Not much has changed now that I'm grown up, but your belief in me made all of this possible.

Chapter One

At well past midnight on an early summer Sunday, I had time on my hands and a dead man on my mind.

I walked down a darkened gravel road, with only the light of a bone-white moon and its dazzling company of stars to guide me. Surrounded by a familiar blanket of night, I pondered the life of a vampire. Before I'd run away from my life and responsibilities in New York to escape to Southern Manitoba, a vampire named Holden Chancery had helped save me from the brink of certain death. During my recovery, the vampire council we both served handed me his death warrant.

I had successfully completed a seemingly impossible job for the council, and as a reward they told me I had to kill one of my only friends. I wasn't sure if vampires understood the concept of stress leave, but it didn't stop me from pulling a vanishing act and crossing international borders.

I stood at the intersection of the gravel road I'd been traveling and the deserted highway it bisected, and hesitated before making my way across the blacktop. I was going to go into the small town on the opposite side of the highway when something caught my eye. It was only a brief flash of movement, but enough to grab my attention.

My whole body tensed. Staying as still as an owl tuned in to a mouse, I listened to the sounds of the night. First I heard only crickets, a distant birdcall and the sway of summer grasses brushing against each other. Then, once I was almost certain I was imagining things, I heard the sound of leaves crunching underfoot and the snap of a dry twig.

I inclined my face to the left and sniffed the air. From my maternal line I had inherited an intriguing collection of gifts. My mother was a werewolf. While I did not have her habit of turning into a wild animal every full moon, I did manage to luck into a few of the less furry traits. Keen senses of smell and hearing were chief among them.

On the air was the pungent stink of cow manure, the wet, mossy smell of damp earthy duff, and from the direction of town the human aromas of gasoline, burnt dinners and stress. I closed my eyes and concentrated.

There. Something animal, but reeking of adrenaline instead of fear. Under that was the unmistakable whiff of humanity. The combination of the two created a telltale perfume. *Were.* And judging by the familiarity of the animal smell, it was a wolf.

I opened my eyes and scanned the tree line again, my heart pounding with a mix of exhilaration, anxiety and guilt. For a hopeful moment I concentrated on the way my mouth tasted. Had I savored a hint of cinnamon or lime, my heart would have tripped with joy. The first flavor would have meant Lucas Rain, King of the Eastern wolf packs, had come to find me. The tang of lime would have had a much more carnal response, because it would have meant Desmond Alvarez, Lucas's second-in-command and best friend, was waiting for me in the woods.

The absence of any taste except for the musky one associated with all werewolves told me whoever was hiding among the trees was not one of my wolves. The presence of a werewolf in this area was surprising enough. If it wasn't someone here to collect me, then who were they and what were they doing here?

Finding a solo wolf out here in rural Manitoba, where I knew there were no other lycanthropes, was a bit of a shock. I needed to know who was in the woods and what their purpose was. If they were up to no good, it was up to me to keep them the hell away from town.

I looked down the road into Elmwood to make sure no other late-night pedestrians were out who might question my next move. Once I was sure I was alone, I sniffed the air one last time to make sure I knew where I was going, then dove off the road and into the ditch.

Sprinting across the field next to the road, it took me a few moments to get my bearings on the uneven ground. My ankle twisted to the side when I stumbled on a gopher hole. Cursing my bipedalism as I crashed down, I brushed the dirt off my palms and knelt on the ground, letting my heart calm itself while I tried to figure out if the sound of my fall had alerted the wolf in the woods that he was being followed.

To be fair, I didn't know the wolf was a man, but about three quarters or more of all werewolves were male. It wasn't that daughters refused the Awakening more often, it just seemed like werewolf parents had sons more often than daughters. Maybe it was an evolutionary thing, I didn't know. But werewolves were predominantly male.

This wolf, male or female, hadn't been able to ignore the sound of a hundred and ten pounds of clumsiness hitting the ground in a flourish of profanity. I could hear them retreating into the woods.

Some stalker I was. Secret McQueen—half-werewolf, half-vampire, hired gun of the underworld—and I couldn't even run across an empty field without alerting one solitary wolf. Truly pathetic. Maybe this was the world's way of telling me I shouldn't have left my day job.

I stood up, dusted off my shorts and listened, then turned to the south and gave chase again.

I reached the heavy tree cover and ducked under the outstretched branch of an evergreen. Underestimating the height of the branch, my head was jerked back when the pine needles tangled themselves into my hair. Ignoring the tugging as best I could, I took an exploratory sniff to relocate my quarry.

Nothing.

I smelled the air a little more deeply, urging my suppressed werewolf nature to engage so my combined abilities could help me locate the mystery wolf. Still, the scent was gone.

"Impossible," I hissed.

Wolves couldn't vanish into thin air. Yet all I could smell was pine, dirt and the cool scents of night. I listened, holding my breath, hoping I had missed something. But I was alone in the woods. Whoever I'd been chasing was gone, taking with them my misguided hopes of some message from home.

I slumped down into the damp moss and kicked the pine tree out of frustration. The tree rattled from the force, shaking some pinecones loose, where they fell to the ground—*plop, plop, plop.* The fragrance of pine now overwhelmed everything else.

No longer able to use the unknown werewolf to distract myself, my mind returned to the thoughts I'd left behind on the road. Holden was now the only thing I was able to focus on. I was going to have to come to terms with the warrant I'd been issued. It was only a matter of time before the Tribunal grew tired of my very un-vampire-like hissy fit and assigned the task to someone else. Someone like my human partner, Keaty, who would have no qualms about killing Holden.

But I couldn't believe Holden had turned traitor. This time I would need a why. Holden had dedicated his afterlife to being one of the lowest-ranking vampires in the council, a warden, for over two hundred years. He'd been given the thankless task of being my liaison, a job no one envied him. And he'd done it all without complaint. So what would cause him to go rogue now? It made no sense.

I got up with moss sticking to the backs of my bare thighs. I flicked it off and started in the direction of the road. Before the chase, I had planned on going into town to waste some time and money at the only bar, but I was no longer in a social mood.

Instead of taking the road north into town, I set my sights south and back towards my *grandmere*'s house.

Chapter Two

I didn't bother turning on the basement light as I followed the stairs to the lowest level of the house. All the windows that had once been installed had long since been removed and bricked over, so the light of the waxing moon did nothing to illuminate the darkness. I didn't need light to find my way through the familiar hallways, passing the laundry room and small bathroom, running my fingertips over the wood-paneled walls until I arrived at the doorway of my own bedroom.

The dark was a comforting blanket to me, and I let myself collapse backwards onto my unmade bed. The cotton was a cool embrace against the heavy heat that had begun creeping into the summer nights. I sighed, and my breath was hot on my lips as I exhaled. Dawn was still an hour away, but I found myself unusually tired. The chase through the woods and the sudden disappearance of the mystery wolf left me dumbfounded and cranky. Plus, chasing anything without catching it was always frustrating.

I stared at the low ceiling, imagining what might bring a lone wolf into my territory, and what motivation led him to be in Elmwood of all places. I chided myself for letting my guard down and not paying better attention during my evening runs for the telltale signs and smells of a new wolf. I shouldn't have relaxed my constant wariness for a second, but being back in Elmwood had caused me to take my safety for granted.

If this wolf was one of the dissenting pack formed under Marcus Sullivan, the wolf I dispatched to an early grave three months earlier, they might be here to do me harm. Meaning *Grandmere* and the whole town could become collateral damage in a war that had nothing to do with them. As far as I was concerned, the war was over. Lucas's position as king was secure, which I'd guaranteed by killing Marcus.

I fell asleep to the nagging thought of how many times I'd been wrong about these things before.

I hadn't dreamed since the night I'd almost died. My daytime sleep usually passed in a comatose stupor, the near-death state of dozing vampires. On the few rare occasions I'd had dreams in the past, there'd been an overtone of premonition to them. Which isn't to say I'm psychic, I sure as hell am not, but when I do dream, it's for a reason.

It had once saved my life.

Because I dreamed so infrequently, and because my dreams were so lucid, I often had difficulty differentiating my dreams from reality. Unless, of course, my dream involved a wedding dress. That was always a dead giveaway to it not being real.

However, in the dream I found myself in that night, I wasn't wearing anything at all.

The first thing that caught my attention, aside from my missing clothing, was the presence of satin sheets. The departure from my familiar cotton bedding was noteworthy.

I splayed my hand out, palm down, and felt the smooth, almost-liquid texture of the sheets. I burrowed my face into the pillow and let out a contented sigh. I could handle dreams about fine bedroom decor.

Then my wandering hand met up with skin that was most definitely not my own. I sucked in a breath and held it. Nothing here smelled like either of my men. There was no taste in my mouth, and nothing triggered the alarm of wolf in my brain. So, who...

Tentatively, I turned my head and opened one eye. I let my gaze follow my arm down to my hand, where it rested on the pale curve of someone's lower back. Pale. So, so pale. Their skin was as white as mine, and mine had never seen the light of day.

I opened both my eyes, and the pair looking back at me was not blue like Lucas's or gray like Desmond's. These eyes were a brown so dark they were almost black, and the instant recognition made my heart seize. My hand spasmed on his back.

"Holden."

He rolled onto his side, propped up on an elbow and took an assessing inventory of my body, which was lying fully exposed on top of the sheets. I let him look, unencumbered by the shy morality of humankind. I was more interested in why he was sharing my dream than why he was checking me out.

"So you can't look at me naked in real life, but in a dream it's okay?" I asked, recalling all the times he'd come into my home and imposed an outdated sense of modesty on me.

"It's your dream."

I made a dismissive grunt and sat up so he was no longer looking down on me.

"Don't be coy with me, Holden, not now."

The vampire gave a sad smile, letting the barest trace of emotion say all the things he could not allow himself to utter out loud. He reached out and brushed a curl from my face.

"Why do they want me to kill you? Why you?" I implored.

For a long time he did not reply, twisting a yellow-gold ringlet of my hair around his finger. I took a mental inventory of his appearance and longed for his returned presence in my life.

He looked tired, which was an impressive feat for a vampire, and his skin was almost translucent in places, which told me he wasn't eating enough. His hair was getting longer, some of the natural curl showing through. It had grown past his ears and now flirted with the base of his neck.

Holden was always vigilant about his appearance. He'd once been an editor-at-large for *GQ*, and I had never seen him look anything less than perfect. He considered his appearance a point of pride, and his pride ran deep.

Mirroring his gesture, I reached out and ran my fingers through his hair, surprised by how soft it was. I trailed my hand from his hair to his cheek, his cheek to his mouth. His gaze didn't leave mine, even as my thumb pressed down on his lower lip. I pressed more insistently, and he let his mouth fall open. His fangs were exposed.

I shivered when his tongue flicked against the pad of my thumb.

"You won't kill me," he said matter-of-factly.

"I have to." I began to withdraw my hand, but he caught my wrist.

"You. *Won't*. Kill. Me."

There was a flash of fang in his words, and a deep chill curdled my insides. He did not release me and instead used the advantage of his superior strength to draw me towards him. With his one hand still in my hair, he forced me to look him straight in the eyes.

I was immune to the vampire ability to enthrall their human victims, known as the thrall, but it felt like that was what he was trying to do. Of all vampires, Holden knew of my immunity the best, so I wasn't sure what his intentions were. I swallowed hard, and he pulled me closer so our bodies pressed together. My skin felt hot where it touched his.

"I need you, Secret," he whispered against my lips. I shivered again, but this time it wasn't from fear.

"Where *are* you?"

"I'm safe, for now." He trailed his fingertips down my left cheek.

"I can't come home."

"You have to. I need you."

"If I come home, Sig will make me kill you."

"Will he?" He had his mouth hovering over mine, his lips brushing the oversensitive surface of my own, bringing a new wave of heat over my body. I was having trouble breathing, and he was moving his hands towards my lower back.

"As far as Sig's concerned…" I trembled, "…it's you or me."

A smile curved his mouth as his tongue traced the outline of my lower lip. "It won't be me," he promised.

Then, with a movement so fast it lasted less time than my alarmed gasp, he dropped his head and sank his ready teeth into my exposed neck.

Chapter Three

"Secret Merriweather McQueen! You put that in a glass this *instant.*" My *grandmere* snatched the old-style glass milk bottle from my hand.

"It's blood!" I exclaimed, reaching out to reclaim my breakfast. "You want me to put blood in your nice glasses?" Of course, this question was ridiculous on many levels. After sixteen years under her roof, I knew that was exactly what she wanted.

"It wouldn't be the first time, baby," she said, practically reading my mind. She was holding the bottle aloft while she rummaged through the cupboards. It was quite the spectacle, seeing my petite grandmother with a bottle of blood grasped in her hand, and keeping me at arm's reach while she searched. Considering I had the physical strength to take the bottle by force, the situation was all the more comical because I did nothing to fight her. It was like a rabbit telling a bear to hang on for a second while the rabbit got him a plate.

She found what she was looking for and, with a satisfied grin, plunked a glass down on the counter.

I gave her a horrified look.

"You're kidding me. How is *that...*" I pointed to the offending object, "...more civilized than drinking it from the bottle?"

She had found an old Sesame Street cup, depicting The Count. His cartoonish fangs beamed at me, and I read the writing on the side which proclaimed, *One... One Glass of Milk!* I wanted to stab myself in the face with the broken shards of my dignity.

Grandmere filled the glass with the bottled blood—pig, based on the small mouthful I'd tasted—and handed it to me.

"I raised a lady."

I let that one go, because I didn't want her to know how far off base she was. I cursed like a sailor, slept with boys I wasn't married to, and was sort of soul-married to two werewolves in a bizarre, polyandrous, metaphysical mess. Plus, I drank my blood straight out of the fridge back home. *Lady* was hardly the first word that came to mind when I described myself. But there was no point in telling all this to my *grandmere*, who I loved more than any human alive.

"It's *blood*," I reminded her again, more insistently. "In a toddler's drinking glass. This is *insulting.*"

"Drink it from that or don't drink it at all." She put her hands on her hips and gave me a stern stare down, which let me know she wasn't fooling around.

I picked up the glass with a little *harrumph* and knew my pouting wasn't going to faze her. It probably only reminded her of the teenager I'd been when I ran away six years earlier. A lot about me had changed since then. I'd grown up, gotten harder and meaner. In many ways I was the most world-weary twenty-two-year-old in history. But I still knew how to laugh.

She sat down at the kitchen table and picked up a small box that had been left there. Something hard rattled inside when she shook it back and forth.

"I have something for you."

I placed my empty glass in the sink, and before she had a chance to remind me, filled it with soap and hot water and washed it out. Blood was a bitch to clean once it dried. With the glass now in the drain rack, I sat in the chair across from her.

Grandmere put the box back on the table and slid it across the wood until it was in front of me. I took off the lid, and inside was a necklace made from a blood red, striped stone with a band of gold flecks running down the middle. It was set with simple gold wire and hung on a gold chain.

I raised my eyes and gave her a questioning look. She was a witch, and witches didn't give away stones without a specific reason.

"It's tiger's iron," she explained. "It wards against evil magic."

I laughed. "Am I expecting to run into a lot of evil magic out here?" The strange wolf flashed to mind, and my laughter died away. "*Am* I?"

"Never hurts to protect yourself, baby." Her halfhearted smile said she wasn't telling me everything.

Taking her hands in mine, I gave her a comforting squeeze. "Thank you."

"Let me help you put it on." She was up from the table in a flash, with the necklace already in her hand. For a senior, she sometimes exhibited supernatural speed.

Her rush to have me guarded against evil made me feel more anxious than anything. She pulled my hair off my shoulders, and for a moment she hesitated. My heart stopped, because in spite of how impossible it would be, I worried she might see Holden's bite mark from my dream on me.

Talk about a guilty conscience.

Grandmere clasped the necklace, and the stone hung around my neck with a foreign weight. It was a big pendant, roughly the same width as an oyster shell. The color was disconcerting, making it look like there was a splash of gold-infused blood over my heart. I held the stone up, and the gold winked at me under the kitchen lights.

"It's pretty."

She let my hair down and placed a kiss on top of my head. "I won't keep you. I know you had plans tonight."

Drinking at a dive bar with a bunch of surly farmers. Some plan. I didn't argue with her, though. I got up from the table and went to the back door to find my shoes, still fiddling with the necklace. From the kitchen, *Grandmere* cleared her throat. Seems she had decided to say everything on her mind after all.

"Secret, sweetie, you know I love you, right?"

"Of course." I stopped what I was doing so I could get a better look at her as she spoke. She was staring out the kitchen window over the sink and didn't turn to face me when I came back into the kitchen.

"Then try not to take this the wrong way."

I raised a questioning brow.

"Baby, I think it's time you went home."

I made the walk to the bar without any supernatural encounters, but this time I was prepared for them. In spite of the necklace to ward off evil, I felt better when I was armed. My SIG 9mm was tucked in the waistband of the black shorts I was wearing. I'd covered the weapon with my yellow tank top, which had just enough give to camouflage the gun. I'd tried to make the casual ensemble into a coordinated outfit by wearing matching yellow flip-flops, but my tangled blonde curls were in a messy bun on top of my head.

The Elm Tree was a slim two-story building whose front window was decorated with neon beer adverts, and whose main sign misleadingly referred to it as a *hotel and bar*. When I walked in, my flip-flops smacked against the sticky hardwood floor like a sloppy kiss, announcing my presence as the only female in the room.

Howard, the sweet, lumberjack-sized bartender, looked up from the beer taps and smiled at me. At least I assumed he smiled because his bearded cheeks moved in an upward direction.

"McQueen," he acknowledged, his voice so rough he might have been swallowing crushed rocks every night.

I loved that no one here called me Secret. To the men of the Elm Tree, who admired machismo and masculinity above all else, there was no need to call me anything but McQueen. Sharing a name with Steve McQueen, King of Cool, gave me an instant pass with these guys, and that suited me fine. I sidled up to the bar and sat next to a man known only as Bear. He weighed about three hundred pounds and stood almost six-foot-eight whenever he found use for his feet. He had a beard so grizzled it made Howard look clean cut.

"Bear," I said with a nod.

"McQueen," he replied into his half-empty pint glass.

I'd often hoped part of Bear's size and appearance was due to genuine ursine shapeshifter DNA. Having never met or even heard of a were-bear, I longed for a story to share with Lucas and Desmond when I saw them again. Selfishly, I also wanted to know I wasn't the only freak in Elmwood. Alas, in three months I hadn't gotten the slightest hint of a supernatural trigger from him. He was as human as they came.

"Rickard's," I requested to Howard, who was already filling a glass for me, tipping it to avoid a heady draught. He slid it down the bar to me, partially because he loved minute attempts at flair bartending, and more so because he knew I'd never miss. "Thanks." I held the drink in one hand and surveyed the room via the large mirror behind the bar.

"Hey, Howard?" I asked. He turned his too-kind eyes towards me. "Who's the crew cut by the jukebox?"

Considering I spent almost every day at the bar, even the irregulars were known to me, along with most of the gossip about the town and surrounding area. I also knew all about the summer forecast for wheat, canola, flax and sunflowers—mediocre to superb, depending on the number of drinks in the farmer doing the predicting.

There wasn't a face that passed through the bar I didn't recognize, or so I'd thought.

Next to the jukebox on which Bruce Springsteen was singing "Thunder Road" sat a man in his mid-thirties. He had an olive complexion, thick black eyebrows over dark black eyes, and his hair was cut short.

"He came in yesterday, took the same booth until close, then left. Came back again soon as we opened tonight. Odd fella."

All-night drinkers were not so unusual here, so for Howard to single this man out as odd gave me an uneasy feeling. I sniffed the air, but all I got was the ripe scent of Bear's armpit sweat and the lingering smells of booze and testosterone. I watched the man in the mirror until he shifted his glance and our eyes locked in the glass. For one long, breathless moment we remained in that stare, until he looked away. My heart was pounding, which was not such an easy feat. His expression had been so smug and unflinching. Something was definitely wrong.

I stared into my beer, my skin suddenly cold and beaded with uncomfortable sweat. The way he had stared at me set off every alarm in the book, and there was a nagging feeling in my bones that I needed to find out what was up with this mysterious stranger. When I turned back to the mirror to check on my scary new friend with the crew cut, my breath caught in my throat.

His booth was empty.

I spun around in my chair, pulse hammering. He wasn't anywhere in the bar. I took a five out of my pocket and put it on the bar.

"Thanks, Howard."

"Leaving already?"

"Yeah, sorry," I said, already halfway out the door. "Thanks."

Outside, the air had grown colder and the town had gone to sleep for the night. A cool breeze ruffled the short hairs at the back of my neck as I stood on the empty road in front of the Elm Tree.

"Where are you?" I asked to myself, listening for any trace of movement. On cue, I heard the soft crunch of gravel coming from the path behind the bar. I hesitated for a moment, knowing it couldn't be so easy. But I had to know who he was. I followed the sound to the back of the bar and took the path as it sloped down a hill to Howard's storage shed.

The shed was on the edge of the forest, but even with my ability to see in the dark, I couldn't discern anyone in the trees.

I walked all the way up to the shed, then stopped. I rested my hand against the rough barn-wood exterior of the small building, hoping to feel the vibration of someone hiding behind or within, but there was nothing. Just like in the woods the night before, all traces of my quarry had vanished. The air smelled heavy with ozone and anxious peat.

Rain was coming.

Closing my eyes, I concentrated harder. I heard the rumble of thunder still miles away but approaching as steadily as a Hun raiding party. I could smell night blossoms turning their hungry faces towards the sound. One by one, crickets and cicadas stopped singing so they could take shelter.

I looked into the blackness of the woods. On a branch, a large barn owl with heavily lidded eyes turned his head to me. I almost dismissed the bird, until I realized he was staring at me.

Staring with a cold, unflinching glare.

Icy fear began at my toes and spread through my whole body in seconds. I wanted to run. Running was the only instinct I understood, but when I tried to move, I found myself frozen in place. My eyes widened with the horror of understanding, and the owl kept its focus on me.

"*Who*," the owl said.

My pulse sped up and blood screamed behind my ears until all I could hear was my body's panic. Without warning, I was bombarded by the fragrance of wolf. The same smell I'd chased the night before. It was so close I should have sensed it sooner, but it seemed to appear out of nowhere, without warning. The wolf was right behind me, but being frozen as I was, I couldn't turn to face him.

The owl stretched his wings, then pushed off from the branch, flying towards me. Mid-flight, a ripple of blue light shivered over the bird and burst outward in an explosion of white-hot radiance and feathers. The air reeked of burning, and once my vision readjusted to the dark, the owl was gone.

Where the bird has been there was now a man. The olive-skinned man from the bar was about ten feet away from me, straightening his tie and smoothing feathers off his suit. There were no bird shapeshifters, which meant he must have performed a transfiguration spell.

"Witch," I spat, my jaw aching from the effort.

Transfiguration was an energy-consuming, high-level spell. *Grandmere*, the best spell caster I knew, had once confessed she was unable to do it. This man had been able to reverse the spell mid-flight and without wrinkling his clothes. The fact he'd managed to do the spell without losing his clothing altogether was all the more remarkable.

"Good evening, Miss McQueen," he greeted, his voice thick with the melodic accent of a foreign country. North African, I guessed. He sounded and looked like he'd walked off the set of *Casablanca*. He came closer and lifted the tiger's-iron pendant from my neck, turning the stone over in his hand before he let it fall back. He smiled.

I growled.

"I have no interest in harming you. I will, however, need you to be on your best behavior in order to conclude our business together."

Business?

"I'm afraid I don't think we can trust you to have a nonviolent reaction, given the circumstances, so I apologize for this next bit. Precautions, you understand."

I had enough time to feel a break in the air over my head, and an instant later something hard and heavy cracked me on my skull.

I saw stars, then nothing at all.

Chapter Four

I'm dead, I thought.

Of course, the ability *to* think negated the content of my thought. But if I wasn't dead, where was I?

My being awake meant it was most likely night. The question then became was it the same night or had more time passed since I'd last been conscious? It couldn't have been more than a day, given my speedy healing abilities, but then again, who knew what this witch was capable of?

Trapping me in a tiny, cramped box, for one. I had enough room I could adjust my position and roll over with a little effort, which ruled out a coffin. If I listened, I could hear the quiet sounds of wind. So, buried alive was off the list too. I tried moving my arms and then my legs, both successfully. The paralysis spell had worn off or been lifted. I checked for my gun, but it wasn't there. When I struck out in frustration, my hand bumped against something, and I peered through the darkness to get a look at it. A tire iron.

This told me two things. The first was I was locked in a car trunk, the second was whoever had put me here hadn't considered what common items could be used as weapons. I tightened my grip around the tire iron and shrank into the farthest quarter of the trunk, waiting.

Waiting dragged into agonizing hours alone in the trunk, anticipating nothing specific. The uncertainty was making me crazy. What did they want? Why would they come all the way to Elmwood to kidnap me?

It sounded like the start of a bad joke. A witch and a werewolf walk in to a bar...

I refused to loosen my grip on the tire iron, and my joints were aching and stiff. My stomach rumbled in protest of its emptiness, and I felt a sharp ache in my gums. If I didn't feed soon, I wouldn't be able to conceal my fangs much longer.

Not that I cared what these hooligans thought I was. As of right now my plan, if they didn't let me go, was to bash in their skulls with the tire iron and then maybe rip out their throats. I was flexible on the details, as long as the end result was two dead kidnappers.

My breathing had slowed to a near stop, and my heartbeat was unhurried and regular. I could wait them out. As long as there was night left, I would wait. Once the sun rose, though, it would be a different story. I hadn't fed enough to keep myself awake after sunrise. Dead to the world I was helpless, but in the dark I was a force to be reckoned with.

Several more hours passed, and a telltale sluggishness began to flow through me. Dawn was on its way, ignorant of my need to stay awake. If I'd had more than just a sip of blood at nightfall, I might have been able to stay awake longer, but as it was my grip started loosening on the iron, and I didn't have much wakeful time left.

I heard footsteps and the heavy metallic noises of the trunk being unlocked. I had the will to fight but was running out of the power to follow through. The trunk lid lifted, and I swung with all the energy I had left.

There was a satisfying sound of metal meeting flesh and a cry of surprised pain. I vaulted out of the trunk, but my foot caught the body of one of my kidnappers, who was now nursing his bloody face, and I fell. I tried to break my fall, but my hands were locked around the tire iron, and I hit the ground face first. Gravel and bits of broken beer bottle bit into my cheek. I pushed myself up with my palms and managed to find more shards of glass when they pierced the dry pads of my hands and jabbed into my fingers. Still, I fought to regain my footing, warm blood dripping off my chin and onto my yellow tank top, creating a grim Rorschach test over my cleavage.

I tried to get a bearing on where I was but couldn't orient myself. The car was parked on an old highway in the gravel lot in front of a motel. My heart sang with hope for help, until I saw the large, aged For Sale sign with evidence of many unsuccessful price reductions.

Abandoned.

Around us was nothing but forest, empty road and the purple threat of sunrise peeking over the trees. My werewolf half told me to run and take my chances in the bush. My more logical, less-impulsive vampire half told me running into the woods meant certain death at dawn, while my captors might actually want me alive.

I slumped to the ground, my limbs unwilling to push me in either direction. This allowed the werewolf I'd smashed in the face to grab me under the arms and drag me towards one of the motel rooms.

"What do you want?" I rolled my head back, loose as a rag doll, to look at him. His face was familiar, but I couldn't place how I knew him. He was young, not even twenty, and had probably been handsome before I'd broken his nose and part of his cheekbone. He had catlike green eyes and a mop of dark hair. He looked away from me, but his expression was calm, not angry.

"I just want to do my job. Are you hurt bad? I'll catch hell if you're hurt." His voice sounded of the South, but not like *Grandmere*'s. He wasn't Louisiana South, more like Texas South. Again, I struggled to remember how I knew him.

His attitude surprised me too. I'd shattered his nose, and he was worried about me? I groaned and moved my jaw. Nothing felt broken, and the glass and gravel were already being forced out of my skin. Healing would be slow this close to sunrise and with no blood in me.

Blood.

I noticed the fresh spill of it on his face in a new, different light as he paused to knock on the door marked 9 but had most likely once been 6.

"I'll live," I whispered, licking my lips. My darkening eyes must have given me away, because he knocked on the door more urgently, not stopping until it opened. The witch was waiting inside and looked a little paler when he saw me slumped on the ground and both the pup and I covered in blood.

"Holy Hecuba," he swore. "What happened?"

The pup grumbled something and hoisted me over the threshold into the dark room.

"Is he here?" the boy asked.

"I think so. But he said to leave her in the room at sunrise and get the hell out." The witch had a suitcase in one hand. "He's going to be pissed about her face."

Their voices were getting slow and deep, like the world was going the wrong speed. I crawled out of the wolf's grasp and towards the bed but only made it a few inches before my strength abandoned me.

"Should we help her?" the wolf asked, giving me a worried look.

I wouldn't know what the witch was about to reply, because a new voice interrupted.

"Leave," was all it said, and I couldn't understand how it came from everywhere and nowhere all at once.

I turned my face on the rug so the uninjured side was against the soft, musty fibers and watched them both leave the room without closing the door. I had to close it before sunrise, but I didn't know how I would get to it. Before I could come up with a plan, a tall silhouette filled the frame and then disappeared when the door shut.

It was mere seconds to sunrise, and I didn't have any time left.

"Secret, my sweet, have they hurt you?" a familiar male voice asked, and my blood ran cold.

I looked up at him, his blue eyes showing cool compassion. His blond bangs were brushed off his forehead. The honeyed tones of an ancient accent sweetened his every turn of phrase.

Seeing Death himself would have filled me with less fear.

"Sig?" I asked, unable to believe he was here.

He touched my face, and I winced. Pulling his hand away, he looked at the blood on his fingers, then placed each impossibly long digit in his mouth, cleaning my blood from them with a smile.

I shuddered.

"Sleep," he ordered. "You're going to need it."

I don't know if it was meant to sound so threatening, but as I slipped into the abyss of vampire sleep, I found myself wondering if I'd ever wake up again.

Chapter Five

I awoke hungry, with only a faint recollection of where I was. Someone had moved me off the floor, and I gathered it was the same someone whose chest my head rested on and whose fingers were tangled in my hair.

My mind went blank, and for a moment I let myself enjoy the feeling of being in someone's arms without worrying about whose they were. Then, bit by bit, the events of the last several days started coming into sharper focus, until I could no longer ignore them. I couldn't pretend I was safe in my current embrace.

"Why didn't you kill me while I was sleeping?" I hadn't opened my eyes yet, so for the time being I could still think of this as a dream. I knew better, of course, because it lacked the surreal, hyperrealistic feeling my usual dreams had.

The motel room smelled stale and musty, and there was a harsh fungal aroma laced in with the decay. The blanket under us reeked of age and stagnation. I was glad to be on top of it rather than underneath.

Sig, on the other hand, smelled clean, like fresh air-dried linen. There was no warmth coming from his body, only the feel of hard, room-temperature flesh. Like a corpse. Sleeping next to a vampire was a strange feeling.

He sighed and stopped playing with my hair. "Now, why would I want to kill you?"

"Why does the Tribunal do anything it does? Why kill Holden?" I opened my eyes and was looking at his stomach, which was covered in a soft, ribbed, gray shirt. I brushed my cheek against it, wondering how it felt. At the same time, putting pressure on my face allowed me to judge how my healing was coming along. A+ on both counts.

"I didn't bring you here to kill you, Secret. It is time for your sabbatical to come to an end."

"Sabbatical?" I couldn't help but make a derisive snort at the word. "That's a polite way of saying 'ran away from home'." I turned my head so my chin was resting on his abs and I could look up to meet his gaze. Without the typical blond bangs obscuring them, his ice-blue irises were alarmingly bright. I'd seen them before, but they looked more serious without the hair to soften their edge.

Sig wasn't interested in softening any blows tonight. He hadn't kidnapped me so we could have a polite chitchat in bed. He meant business.

"Sig," I began, my voice losing its childish sarcasm. "I can't."

He closed his eyes and leaned his head against the wall, sighing. You haven't heard a sigh until you've heard one two thousand years in the making. All the frustration and angst of a hundred generations worth of lives was compressed into that escape of air. It did what it meant to, because I felt guilty. Overwhelmingly guilty for telling him I couldn't kill my best friend.

"Maybe..." As I started again, he opened one eye. "Maybe if you could tell me why?"

I still had no idea what Holden stood accused of. At first I'd believed he was being punished for refusing to abandon me at the brink of death, as a council representative had demanded he do. But his loyalty to me wasn't the cause for the warrant. I'd learned that much by bombarding my immortal caretaker, Calliope, with ten thousand questions until she confessed what little she knew. Holden had betrayed the council somehow. And it was for something much more serious than being a dutiful friend. With Sig here, I thought I might be able to get real answers.

Now he was fully focused on me with a chilling stare. His hand tightened into a fist in my hair, and the extra pull hurt.

"Why?" He tugged my head back so I couldn't look away. I found myself both fascinated and terrified. I'd never seen Sig angry. He had a particular gift, which was to make those in his presence feel at ease. Intuitively I knew I should be terrified of what a two-thousand-year-old vampire could do to me, but with him this close I had to fight against the unnatural calm washing over me.

I shivered, and my whole body trembled from it.

I couldn't back down now. He'd already claimed he didn't want to kill me, so why shouldn't I ask him what I wanted to know?

"I need to know why you put a warrant out on Holden. I need to know or I can't kill him."

"It is not your place to know *why*," he said flatly, pulling me into a sitting position so we looked at each other face-to-face. "You've never needed or wanted to know why before."

"This is different and you know it." I put my hand on his, where he was locked into my curls, and attempted to coax his fingers to relax. I didn't have any vampire gifts, so I couldn't force him to do anything. I was simply hoping for a reprieve from the growing ache on my scalp.

"I can't tell you why."

"You're the Tribunal leader, Sig. You control everyone. Don't tell me you can't."

He released my hair but didn't look away. My heartbeat quickened, and it was so loud he must have been able to hear it, but he did nothing to acknowledge the change.

"There are laws. Laws even I am bound by. Once a warrant is issued, it's final, and its reasons are for those who issued it to know and for them alone. The Tribunal is signed into silence once we issue a warrant."

"You can't tell me *anything*?"

"I can tell you that if I do not bring you home, Juan Carlos has no qualms about issuing a new warrant. One with *your* name on it."

The mention of Juan Carlos brought the reality of the situation into sharper focus. Left in the hands of Daria and Sig, I suspected my lease on life would be a little longer term. But Juan Carlos hated me. Not in the passive way people hate spiders or little kids hate eating vegetables. No, Juan Carlos hated me the way the families of murder victims hate the killers. He hated me the way the people of Europe hated the rats who brought them the bubonic plague.

He hated me the way women in New York City hate finding out about a clearance bridal sale at Kleinfeld the day *after* it happens.

Not only did he want my lease on life to expire, he wanted to evict me before the final notice. I wasn't sure if it was because I was alive and Sig had accepted me as one of the fold, or if it was because I never showed the Tribunal the appropriate level of respect, or if it was because I was so willing to execute other vampires, but Juan Carlos didn't like having me around.

He was also seriously scary. He'd been a Spanish Conquistador in life, which wasn't a fluffy day job. Before he'd been turned, he'd met the wrong end of someone's sword, and it had butchered up the side of his face. His lips had healed together wrong, and the mangled side of his mouth gave him a constant sneer. The combination of that sneer with his fangs, and the look of absolute hate in his eyes, made him one of the scariest vampires I'd ever encountered.

I never, *ever* wanted to be on the wrong side of a fight with Juan Carlos.

"Well gosh." I lay down again and placed my head back on his stomach. "If Juan Carlos wants me home, I guess that's all the invitation I need." I'd rather not let my fear show to Sig. He already knew I was scared, but there was no reason to flaunt my unease.

Sig was the only member of the Tribunal who knew what I really was. It was in my best interest to stay on his good side rather than tempt fate by poking an angry bull.

"I'll go back," I said after a long pause.

He remained quiet. The room was filled with a literal dead silence. He didn't move until he began to stroke my hair again. Like before, I let myself enjoy it, even though it reminded me of how Ingrid, his daytime servant, once said Sig thought of me as his pet.

"Sig?" I asked, wondering if his silence meant he hadn't heard me.

"Shhh," he replied. "Secret, the last time I slept next to someone with a pulse was the year seven." I waited for him to finish, but he didn't, and it dawned on me he meant the year 7 A.D. "That someone was my wife, and it's been over two thousand years since anything has reminded me so much of her. So *shhh.*"

I took that in the best way I could and tried to remain silent for as long as possible, but my curiosity reached a boiling point and I could no longer contain it.

"What was her name?"

"Ingaborg." He was still stroking my hair.

"Is that why you singled out Ingrid? Because of her name?" Vampires had done things for more ridiculous reasons before, so it wasn't out of the question he would base his choice for a daytime servant on name alone.

"No. By the time I met Ingrid, Ingaborg was the shadow of a memory to me. I was an angrier man in Germany during the Middle Ages."

"Did you have any children?"

"Yes."

"How many?"

"Ingaborg gave birth to eleven children. Seven lived past their infancy. While at war, I fathered another. I know nothing of what became of her." He said these things like they were footnotes in a history text. To him, they must have been. Could someone still love a child who had died before Western civilization was a reality? Sig's children might have died before Jesus.

Sig's children might have *killed* Jesus.

I reminded myself Sig was Finnish, and it was pretty unlikely any of his spawn would have traveled across Europe to kill a trouble-making Jewish carpenter. I was also putting *way* too much thought in to this. I had to admit, though, it would be cool if one of his children had played a famous part in history. Asking him about this seemed frivolous, so I didn't.

"What happened to your family after you were turned?"

"I do not know."

"Why?"

"I was turned in 9 A.D., during the Battle of Teutoburg Forest, in what is now Germany, but was then simply Roman land in need of leadership. I had come from the North two years earlier to help prevent my brother's settlement from being overtaken by the Romans. This, ultimately, proved unsuccessful, but we did manage to hold them off at the time. It was a special kind of day to be turned. September ninth, in the year nine. A lot of nines. Of course, the modern system of dating didn't exist then. I only learned that date later when the history books wrote about our war, and I liked the symmetry of it. All I knew then was that I was seized one night from the camp, and the next night I had to dig myself out of a shallow grave."

I was starting to be sorry I asked.

"The reason I don't know what happened to my family was because I didn't go back to Finland for almost forty years. It took me a long time to learn how to control myself and not be the killer who emerged from the woods that night."

"I'm sorry."

"You needn't be."

"Do I remind you of her?"

"Of Ingaborg?"

"Yes."

"No, my sweet. Only in your breathing and your pulse. The nearness of someone alive feels marvelous. It makes me feel almost human, and I haven't felt that since I died," he admitted. I raised my face to look at him, and he smiled down at me even though his eyes were closed. "Ingaborg was very...womanly. Not all bones and angles like you girls today. She was unbreakable."

I found it hard to imagine Sig married to any woman, especially a curvy, motherly type with a brood of babies all around. But the way he smiled when he talked about her made me shut my mouth fast. Love is love, and though she was nothing but history now, Sig had obviously loved his wife.

We lay like that for another hour, and then it was time to leave.

Chapter Six

I knew Sig could wake before sunset, but I'd never known before that being near him would make it easier for me to do the same. It had still been light out when we'd had our chat in the motel room, and now the final minutes of sunset were upon us.

When Sig pulled his navy blue Lexus out onto the old highway with me in the passenger seat, I didn't look back at the motel. The sun had dipped below the horizon, and the whole sky was glowing a deep peach-pink. I was too busy enjoying the briefest glimpse of day to spoil it with remembrances of how I'd gotten here.

When we arrived at the main highway and began driving east, the last traces of twilight vanished in the rearview mirror. We drove in silence, and I didn't attempt to make small talk. What could a twenty-two-year-old say to a two-thousand-year-old vampire that wouldn't sound completely vacuous?

I pressed my temple to the cool glass of the passenger window and watched the darkness set in while the scenery whipped by in a nauseating blur. Vampires always drove too fast.

Before I had time to think too much about my return home, we were in New York State. I hadn't yet let myself think about what I would do when we got back to the city. Foolishly, I'd assumed we must have been several hours away from home. Worry yielded to reality as the road signs began to read shorter and shorter distances to New York City. The pretty, wooded spaces of upstate New York became more populated and urban, and at last the glow of the city skyline came into view.

"Where am I to take you, pet?"

I didn't have much time before we'd be in the heart of Manhattan, and my gut was a clenched fist of nerves. Did I want to go to the office and see Keaty? Or perhaps have Sig drop me at the 52nd Street Starbucks? It was a short walk from my apartment but also a gateway to the unique reality inhabited by the Oracle, Calliope. Certainly the half-god/half-fairy would have a thing or two to tell me about what my arrival home meant. Did I maybe, instead, want delivery to Rain Hotel, where my coveted black keycard would give me direct access to the three-story penthouse?

Unless my access had been cut off.

I swallowed hard.

"Take me home."

For a moment I swore he smiled, but just as fast, it was gone.

"Of course."

Without time for further thought, we were on the four hundred block of West 52nd Street and stopped in front of my slender yellow apartment building. The lights in my basement suite were dark, and I let out a breath I hadn't realized I was holding.

Who had I expected to be there?

Neither Desmond nor Lucas would be there like obedient dogs, awaiting my return. Nor could I expect Holden to be inside, inviting me to capture him for his mysterious crimes.

Behind our idling car, an impatient driver honked.

"You may need these." He handed me a familiar-looking bundle. It was my gun and the small wallet I'd had with me at the Elm Tree. The only keys I needed for anything were inside the zippered change compartment. I took them tentatively. I'd never noticed the wallet was gone. The car honked again.

"Thanks, Sig."

"Do not be so quick to thank me, Miss McQueen." His smile was unmistakable, but before I could make sense of it, I was standing in the street, smothered by the humidity of the July night. I eyed my building with suspicion as several cars sped by.

"Home, sweet home," I sighed.

Inside, things went from odd to completely insane.

I unlocked my front door and didn't give my eyes a chance to adjust when I stepped over the threshold, taking for granted my familiarity with my own apartment.

Once I put my gun and wallet on the table beside the door, I tripped over a pair of Steve Madden peep-toe pumps. I caught my balance before falling but was rewarded by snagging my flip-flops on the pointy heel of my strappy gold Jimmy Choo cage sandals.

My shoe collection was like other people's art collections—a demented passion that had almost no use in the real world. My chosen career required *a lot* of running, and though I could run in Manolos if need be, flats or running shoes were much less risky.

When my eyes adjusted, I could see the contents of my hallway shoe closet strewn across the entranceway and spilling over into the living room. T-straps, Mary Janes, cage sandals and wedges, the shiny, expensive debris of a fashion hurricane. I plucked my glossy black Louboutins from where they'd been hurled and clutched them to my chest.

On the living-room table I noted several empty blood-donor bags. In the hall I reached for the light switch, but turning it on yielded nothing.

My power had been shut off.

Something small and fluffy passed in between my legs, and I resisted the urge to assume it was of demonic origin. The furry thing introduced itself with a *"Brrr-eow?"*

The tiny white kitten looked up at me, and I hugged my shoes tighter. Cats. Close enough to demons. As if it had read my mind, it began purring and rubbed itself against my ankles. Until that instant I had forgotten about who I should have expected in my apartment all along.

"Brigit," I screamed, startling the fur-demon so badly it shot off like a bolt and hid under the armchair.

My bathroom door opened and steam spilled into the hall. At least she'd paid the water bill.

"Oh. My. *Gawd!"* Wrapped in one of my towels, with her blonde hair sticking to her slick, wet skin, Brigit Stewart looked surprised to see me.

The baby vampire had been assigned to me as a ward by Sig before I left. The decision had given me a pretty impressive promotion within the council, and also made the ditsy ex-beauty queen a giant, and permanent, pain in my ass.

The kitten came out from under the chair, and I kept it at bay with one foot while continuing to cradle my shoes, all while I avoided tripping over the explosion of footwear on the floor. I fixed Brigit with a deadly serious glare.

"I wasn't expecting you!" she said, half-smiling and shrugging as if to say *what can you do?* I understood how, in life, Brigit had managed to get everything she wanted. I was not about to play games with her, however. If she was my charge, maybe it was time for her to start respecting my position as a warden.

"What the *hell,* Brigit?"

"Well." She eyed the scene, trying to assess it as I must be seeing it. "Umm?" Big round blue eyes and an innocent smile were all she offered.

"And what the *fuck* is *that?"* I pointed a five-inch heel at the purring, evil cotton ball rubbing its face against my flip-flop.

"Ohmigod, so cute, right? I got her from some homeless guy, and I was totally gonna eat her." She snatched up the kitten, almost losing her towel in the process, and for a moment I thought she was going to turn the thing into a Happy Meal. Instead she held it in my face, apparently for my approval. "But how could I eat something so *cute*?" The cat's purring was loud and constant. Brigit rubbed the kitten against her cheek and giggled. "Her name is Rio."

I was dumbfounded, and it was only getting worse. "Excuse me?"

"Rio." She forced the kitten into my hands, so I was holding it as well as my shoes. "I named her that for you!"

"Because of my deep-rooted love of Brazil?"

She looked at me like I was retarded. "Uh. No. From that song. By that band. Oh, you know."

"Clearly I don't."

"You know." She searched her memory. "Depeche Mode! The song about the wolves." She winked at me. "Because you *loooove* wolves."

I was appalled by both her cavalier reference to my werewolf consorts and her flagrant disregard for eighties pop culture.

"Duran Duran," I sighed.

"Hmm. I know all your boyfriends had names that started with a D, but wasn't the cute brunet called Desmond?"

I set the cat on the yellow loveseat and placed my shoes on the mantle above my fireplace. "Duran Duran is a band. They *did* sing a song called 'Rio', but the song about wolves was 'Hungry Like the Wolf', and it was more of a metaphor than an anthem." I plopped down on my overstuffed, oversize armchair and stared at the ceiling, trying to will myself back to Elmwood.

"Oh." She adjusted her towel. "Well, we can't really call her that."

The cat was staring at me. This was all a little too much for me to handle so soon after getting back. I kicked off my flip-flops, then stood back up and grabbed the Louboutins, stepping into them and enjoying my new height.

Ignoring Brigit's inquiring stare, I picked up a small purse from the floor, then took the only two things I needed off the table next to the door.

A gun and my keycard for Rain Hotel.

Chapter Seven

I caught a cab a few blocks away from home, and in those short blocks I was already reconsidering my plan. Admittedly, I was chickening out on seeing Lucas. We hadn't left our relationship on the best footing when I ran away. First, there was the small problem of me also being connected to Desmond and the teeny-tiny issue of me having slept with him. Then there was the real problem—they both now knew I was part vampire, and Lucas had made a huge sacrifice to save my life when he shared his blood with me.

We hadn't had time to discuss the ramifications of that particular revelation. I'd needed to heal, and then I'd needed a lot of time to clear my head. All of this was time spent apart from them. The wolf king was a patient man, but he was probably having to field a lot of questions at home about what had become of his Southern wolf princess.

The pack within New York was small, only twenty-four wolves. Twenty-four people were not likely to forget their leader telling them he had met his mate.

I sighed.

"Lady, this ain't a sitting room. Where you wanna go?"

If the cab were a sitting room, it would have been one in a sauna. There was no air conditioning, and the bitter tang of sweat was rolling off the potbellied, wifebeater-clad cab driver. If it was still legal to smoke in taxis, I was willing to bet he'd have a cigar dangling from his meaty lips. His singular eyebrow was dipped in a scowl in the rearview mirror.

I was about to say SoHo, but it came out as a sibilant breath. No. I wasn't ready, not yet. He must have seen the slight head shake, because he coughed with a phlegmy rattle and spit something out his open window. A cyclist cursed and the cabby snarled at him.

"*Lady.*" He drew out the word, emphasizing his impatience.

I gave him an address in the West Village, northwest of Rain Hotel, and he put the car in drive before I listed the cross street. As we drove, I pulled my cell phone out of my purse and dialed a number I almost never had cause to use.

"Miss me so soon?"

"Sig," I said, no friendliness in my tone. "We need to talk about Brigit."

"Yes?" As if he had no idea what I meant.

"She needs to go."

"She is your charge."

"I never had to live with my warden."

There was a long pause. I hadn't mentioned Holden by name, but it hung unsaid in the air.

"You will continue to monitor her. She is your responsibility."

"She can be my responsibility somewhere else. Somewhere I am less likely to shoot her in her sleep. I got home and my *shoes* were everywhere. My power's been shut off."

I was thankful I'd had the foresight to pay up my rent until the end of the summer, especially now that I knew the newbie vampire hadn't spared much thought for the little things, like bills.

"Shoes," Sig said with a laugh. I don't know if I'd ever heard Sig laugh, and it made my pulse trip. "Very well, Secret. I will have Ingrid make arrangements for Miss Stewart. And I will make a call about your power." His tone told me he was less than thrilled about having to deal with such trifling issues. He hung up without any further comment.

The streets slid by slowly, and I watched as groups proceeded along the sidewalk to find their place in the Manhattan night. Girls in too-short sequined dresses and too-high heels moved in giggling packs. Men in cheap suits were leaving happy-hour pubs and advanced on to more promising nightspots. A red double-decker tour bus snaked past the cab, and groups of wide-eyed city virgins snapped endless photos of the glittery face of the city. New York was a shameless showgirl who never took off her makeup and always had a little too much leg showing. She was dazzling and unrepentant. I smiled, feeling like I was well and truly home.

We turned onto Christopher Street and followed it for a few moments until we arrived at Carmine, where the cab stopped in front of a short strip of brick buildings. I got out at a bakery called Sweet Jean's and thrust some crumpled bills at the cabby. The air outside was cooler than it had been in the cab, and I enjoyed the slight turn of breeze that smelled like hot brick and the promise of a dirty night.

Beside the entrance to Sweet Jean's was a small alley where a wrought-iron gate was the only indication something lay beyond. I squirmed down the pass and found the door buzzer next to the locked gate. After a short run of rings, a female voice asked, "Yes?"

"Cedes?" I knew it was her, if only because of the peevish, tired tone in her voice. Mercedes Castilla was a homicide detective with the NYPD. She knew I was a little wolfish, but that was about it. She was the only human I knew, aside from Keaty, who believed in monsters.

"Secret?" So many question marks, so few actual questions.

"The one and only."

"You wily little skank. Stay right there."

The buzzer fell silent, and I watched a couple walk by the mouth of the alley, laughing at a joke I had missed. I heard the fall of her footsteps raining down the inner stairwell, and then with a click of bolts being turned, she emerged on the other side of the gate, pushing it open to get a better look at me.

Her unruly, curly black hair was swept up into a bushy ponytail, and she wore a gray NYPD shirt that was one size too large over a pair of jean shorts. Her face, as usual, looked worn and tired, but her eyes were bright and her skin was fresh. I couldn't help but smile at her as I said, "Hi."

"Hi?" She laughed at the statement and pulled me in for a tight hug. "I can't believe you. Do you know how crazy people have been going about you?"

Mercedes and Keaty were the only people who knew where I'd gone. I figured it would be best to tell her outright rather than deal with the fallout if she launched a manhunt for me. I hugged her back, enjoying the sweet, fruity scent of her shampoo and the warmth coming from her small, muscular body.

"Come on," she said as she locked the inner door and gate behind her. "We have some catching up to do."

We found ourselves at a small bar within walking distance called Fat Sam's. The bartender was a slim, tall man who smiled at Mercedes in a way that suggested more than passing familiarity. Her color darkened the slightest bit, but she gave no other indication of how they knew each other.

"Evening, Detective," he said warmly.

"Owen." She nodded and held up two fingers, then added, "And keep 'em coming."

We slid into a booth with cracked leather seats which sank beneath our individual weights so we were at an almost comically low height with the scarred wooden table. Owen came over carrying a tray and threw down two Newcastle Ale coasters, then put a pint glass down on each one of them. Next to the pints he gave us each a shot glass brimming over with strong, old-smelling whiskey. He eyed me the way bartenders often do when they suspect someone of being underage. Cedes touched his forearm and smiled sweetly, something I'd never seen her do before.

"She's on the level, Owen, I promise."

"You're the cop." He turned back to the bar where a group of college-aged man-boys in NYU sweatshirts were waiting. He ID'd them right away, and I felt a little guilty knowing it was me who'd set off his radar.

"Owen?" I asked, smirking at her.

"Shush. We're here to talk about *you*."

"Are we?" I leaned back in the booth, trying to act as casual as possible. "What did you mean when you said people were going crazy about me?"

She was drinking from her pint, and I could smell how robust the stout was. She held up her pinky to silence me a moment while she continued to drink, and then licked the foam from her top lip before speaking again.

"People came to see me. At work. About you." She pulled the ponytail out of her hair and shook it loose, letting the dark curls settle around her face. I could see some of her hair was still damp, which explained the strong, lingering smell of her shampoo. My own hair was greasy, and the curls always looked extra heavy when that was the case. I also was increasingly aware of the fact my shirt was still covered in dry blood, and no one had commented on it yet.

Perhaps Brigit was too dense. Mercedes, on the other hand, must have assumed it belonged to someone else. I picked at the front of my shirt uneasily.

"I was gonna ask you about that." Her voice gave no sign of any worried edge. If I was in trouble, she knew I would tell her.

"I forgot to change when I got home."

"You thought to put on fuck-me pumps but not to change your bloody shirt?" She laughed, slapping her palm on the table. I saw Owen turn, his gaze fixed on her, an admiring smile on his lips. "Owen!" She looked at him, failing to realize he'd been watching her the whole time. "You still got those shirts Sam used to make the weekend girls wear?"

I didn't like the sound of that.

He rummaged under the counter without asking her any details and came up with a tank top in his hand. He walked over to us and held the shirt out for her assessment. It was a skimpy spaghetti-strapped black tank with white printing that read—*Fat Sam's: Helping People Forget Their Problems Since 1964.*

"Jesus," I hissed.

Owen left it on the table, and Mercedes pushed it towards me. "It's that or walk around looking like a crime scene." She pointed to my chest, which could have given a blood-spatter analyst a hard-on.

I glared at her, then tossed back my shot for a hit of instant courage. Without waiting to see if the coast was clear, I stripped off my ruined yellow shirt and was in the process of putting the new one on when I heard the chorus of appreciative cheers from the boys at the bar. One of them looked Owen dead in the eyes and said, "This is the greatest bar in the world."

At least I had worn a bra.

Mercedes grinned and saluted me with her pint glass.

"Now tell me who came to see you," I said, getting our conversation back on track. Alcohol from the shot was whipping through my system at breakneck speed, making my head feel light. One of the blessings of my condition was that things like alcohol and coffee, the two greatest legal drugs on the market, acted extra fast. They also lasted for far less time, so I almost never got a chance to feel the hangover dregs or caffeine crashes.

"Lucas Fucking Rain, for one." She said it like *fucking* was actually his middle name. "He nearly gave the front-desk girl a heart attack when he told her his name."

If it was the same front-desk girl I'd met on several occasions, I was sorry he hadn't finished the job. She was a snotty little thing, and there was no love lost between us.

"Must have made you popular."

"Lucas Rain comes to the homicide department to ask about a missing girl? Yeah. Some knob in my department seemed to think that particular tidbit was fair game for Page Six. Poor Kellen Rain was the target of some pretty scandalous blind-item gossip. Something like *Real Estate Heiress's Brother Talks to Cops: Bad News Beauty in More Than a Little Trouble?*"

From what I'd read about Kellen Rain, she was no stranger to being the center of attention. Page Six worshipped her antics, and she put most other spoiled party girls to shame with her drinking, sleeping around and general destruction of public property.

"What did you tell him?"

"I told him you were safe and you'd come home when you were ready."

"And he left it at that?"

"He's a proud man, Secret, and he's richer than God. He didn't try to bribe me, but I think he was testing the water to see if I might bite if he did."

"Cedes, he could have bought you a penthouse on Central Park West without blinking. You should have *let* him bribe you."

She laughed again, and I took a long swig of beer. It was cold and dark, and I could almost hear Irish tin whistles while I drank. It felt thick and cloying on my tongue. I loved it.

"He certainly didn't like it when I sent him on his merry way without any information. For the life of me, I don't know why you would run away and not take him *with* you. He is one hell of a good-looking man."

I smiled and drank a little more but said nothing one way or the other.

"And your vampire came by a few days ago."

I coughed and beer actually came out my nose as I attempted to stop choking. Had I heard her right? There was only one vampire Mercedes could be talking about, the only one I'd ever introduced her to and vouched for. She hated vampires, so he would also be the only one she would allow around her, all because I told her he was safe.

Holden had gone to see Mercedes, knowing she hated him, to try and find me?

Or, if he was a rogue like the Tribunal was claiming, was he finding people close to me and stalking them to smoke me out? Was his visit to Mercedes a veiled threat on her life? Was Holden telling me I needed to be on guard?

The thought of people I cared about being at risk because someone I once trusted might be turning his back on me sent a chill into my core. I used my old shirt to wipe beer off my face, and Mercedes stopped laughing when she saw the seriousness of my expression.

"What? I thought he was your partner or something."

I shook my head, the chill refusing to leave me. "What did he say?"

"He asked if I knew where you were, like Lucas had. When I said I didn't, he asked if I would give you a message."

I laid my palms on the table and leaned in close, waiting for the words just behind her lips. "What did he say?" I repeated.

"He told me to say, 'Tell Secret I'll be seeing her soon.'"

Color drained out of my already-pale face.

"What's so bad about that?"

"I have to go." I stood up from the table, swaying a little as the alcohol swelled inside me.

"Secret? What's the big deal?" Her voice was filled with worry.

"Nothing. Nothing. It's fine." I looked back at her, unable to tell her what I should have—to watch her back. There was no sense in worrying her. Nothing would happen to her now that I was home again.

"I have to go find Lucas," I added, and she smiled knowingly, concern vanishing from her face.

"*Yeah* you do." She emphasized the first word. "Anything you want me to tell the bloodsucker if I see him again?"

I wanted to tell her to run if that happened.

"Just tell him 'Not if I see you first.'"

She shrugged, and I was gone before she could ask anything else.

Chapter Eight

I hadn't lied when I told her I had to see Lucas. My restored need to find the wolf king was threefold. First, I intended to warn him about Holden; second, I really wanted to see him again; and third, I was drunk.

Rain Hotel was exactly as I remembered it—glossy, sleek and expensive looking. The interior was inviting, and I took a moment to enjoy the array of chandeliers and the full-wall fountain. The harpist was still in her hidden nook, only tonight she was playing "Bohemian Rhapsody", which was quite a shift from the chamber music she used to play. The slick marble floor would have been hazardous to most women in such high heels, but I marched across the long lobby without any hesitation and pressed the elevator's up button.

My head was swimming, and I probably should have let myself sober up before seeing Lucas, but I had to admit I needed the extra courage the booze had given me. As I waited for the elevator, I heard a loud, intentional cough from the desk.

"*Excuuuse me*, miss, do you need help?" The voice was shrill and annoying, and I knew right away who it belonged to.

During my second visit to Rain Hotel, I'd been accosted by an unpleasant desk clerk named Melvin. Melvin was a were-ferret, which made him the first of such I'd heard of, but he was weaselly enough to fit the bill. I turned my head and fixed a withering glare on the shrewd-looking little man. His mouth fell open and his eyes widened.

"No, Melvin, I don't believe I'll be needing any help from *you.*" I waved my black keycard at him and faced the elevator.

"Apologies, Miss McQueen. We weren't expecting you."

I grunted and the doors swished open. "No one ever expects the Spanish Inquisition." It was a foolish reply and I almost regretted it, but I was too busy chuckling to myself to let it show. His face was red.

I punched in my penthouse access code on a hidden keypad above the regular numbers and gave Melvin a satisfied wave as the doors shut between us.

The elevator whirred to life, which put at least one fear to rest. My key code hadn't been revoked. The higher the elevator numbers climbed, the more my heart sank until it was swimming in my stomach, doing backflips in the beer. I let out a shaky sigh as the ride came to an end with a slight jerk and the doors opened into the foyer of Lucas's penthouse.

The main hall was dark and quiet, and I stepped into the hallway, listening for any sign of life. All I could hear was my own breathing. I followed the hallway for a few steps and saw a light on in a room I remembered being a small office. With as much stealth as possible given my shoes, I moved towards the light and, after a moment's hesitation, pushed the door open an inch, asking, "Lucas?"

"No, he's not..."

The speaker and I both froze simultaneously and stared at each other from across the dimly lit room. I didn't need more light to know who it was. I had known the second I opened the door and was assaulted by the tart, bright flavor of limes. My eyes watered from the overpowering emotional response to the taste.

"Desmond."

"Secret?" He didn't seem to believe it. He put down the book he'd been reading and stood by the far wall, licking his lips tentatively. I tasted sweet to him, like crème brulee or spun sugar, and he was probably checking for the sweetness. With that much flavor in the room, there was no way for him to pass my presence off as a flight of imagination.

He looked different somehow. His dark brown hair had grown out but was cut more evenly, so instead of being short in the back and longer in front, it was uniformly shaggy and had been left to hang in his face. His big violet-gray eyes held a hint of pain that tore at my insides and sobered me up better than a cold shower. It was the same way he'd looked at me when he thought I might be dead. He was wearing dark jeans cut to show off the muscular build of his lower body, and a crisp white dress shirt, rolled up to the elbows, paired with a skinny black tie, loosened enough he had undone his top shirt button. Under the lime, I could smell a musky cologne on him, and the combined package made me take a step closer.

In response, he moved backwards.

"What are you doing here?" The words were loaded with unspoken accusation. I had anticipated it, but nevertheless, it stung.

"I'm back," I replied. "I'm home."

His face clouded with anger. "Lucas isn't here."

I looked around the room, as if he meant here with us, which seemed obvious enough. Then I realized he meant in the penthouse.

"Where is he?"

"He's upstate, dealing with pack business. He's had to do a lot since you left. There was a big mess to clean up and no one to help him with it."

I couldn't imagine exactly how my killing Marcus Sullivan might result in a *big mess* for the king, but I suppose there were a lot of things about the pack I didn't understand.

"Oh," was all I could say.

"Is that all?" His tone was cold and painful for me to hear. I stepped closer to him again, and this time he didn't retreat, though I could feel anger coming off him in hot waves.

"I'm so sorry, Desmond. For everything."

He growled a little, still glaring, but he didn't stop me from edging towards him. I was within inches and could feel his rage in a searing, red aura. He was shaking.

"Why?" he asked.

"Why what?"

"Why?" He looked beyond me. "Just...why? All of it."

"I left because I was scared. I didn't know what you and Lucas would think. And more than that. The vampire council came to me at the Oracle's and gave me a job I was too scared to deal with."

"Is that why you're back?"

"That's part of it."

He raised a hand as if he wanted to touch me, but reconsidered and let it drop.

"I didn't mean to hurt you." I lowered my voice and found I couldn't look at him. "I missed you. I missed the taste of you." I didn't mean it in a sexual sense, though I had missed that too. With the sweet limey taste on my tongue, I was able to accept how much I missed the literal flavor of him.

Desmond made a small sound, somewhere between a whimper and a sigh, and then his mouth was on mine. His large, warm hands cupped my face, and he was imploring my lips to open. I sighed against him and wrapped my arms around his back, feeling the heat of his body through the thin layer of his shirt.

He pulled back again, holding my face, and looked at me with dark seriousness. "Don't you *ever* leave me again."

I nodded, no hesitation to my agreement. I'd longed for the warmth of his touch every night while I'd been gone, and now that I was with him once more, I never wanted to leave. "Shut up and kiss me," I demanded, and he didn't wait to be told a second time.

Picking me up, he walked us over to the desk and put me down on the hard wood surface. The few items that had been there—a phone, a penholder, a stack of papers—were showered onto the floor as he climbed onto the desk with me. I lay back and his body covered mine. I worshiped the heat coming off him as we kissed each other with the pent-up desire of a long separation. He clipped my lip with his teeth, breaking the delicate skin, then pulled back and gently sucked the blood off my lower lip.

I shuddered, and my lids fell closed as he tilted my head back and trailed kisses down my jaw, to my neck, then to my throat, then almost to my...

"Secret?" He stopped.

"Uhn?"

"This is the stupidest shirt I've ever seen."

It took me a moment to realize what he was talking about until I looked between us and remembered the shirt I had borrowed.

"Oh. My other one was covered in blood, so I—"

Desmond froze. His body went rigid on top of me, and not in the way I would have hoped given our position. He slid back and climbed off me, standing almost out of reach and looking at me with a frightening expression. I sat up, shimmied to the edge of the desk and took his limp hand in both of mine.

"What just happened?" I asked.

"Why was your shirt covered in blood?"

Oh, yeah, I probably could have worded things a bit better. "Um. I guess I haven't been entirely honest about what brought me back. It wasn't really my decision."

"What does that mean?" He took another step closer and placed one hand on my wrist, brushing his thumb down it.

"I was kidnapped?"

"You say that like it's a question."

"Well, it wasn't a *kidnappy* kidnapping. It was more like the time you guys kidnapped me, you know?"

He raised an eyebrow, and I couldn't blame him. I tugged him closer and wrapped my legs around his waist. He was still hard, but he didn't take the bait. He didn't pull away either, and I was happy just being close to him again.

"Sig needed me back, so he sent some people to come and get me. The teen wolf and I got into a bit of a scuffle, and we both got a little bloody, that's all."

"That's all?" He cupped my chin and moved my face from left to right, most likely checking for any signs of damage. He seemed satisfied my healing had done its job, and let his fingers trail down my face and rest on my shoulder. "Teen wolf?"

"Yeah, some kid. Definitely a wolf and seemed familiar. Might have been cute before I got him in the face with a tire iron."

"That's my girl." He smiled. A part of him was trying to piece together everything I'd told him, but a more substantial part of him was pressed against my pelvis. Now that his worry had faded, I was more likely to get what I wanted most out of the situation.

"Desmond?"

"Yeah?" He was absently rubbing his hand from my clavicle to my throat and back down again, making my pulse sing.

"About the shirt?"

He looked at my shirt and made a face.

"If you hate it so much, maybe you should take it off."

Chapter Nine

My shirt was off before I'd finished the sentence. His was much less patiently removed in a tinkling shower of buttons hitting the floor and the satisfying sound of shredding cotton.

"I liked that shirt," he said with a laugh as he pushed me back down onto the desk and kissed my exposed stomach. I grinned and ran my hands over his smooth, warm back.

"I'll buy you a new one."

There was little opportunity to joke around once he kissed me again. I fell into the abyss of his attentions, drowning in each deep, probing kiss. I dragged my fingers through the new length of his hair as he moved his hands between us and undid the button on my shorts. He found his way to the waistband of my underwear, and his sly fingers slipped under the cotton. He slid one finger inside me, and I gasped from the unexpected roughness of his warm skin.

He drifted away from my lips, peppering kisses over my breasts. I didn't want him to stop what his probing fingers were doing, as first one, then two found a slow, deliberate rhythm inside me, making my head swim. With a faint grasp of how to use my hands, I undid my bra and shucked it to the floor. It was still dangling from my fingers when his hot mouth latched on to one peaked nipple, dragging a ragged sigh from my lips.

He pushed my shorts off, and they fell to the ground with a soft sound. I felt his hardness, trapped in his slacks, against my inner thigh. I let out a moan, drowning in the urgent need to have him inside me again. I had both hands on his lower back, imploring him to come closer, when I had a flash of memory.

For a moment I thought I was remembering our previous times together, and then, as he put a third finger inside me and his tongue swirled around my nipple, I was overcome by a disorienting dizziness. When I opened my eyes, I found myself in bed with Holden.

I blinked, unable to understand where the desk, Desmond and all of my reality had gone. And why it had been replaced with a missing vampire in a satin-sheeted bed.

My hands were on Holden's lower back and his mouth was at my neck, and I caught my breath when his teeth dragged over my skin. The change in my breathing made my throat tighten, and the sharpness of his fangs pressed over my throbbing artery. Desmond was forgotten, as were all of the worries of my real life. When I touched Holden our bodies created steam where his cool skin rubbed against my own feverish exterior. His touch was as real as anything I'd ever felt, and the only thing my body understood was a growing desire that needed to be fed.

As far as my animal desires were concerned, one hard cock was as good as another right then. I shivered in anticipation of what was to follow and arched my hips against him.

"*Yes*," I purred.

I was back on the desk with Desmond, and his pants were now undone. He ran his hands down my waist and grasped my hips as his mouth reclaimed mine for a jarring kiss. Without his fingers inside me there was a pulsing ache that demanded attention. I growled against his lips and nipped at his tongue. The rational parts of me were no longer in control, otherwise I would have been wondering what was happening to me. A wave of tension trembled through his body as he pushed himself inside me. I broke free of the kiss with a gasp, digging my nails into the skin of his back. I'd forgotten what it felt like to have the hot length of him fill me up. My eyes rolled back and then...

Holden's body rocked against mine, and the heat of Desmond was replaced with a coolness so soothing it felt like a full-body sigh. The vampire drew me upright so I was perched on his lap. He held my hair away from my neck, and his tongue teased the delicate skin until my pulse raced with the breakneck speed of my overeager heart. With his free hand, he brushed his fingers down my back and over my bottom, where he lifted me easily, then lowered me, repeating the action until my hips took up the rhythm naturally, and I swayed with him as we built towards a fever pitch. As my cries grew louder and more frantic, my body shook. Teeth sank into my neck, and I heard myself call out in both realities from the combined pleasure of what was happening on both planes.

I clawed at the desk but felt satin instead. I reached for Holden to push him away and met with the warmth of Desmond. Closing my eyes seemed to make it worse, so I opened them and hazily fixed my gaze on Desmond, who was looking down at me as he moved.

The sensation of him pounding inside me and the way it tasted when he kissed me was almost too much to bear, and I couldn't help but shut my lids for a moment. In that instant I was back with Holden. He stopped biting me and pulled his head back with a look so satisfied it gave me a chill.

"Soon," he said, tracing his thumb over my raw lips.

I wanted to reply, but my eyes flew open when Desmond pulled my hips closer to the edge of the desk and found his way deeper within me with a fierce thrust. I gasped, my mind reeling, and when he finished, I let him lay on top of me, breathing softly, while I stared at the ceiling, terrified to close my eyes.

I needed to find Holden Chancery.

Once I was back in my right mind, I felt violated. I buttoned up the dress shirt Desmond had brought me, trying to understand what had just happened. Seated on one of the leather chairs in the study, I was being too quiet, and it seemed to be making Desmond worry. I didn't want him to think he'd done anything wrong, but he couldn't know about the weird subconscious threesome we'd just had.

I didn't know how to reconcile what I'd just experienced, so how could I expect him to understand? If I tried to explain it, I doubted I could make it sound like anything other than *I was thinking about a vampire while we were having sex.*

Desmond sat down in the chair across from me and gave a tentative half smile. You would think I'd just lost my virginity or something, with how careful he was being.

"Secret, I think I know what's wrong."

Startled, I looked up at him, and my breath caught in my throat. Had he been able to feel it too? Had he seen what I'd seen? God, I hoped not.

"You still need to see Lucas, and this unexpected...delay is making you feel guilty."

"Oh." I looked down at my hands and debated his words. Lesser of two evils. "Something along those lines, yeah."

He knelt on the ground in front of me and wrapped me in his strong arms. I hesitated, scared to close my eyes, but when I did I found nothing there but darkness. So I let myself indulge in Desmond's embrace. I breathed in the smell of him as deep as I could, and the wolf part of me stirred, like a dog stretching after a long nap. It had been a long time since I'd felt her as anything more than fractured senses or abilities. Or animal needs.

To know she was still there, a whole entity, a being unto herself who could still feel things through me, gave me both a chill and a shock of delight. It seemed like I could only feel my wolf as her own entity when I was with Desmond. When I was with Lucas, she merely felt like liquid heat bubbling below the surface. Desmond awakened the animal within.

I pulled back. "Thank you."

"For what?" He brushed a hair back behind my ear.

"For being so damned understanding all the time. I don't know how you do it."

"I do what I need to do in order to keep you." The sadness in his voice was heavy. I think it was the first time I let myself appreciate that neither he nor Lucas liked the situation they had found themselves in any more than I did. Who wanted to share their soul mate? They were no more interested in sharing me with each other than I was interested in being soul-bonded to two men.

As if love wasn't complicated enough without the supernatural getting involved.

"I *do* need to go see Lucas," I said.

"I know. I called one of the cars while I was getting the shirts. It's a bit of a drive, but if you don't get too distracted, you can make it there and back well before sunrise."

"Thank you, Desmond." I kissed his cheek, then his mouth. "I don't deserve you."

"Ha," he said with no humor, looking me in the eyes with that serious expression of his. "Can I ask you something for next time?"

"Of course."

"Next time I want all of you here with me. I don't want your mind off somewhere, or with *someone* else."

I swallowed hard. He thought I'd had Lucas on my mind.

"I want that too," was all I managed to say.

In the car, I tried not to think about what had transpired in Lucas's penthouse but found it impossible. It wasn't so much the sex part that was bothering me, because I had to admit it had been phenomenal, if bizarre. Rather, I was getting more and more concerned about the connection Holden and I seemed to share inside my mind. It was no longer restricted to dreams, and that made it unlike anything I'd ever experienced.

I was immune to the thrall, so it couldn't have been that. Was there some other kind of vampire magic I was unaware of that could let Holden enter my dreams *and* my waking mind without permission? The dream I'd had in Elmwood could have been dismissed as one of my typically weird nocturnal ramblings. But what had happened tonight was something new. The part of me with Holden had felt as real as the physical part of me with Desmond. And when the vampire had bitten me...

My hand went to my neck, and I half-expected to feel something there, but the skin was as smooth as ever. There was nothing to indicate I had ever been bitten.

I sat back in the leather seats of the town car and sighed.

"Almost there, miss," the driver announced, obviously misunderstanding my sigh as one of impatience. The driver was human. I couldn't smell anything lycanthropic or otherwise on him. Lucas must have kept him around for jobs requiring legitimate ignorance.

"No rush," I lied.

The drive to upstate New York took a little over an hour and a half, and much of it was through picturesque wooded areas and nice-looking towns and small cities. These were the places people went to escape the bustle of the city. I don't know why, but I'd assumed Lucas's family mansion would be somewhere in the Hamptons. The more I considered it, though, the more ridiculous that option showed itself to be. If the mansion was where pack business was worked out, and where the pack went to meet on full moons, then having it on a tiny, overpopulated peninsula in Suffolk County was just about the stupidest idea ever.

The mansion we pulled up to was as secluded as one could be within driving distance of New York City. It was a good fifteen minutes beyond the last house we'd seen, and twenty-five minutes or more since the last settlement anyone could call a town. Yet it still wasn't at all what I'd expected.

The house rested on top of a hill, and around it were acres of plain, sprawling lawn, interrupted only by meticulously landscaped English-style gardens. I guess I'd thought the getaway spot for a pack of werewolves would have more trees. Not that there was any shortage of woods surrounding the estate. It seemed like the entire lot across the highway from the mansion was nothing but forest. Yet the lawns of the giant mansion seemed to go on forever and offered nothing in the way of hiding spots.

As if he'd read my mind, the driver said, "Wait until you see the back. He has a legitimate hedge maze back there."

"Excuse me?"

"Straight out of *The Shining*. It's the craziest thing."

He pressed a button on the visor over his head and the huge wrought-iron gates swung open. Above each red brick pillar on either side of the driveway, a large stone gargoyle was perched, guarding the entrance to Lucas Rain's kingdom. The town car followed the winding gravel driveway up the hill at a slow enough speed for me to marvel at Lucas's home.

The Rain mansion was incredible. It had the look and feel of an English Georgian-era manor home, with gray stone walls and dozens upon dozens of windows. There were none of the peaks and turrets I would have imagined a werewolf home to have. I guess, in my head, I'd pictured something a little more Gothic for the wolf king. It was still a grand home and big enough to suit a billionaire's lifestyle.

The car stopped outside the front doors, and the dutiful driver got out to open my door. With a tip of his cap—yes, he was actually wearing a driver's cap *and* gloves—he got back in the car and drove off, leaving me standing at the foot of the entrance stairs wondering what to do next.

I knocked on the front door, but after a long pause there was no reply so I let myself in, somewhat shocked to find the door unlocked. Inside, the house was dark and eerily quiet. I could see a few lights shining down each upstairs hallway but nothing else to indicate anyone was up there. The house's interior was wide and spacious, and even in the dark I could tell it was decorated to feel inviting rather than stuffy.

Somewhere in the rear of the house I heard a masculine voice and a loud, familiar laugh. My heart jumped at the sound of it. I passed through the kitchen and out onto a well-lit stone patio behind the house. There was a full kitchen set up outside as well, built from the same patinated stone as the rest of the patio. Sitting on one long section of counter, next to a built-in barbeque, was a large wooden serving slab that contained the evidence of a massive steak dinner. Wineglasses were scattered all over the patio, some still partially filled with a beautiful, deep red vintage. I was willing to bet this mansion had one hell of a wine cellar.

Aside from the dinner layout and all the wineglasses, there was little else to indicate some sort of party had recently occurred. I followed a trail of lights down a stone path and past the hedge maze the driver had told me about. The walls loomed twelve feet high, and in the dark the maze was sinister looking. I heard the laugh again and was thankful it wasn't from within the foreboding depths of the maze.

The stone path continued, and the glowing turquoise-blue light of a swimming pool appeared ahead, along with a well-lit white pool house with large floor-to-ceiling glass windows. Then I saw Lucas.

The wolf king was standing beside the pool, wearing khaki trousers and an unbuttoned white shirt that looked remarkably similar to the one I had borrowed from his penthouse. He was barefoot, which I had come to realize was one his secret comforts. His blond hair was still short and tousled, but in the three months I'd been gone he'd grown a beard. It was short and well groomed, but it was odd to see his handsome, youthful face covered in fine blond fuzz. It made him look older, more mature, and that was probably the point.

He was talking to a girl with straight brown hair. She faced away from me, but her lean figure was clad in a backless orange sundress. She too was barefoot. Lucas said something to her I couldn't hear, and she tossed her head back and laughed, her hand touching his upper arm as she did.

I stepped into the light and waited until his gaze moved past the girl in the sundress and found me. Me, wearing my borrowed shirt with my unwashed hair and ridiculously overdressed heels. I stood at the edge of the pool's patio and met his wandering gaze across the distance, unsure of how he was going to react.

For a moment he stared. The girl's hand dropped from his arm, and she turned to see what he was looking at. She was fresh-faced and pretty, her skin glowing from a day out in the sun. She didn't look pleased to see me, although I didn't think we'd ever met.

"Secret?" Lucas asked.

"Hi."

He brushed past the girl like she wasn't there, and a part of me was glad he hadn't replaced me, while another small part of me felt bad for her because she had been so easily forgotten. Lucas was halfway from her to me when a twig snapped from the bushes next to the path. I turned, and out of the garden stepped someone I'd never expected to see again—the young wolf who had helped kidnap me.

The wolf and I froze simultaneously, and then both looked away from each other and to Lucas. The young man took another step out of the garden and moved towards Lucas, who was staring at us with great confusion.

I panicked. It seemed like my kidnapper was back and this time he wanted something from the king. Frantic, I screamed, "*No.*" I dove towards Lucas, and before the other wolf could reach him, Lucas and I were falling backwards into the pool.

Chapter Ten

When we resurfaced, two dozen puzzled faces were gazing down at us, including those of the pretty girl and the young wolf. Lucas was already climbing out, looking remarkably graceful for someone who'd been knocked into the water. In addition, a familiar blond was smirking down, extending his arm to help me out of the pool. I grabbed the hand Dominick, Desmond's brother, was offering, and let him pull me up like I weighed nothing. He was a small man, not much taller than me, but he made up for it in strength. Not to mention personality.

"So, Secret," Dominick said, his smirk widening. "You haven't forgotten how to make an entrance, I see."

The other people had stepped back to allow Lucas and me room to get out, but I could see a few of them moving into a defensive stance near him, clearly thinking I was crazy enough to try it again. That none of them seemed worried about the new wolf made me feel foolish and very aware of the mistake I'd made.

"What's *he* doing here?" I pointed an accusing finger at the young man. Now that his face had healed from my attack at the motel, the familiarity of him was driving me crazy.

"Jackson?" Dominick asked. All I needed was to hear his name, and then I remembered why I recognized him. He'd been one of the werewolf guards I'd left alive while trying to take down Marcus. Dominick continued without being aware of my discovery. "Jackson is from Albany. When the dissenting wolves were banished, he was one of the only ones to stay loyal, so we moved him into the city so he could be with our pack. He's been living out here with Lucas." He seemed to remember something else and laughed a little. "Oh, yeah. I guess you've met Jackson."

"What does *that* mean?" This I directed at Lucas. I couldn't tell if Dominick was referring to my previous interaction with Jackson at the Orpheum theater, or if the bodyguard knew about Jackson's part in my kidnapping. The wolf king would have my answers.

"We'll talk about it inside," Lucas said.

"I'd like to talk about it now." I know I sounded petulant, but it was hard not to be when I'd just found out someone who'd kidnapped me happened to be living with my boyfriend.

"Secret." His voice had taken on the authoritative tone of his royal position. "We will discuss it when we are alone." The wolves around him seemed hesitant to stand down until he said, "You all remember Secret McQueen, of course."

A murmur of uncomfortable hellos moved through the crowd, and finally those nearest the king stepped out of the way so he could come towards me. He put a wet arm around my shoulder, and when he pulled me in, our embrace was exactly how I imagined it would be all those lonely months. In my mouth, Desmond's flavor was gone, replaced now by the spicy bite of cinnamon. Being this close to Lucas, I could taste our combined flavors, and the result was like biting into a fresh cinnamon bun.

"I've missed you so much." He spoke into my hair. "Please come inside."

"Lucas, aren't you forgetting something?" This from the pretty brunette he'd been speaking to. She'd balled her hands on her hips and looked none too happy about any of this. Lucas frowned at her, clearly displeased to be scolded in front of his pack by someone who was his inferior. The girl had balls though, and that gained her instant respect in my book.

"Of course." He sighed and held out his hand to indicate I should focus my attention on her. "How rude of me. I'd like to introduce you to someone."

I hesitated. If he planned to tell me he'd been soul-bonded to someone else while I was away, I was so out of here. I didn't need any more wolf drama in my life. Really, I didn't need any more of *any* drama in my life.

Ignoring my cold response, he continued. "Secret, please say hello to Kellen." He looked at me to ensure I had made the connection—I had—but in case I was oblivious—which I was not—added, "Kellen Rain. My sister."

The girl now seemed satisfied she hadn't been overlooked and reached out her hand to me.

"It's nice to finally meet you." Her whole demeanor had changed. "I'm hoping now that you're back it means Lucas will shut up about you." Kellen's smile was sweet, but her words betrayed a small amount of genuine annoyance.

"I find that unlikely," Dominick said, which got him a warning glare from Lucas and a smile of appreciation from me.

"It's nice to meet you too. I guess it's true what they say, you shouldn't believe everything you read."

Her smile faltered a little, and she raised a well-shaped brow. "Meaning?"

"Well, I was led to believe when I met you you'd be buck naked, riding a New York Jet or three, and that you had found a way to replace oxygen with vodka. And here I thought Page Six had a fact checker."

There was a long pause where everyone waited to see what her reaction would be. Bad press or not, it was no secret Kellen Rain had a short fuse. Then, in an instant, her face lit up and she laughed so loud it surprised me. She continued to laugh until the people around us began to as well, proving I hadn't overstepped.

"I'm more of a Rangers girl, Secret. At least in their off season." This made Lucas frown, until she added, "I like her, Luke. You hang on to this one."

"I intend to try, but she doesn't make it easy."

Kellen smiled at me. "The good ones never do."

Inside the house, Lucas led me upstairs to the master suite. Dominick, ever the dutiful bodyguard, trailed behind us at a reasonable distance, then settled onto a loveseat in the hall outside the room. I guess my display at the pool hadn't proven I was ready to be trusted with the king. At least not out of earshot.

As soon as the door closed, I turned to him and tried to speak, but I found he wasn't interested in chatting. He had removed his wet shirt, and his damp skin glistened in the low light of the room.

"Oh."

He crossed the distance from the door to me in a heartbeat, and I was in his arms as he held me tight and met my lips for a long, soft, painfully deliberate kiss. It was nothing like the way Desmond and I had kissed earlier. In fact, apart from both being wolves who were soul-bonded to me, there was almost nothing similar in the relationships I had with my two men.

Lucas's kiss was gentle, inquiring and exploratory. He hugged me tighter, keeping me close to his body, and lifted my feet off the floor entirely. The last time he'd done this I had tangled myself around him, but tonight I was still too hyperaware of having made love to Desmond and the strange overlap that had shown up with Holden. I wasn't ready to go through it again. I also wasn't quite ready to be the kind of girl who could have sex with two different men in one night. At least on the physical plane.

Call me old-fashioned, but having two boyfriends was already hard enough for me to wrap my head around.

He continued to kiss me, and I let him, enjoying each delicate kiss we shared. The way his tongue tasted like cinnamon hearts when he licked my lower lip was a small treat I had forgotten, and it made me long to make each kiss more lingering. But the beard was weirding me out a little, and I couldn't ignore every other part of the evening.

I was also acutely aware this bedroom was smaller than the one he had in the city, and we were a hell of a lot closer to the bed. I didn't want to tempt fate too much, and the longer I let him kiss me like this, the more likely I was to say *fuck it* and, well, fuck it.

"Put me down."

He ignored me, holding me closer and kissing my earlobe.

"Lucas, please."

He stopped, pulled his head back and looked at me with those searing light-blue eyes. They didn't hold the same kind of pain Desmond's always seemed to, but Lucas's were now less innocent than they had once been. I didn't want to think about the last time I'd looked into his eyes. He lowered me back to the ground, but he didn't let me go. He put one hand on either side of my face and kissed my forehead.

"I'm glad you're back."

"About that." I looked up at him and tried to ask the question that had followed us in from outside. I still wasn't sure how to word it. "Jackson?" It was the best I could do.

"You don't want to know about that, Secret." Lucas let his arms drop and stepped away from me. The disappearance of his body heat left me chilled in my soaking-wet shirt. Or maybe something else was leaving me cold.

"I wouldn't ask if I didn't want to know. Do you know what Jackson did to me?"

"Yes."

It wasn't the answer I was expecting. "You do?"

"Of course. Your boss, your vampire boss...the blond one?"

"Sig?" Why was that name coming up everywhere I went tonight?

"He came to me, and we had a little chat about a mutual friend of ours." He shot me a meaningful look. "It seems he was very grateful to me for saving your life."

"Oh?" This was an interesting turn.

"Yes." Lucas sat on the edge of the bed, but I chose to remain standing closer to the door. "He asked me if it would be of any interest to me to help bring you home again."

"I beg your pardon?"

He raised a hand, and I let my question hang unanswered. "I'd tried to find you, I even went to see your friend Mercedes, but she wouldn't give me anything. Then Sig came to me and told me that with a little help he was certain he could bring you back. He said all I needed to do was let him use one of my wolves, someone you didn't know well. He said he had someone close to you who would take care of the rest."

My mind began to spin. Of course, I'd been totally naive. Any fool could see the whole kidnapping was a setup, but I had assumed Sig had worked alone to facilitate it. Sometimes lone wolves worked with vampires for the money, and I'd assumed Jackson had been one of them. But he was part of the pack, and Lucas had asked him to kidnap me. That meant the shape-shifting witch was on someone's team too.

Someone who knew a thing or two about how hard transfiguration magic was. Someone who had told me the very night I vanished how she thought it was time for me to go home. My hand flew to the necklace dangling from my throat. *Ward against evil, my ass.* My *grandmere* had led them right to me.

I slumped to the floor, and in an instant Lucas was crouched in front of me. He tried to help me up, but I pushed him harder than I meant to, and he stumbled backwards onto the floor.

"I spent an entire day locked in the trunk of a car." I glared at him. "I smashed that kid in the face and got my own split open in the process."

His eyes went wide with sudden rage. "Did he—?"

"No. God, do you think that scrawny thing could have beaten me up? It was an accident, and I healed. But that's not the point, Lucas. You helped the head of the vampire Tribunal kidnap me. And you know who was helping him on my end? My own goddamn grandmother." Out of frustration, I began unbuttoning my shirt, unable to stand the feel of the wet cloth on my skin anymore. I stood and threw the shirt on top of his on the floor.

"I'd like to go home," I said bluntly. "Your driver left, and I'd like to leave."

"Secret—"

"I have a rogue vampire to find. Apparently it's so important that everyone I trusted snuck around behind my back and dragged me home against my will. So I should probably get it done." I was standing in my bra, dripping wet, but I managed to make my point serious enough he didn't question it.

"I'll have Dominick bring you a car." He moved past me to open the door.

"Lucas?"

He hesitated as the door swung open.

"I did miss you. I really did. And I wanted to come home. But you should have let me do it my way. I needed time."

"I know. But, Secret, we needed you here. We're your friends."

"Yeah. With friends like you, who the hell needs enemies?"

I slammed the door behind me.

Chapter Eleven

I knew Lucas was up to something the second Dominick showed me to the garage.

The smirking blond bodyguard had been gracious enough to loan me his leather jacket, and because of his slight build, it fit me perfectly. Plus, thanks to the DNA he shared with his brother, it smelled comforting and familiar.

"This one is yours," Dominick said, indicating a pristine yellow BMW convertible.

Like all the other cars in the garage, the BMW Z4 was meticulously detailed and polished within an inch of its life. Something about this specific one, maybe the color, or some type of new-car magic, made me certain this car was more than a loaner.

When I shot Dominick an accusatory glare, he raised his hands and added, "Messenger."

"Harrumph."

"Will you feel better if I call it a loaner?" he asked, obviously picking up on my discomfort.

"My pride will."

"You live in a special country of denial, Secret."

"Have you met me? It's more like a planet." I couldn't help but smile at him.

Dominick tossed a set of keys at me, and I tested the weight of the new object in my hand. It felt foreign but not unwelcome.

"Is it gonna blow up?"

Dominick laughed. "I doubt he'd go through all the effort of getting you back only to kill you."

I opened the unlocked driver's door and let the scent of new leather waft out. I'd never owned a new car before.

Just a loaner, I reminded myself.

"Dominick?" I stopped before climbing in.

"Mmm?" As always, he was grinning and his blue eyes were alight with some inner mischievousness.

I reconsidered my question, opening my mouth to speak, then looked away from him and into the car so I wouldn't have to see his face change.

"Was it bad? When I left, I mean."

He was quiet for so long I had to look back to be sure he was still there.

"For which one?" he asked, just as I was certain he wasn't going to respond. When I couldn't answer, he came and stood on the opposite side of the open car door and fixed a serious expression on me. I couldn't turn away. "It was different for both of them. For Lucas, he was so busy trying to hold the pack together, if he was hurting, he didn't let it show. But he needed you here. You killed Marcus, and whether you know it or not, that puts you in a pretty important position within the pack. I mean, like, Desmond-level importance."

"What? How?"

"You risked your life for the pack. You killed someone who meant to kill the king, and you defended the pack from total collapse. It makes you a pack protector."

"Is that a job title?" I didn't mean to sound so stupid, but there was still so much I didn't know about the world of the pack. I knew if I offered my protection to individuals, they became my responsibility under pack law. *Grandmere* had told me that was why she was able to live among werewolves even though she was human. But I wasn't aware the same rule applied to the pack as a whole. Had I made the entire pack my responsibility when I killed Marcus?

Dominick had waited for me to connect the dots, watching confusion change to understanding in my expression.

"You're pretty much the den mother now, Secret."

"So when I bailed, I wasn't just leaving Lucas."

"You were leaving the entire pack."

"Damn."

"Yeah."

I ran an open palm over the top of the car. "What about Desmond?" I didn't want to hear the answer, but I needed to ask.

"He's been waiting at the penthouse for you for months. He refuses to come out here and says protecting you was his responsibility and he failed. When he saw you in that basement, it took something out of him. He thought he was going to lose you."

I couldn't say anything. The difference between my two wolves became clearer every day. When I left, Lucas lost his mate, his partner in the pack. For Desmond, my running away meant he had watched me escape death only to lose me all over again, this time by my own choice. Lucas needed me to help him lead, but Desmond needed me for entirely emotional reasons. I regretted leaving him in Manhattan to come out here.

"Lucas still should have let me come back on my own."

Dominick barked a laugh. "He's royalty. Have you ever known royalty to wait patiently for anything?"

I smiled, only a little, but enough that the heavy thoughts around us seemed to lift.

"I missed you, Dominick."

He scooted around the door and wrapped me up in a warm, brotherly hug. He smelled like moss and sunshine. I hugged him back. It was nice to be close to another wolf without dealing with a riot of flavor in my mouth or the intense desire to be ravished. Dominick was comforting to me because he felt like the family I'd never known.

"It's good to have you home. I never got a chance to tell you I was happy you didn't die." He planted a light kiss on my forehead. "Give the boss a break on this one. You're good for him. He didn't know any better way to get you back."

"I need to make him sweat it out a little longer."

"You wouldn't be you if you caved too soon." He hugged me again, then added, "But go easy on my brother."

I wanted to make a joke about just how easy I'd been on his brother, but I stopped myself. "I'll be good."

"Well we both know that's not true." He smiled and let me get into the car, then closed the door behind me.

Outside the garage, I paused to put the top down. The car's engine purred while it idled, and I let myself enjoy the view of the stars. I'd wondered about the logic of giving a convertible to a half-vampire with an allergy to the sun. My concerns were resolved by the open air and the view of the night sky.

I was about to continue my course down the long driveway when a body vaulted itself over the passenger door and into the seat next to me.

"Hey." Kellen Rain was beaming like a lunatic. Her blue eyes were like her brother's, only they weren't tainted by the worry of leadership.

"Uh."

"Good thing you're taking the car. I was super close to convincing Luke to give it to me."

"Luke." I'd never heard anyone else call him by the abbreviated form of his name, and Kellen used it so easily.

"Oh man, Secret, I swear to God, I've never seen anything as funny in my life as you knocking him in the pool tonight. I thought I was going to pee." She looked away from me and to the driveway. "Are we gonna go or what?"

"Go?"

"Yeah, you know? Drive? To the city?" She pointed at the driveway. "Isn't that where you're going?"

"Yes."

"Then you wouldn't mind me tagging along, would you?" She obviously didn't expect any other answer than yes, because she was already buckling her seat belt. I stared at her for a moment longer, until she looked back at me with a bright smile and her altogether-too-familiar eyes. I shifted the car into gear and started to drive.

As we passed the main gate and the car eased onto the main highway, I broke the silence.

"Isn't there some sort of pack meeting in progress?"

"Sure. There always is this close to the full moon."

"Is it okay for you to leave?"

"Why wouldn't it be? You'll be in more trouble for leaving than me, considering you're pack protector. And, you know, future queen."

"Mmm," I grumbled, then remembered what Lucas had told me about Kellen months ago. "Wait, you're not a werewolf, are you?"

Kellen grinned and tapped her temple. "Bingo. No, I was never 'Awakened'." She made condescending little air quotes around the word. "I feel plenty awake though."

Awakening was the werewolf coming-of-age process, in which a young man or woman who carried the gene that would activate lycanthropy in them allowed themselves to be bitten by a full-fledged werewolf, thus becoming a werewolf themselves. It was an important rite of passage for werewolf families, but the choice was always up to the youth in question. Lucas opted to follow the family line, and Kellen chose to stay human.

In royal werewolf families, like the Rains, it was expected for the next generation to follow suit so the family would remain in power. Kellen had probably caused quite a stir in her family when she declined to be Awakened. It didn't seem to bother Lucas at all.

The car headlights cut a vibrant white swath across the black highway, and yellow lines flicked by us at an alarming speed. I was going too fast, but that was the vampire in me. Overhead, a strip of stars twinkled in the purple-black sky. Stars were a rare treat when you lived in New York City, but I'd gotten used to seeing them again while living in the country. Tall trees encroached on the highway, creating an ominous coniferous hallway of nothing but blackness.

The light from the headlights also made it difficult for me to discern if anything was lurking in the dark, one of many reasons I usually walked or ran instead of driving.

"Can I ask you something, Secret?"

It took a moment for me to shake out of my distraction. On top of the varied lighting, the scents sailing by me were overwhelming. Driving with the top down was a sensory overload.

"Sure."

"Do you love my brother?"

The car briefly swerved into the wrong lane before I caught myself, steadied the wheel and corrected the direction. "Wow."

"I'm sorry, I just wanted to know."

"I don't know, Kellen." I gripped the wheel a little too hard. "I haven't known him all that long."

"But he's courting you, you know?" The word courting sounded strange coming from the lips of a nineteen-year-old club kid. I knew what she meant, but it was still difficult to put the concept together with the person speaking it.

"I know."

"And you're soul-bonded."

"Yes."

"So, don't you, like, love each other by default?"

I stared at the highway. An updraft caught my hair and blew it across my face, then back up and over my head. It tickled the back of my neck. The air smelled like rain, but it wasn't close enough to cause immediate worry.

"I care about him."

"And what about Desmond?"

"We're not discussing this." I froze up, all my defenses locking into place. "We're *not* discussing my relationship with Desmond."

A thin smile spread across her lips, and I knew I'd given her all the answer she needed.

For the next hour we didn't speak. She found the radio and contented herself with a pop station. I hated every other song, but I didn't argue because it meant she wasn't asking me anything. When we were within view of the city skyline, she dropped a bomb on me.

"I used to be in love with Desmond."

I slammed on the brakes before colliding with a car that had slowed to a stop ahead of me. No longer moving, I turned and fixed my eyes on her.

"What?"

"Desmond. I was in love with him."

"Why are you telling me this?"

She shrugged. "It's not like it means anything. I was only fifteen, and he wanted nothing to do with me. We grew up together, so I was like a sister to him. But I guess I know what it's like. Loving him, I mean."

I didn't think Kellen had any grasp on what it meant to be soul-bonded. She was human, so she'd given up her claim on experiencing the werewolf version of finding one's soul mate. I doubted her fifteen-year-old schoolgirl crush on a then twenty-something Desmond was anything like what I felt for him. But how do you tell someone what they feel is wrong?

Chapter Twelve

After dropping Kellen off on the Upper East Side, I returned home. I walked into the apartment expecting to trip over shoes. When I didn't, I hesitantly took off my Louboutins—now destroyed from their foray into the pool—and dropped my purse on the floor. It fell with a loud thunk where the gun met the carpet. At least the gun hadn't gone swimming with me.

The apartment still smelled of vampire, and I sighed. Sig had said he would take care of the Brigit situation for me. Stupid, unreliable vampire.

"Brigit? Are you here?"

Rio the kitten plodded over and started rubbing against my bare ankles again. If the kitten was here, the blonde vampire couldn't be far. My vision had adjusted to the darkness, and though there was no one else in the room, it felt like I wasn't alone.

I shooed the kitten away with my foot, which seemed to please her because she began to purr. Hopefully Sig had fulfilled his promise about the power, because even though I could see in the dark, I didn't necessarily want to live without light.

I found the switch on the wall and flicked it up, expecting nothing. Instead, the room was flooded with warm light, and I could see my apartment for the first time since I'd gotten home. At least Sig had been true to his word on that point. There was still the matter of the vampire I smelled, though.

"Brigit? Seriously, I'm getting annoyed. More than usual."

I moved towards my bedroom and started to think I was a little crazy. The smell must have just lingered from all the months she'd been living here, because Brigit wasn't anywhere to be found. In my bedroom, the invitation of my bed was almost too strong to avoid. But first I needed to shower.

Feeling restored once three days' worth of blood, sweat and pool water had been cleaned off my skin and out of my hair, I towel-dried my curls and threw caution to the wind by not blow-drying them. Tomorrow my hair would be a mess, but I didn't have the energy to dry it tonight.

Wrapping a towel around me, I walked to my room with the carefree manner of someone who was truly alone for the first time in months. The second I crossed the threshold into my bedroom, I knew how wrong I'd been to ignore my initial instincts.

There was no time for me to react once I realized I wasn't alone. In one instant I was aware, and before I could open my lips to express shock, I was pushed hard against my bedroom wall with a hand covering my mouth and a strong, cool body pressed onto me.

The dark eyes and pale face looking back at me were so familiar I swore for a moment I must have been dreaming. But there was nothing erotic about this situation. Holden Chancery was in my bedroom, but this time he was altogether too real. My eyes were wide, but my pulse was slow and even. I was surprised, but at this point I still wasn't afraid.

I was, however, wishing I had on more than a towel.

When I didn't struggle, he stopped holding me so hard, but still firmly enough I couldn't get away. I may have been strong, but most vampires were still stronger. Conversely, I could kick most werewolves' asses in a fair fight. Maybe I was the perfect pack protector.

"Are you going to scream if I move my hand?" he asked.

I glared at him as if to say *you're kidding me, right?* He pulled his fingers away.

I took a deep lungful of breath, now that his hand wasn't blocking my mouth. I looked at him, trying to connect the man in my room to the Holden I knew. He was paler than usual. His skin had taken on a worrisome gray tone beneath the standard vampiric white. His brown eyes, which were always dark, were now almost black, and his pupils were huge. His hair, like in my dream, was longer than I remembered and too wild for him.

"Holden?"

"Welcome home." There was more than a little sarcasm and anger in his voice.

"Are you *insane?* You know Sig was here earlier, don't you?"

He took a step back, so he was no longer pressed against me, but he was still close and still holding me against the wall. He didn't want me going anywhere.

"I waited until Ingrid took Brigit away before I came in. I've been watching."

Rio had entered the room, but something about Holden upset her, because she was puffed up to twice her usual size and was making a weird howling noise low in her throat. Coming from a kitten, it sounded like the air being let out of a balloon. Holden ignored her.

"What are you doing here?" I put a hand in between us when he loosened his grip so I could keep my towel together.

"Did you come back to kill me?"

Now that he was here with me, I had the perfect opportunity to get the answers to the questions that had been nagging me for months. "What did you *do*, Holden? Why do they want me to kill you? Did you really go rogue?"

He snorted and rolled his eyes. "Honestly, Secret." But in spite of the cavalier tone, he didn't relax, and he was wound tighter than a spring. The whole room filled with tension.

"Holden."

"Do you think so little of me?"

"Don't answer a question with a question."

He moved back and took the few short steps to my bed, where he sat down and put his head in his hands, raking his fingers through his thick, dark hair.

"I didn't go rogue," he said finally.

"Then why are they saying you did? Why did they contract me to kill you?"

"I knew I was in trouble when someone told me you'd gotten the contract. The Tribunal only contracts you when they mean business. But then you left. I didn't know if I should be waiting for you to help me, or if you were letting me put my defenses down before you came after me. I reached out the only way I knew how. I needed to know what you planned to do."

I froze. "You mean by coming here tonight, right?"

"You *know* what I mean."

I pulled the towel tighter and started looking for something else to cover myself with.

"There's no point, I've seen it all already," he reminded me.

I glared at him and grabbed a robe off the arm of the chair by my door. It smelled like Brigit, but I didn't care right then. I put it on and let the towel drop.

"You invaded my dreams?"

"It's only an invasion if the receiving party fights it. You..." he looked right at me, "...didn't fight at all. You were so open, in fact, I got back in while we were both still awake."

So my awkward moment earlier tonight hadn't been my imagination. I shuddered from the deep feeling of violation. Worse still, according to him, I'd *let* him in.

"How?" I should have asked why, but it wasn't what came out.

He shrugged. "I was your warden. Wardens have a pretty unique connection with their wards. Before shit hit the fan, my power increased. I think I was about to advance to sentry. The extra power meant I could take better advantage of our connection. It didn't hurt when they advanced you to warden. The more power both parties have, the better the connection is. Or so I'm told. Getting into your dream earlier this week was my first attempt. And tonight, well—"

"*Never* again," I shouted. "You violated the most private experience. I should kill you for that."

"You could try. But you're unarmed right now. I'd kill you."

I couldn't stop myself. I crossed the room without thinking and punched him as hard as I could right in the face. It made a satisfying crack, and his head snapped back. Then he sat up straight, tentatively touching his nose, and a pinpoint of pain in my hand exploded to a full-blown searing agony. The crack I'd heard had been from one of my knucklebones breaking. I'd never broken my hand punching a vampire before. I was out of practice.

Broken hand or not, I hauled back to punch him again, but this time he saw it coming. He grabbed my wrist and pulled me easily onto the bed. I kept trying to lash out at him, until he climbed on top of me and held both of my hands above my head, sitting on my legs to keep me from attacking him with any well-placed kicks.

"*Calm down*," he snarled. "Jesus, Secret, I'm *sorry*. I opened up the connection with the dream, but I didn't know it would stay open. It wasn't intentional."

"You *bit* me." I still struggled against his hold, the desire to claw off his face now all I seemed focused on. "*You fucking bit me.*" If we were going to argue semantics, he actually bit me *while* we were fucking. But neither of us brought up that point.

"It was a dream," he reminded me.

"So? If you bit me in a dream, you probably want to do it in real life."

"You *let* me do it in the dream. Does that mean you want to do everything we did in the dream in real life?"

I stopped struggling. Goddamn vampires, how could they be so logical all the time, no matter the situation? The problem was I didn't know what the dream had said about me or what I wanted. I really didn't need him to know that. Sensing the fight had started to seep out of me, he released my arms.

I slapped him with my unbroken hand, but it was more of a statement than an actual attack. "You're an asshole."

"I needed to know if you were going to go through with the contract."

"I kind of want to now."

"You're not going to kill me because I was the *interruptus* to your *coitus.*"

Sighing, I looked up at my water-stained ceiling. He was still sitting on my legs, so I couldn't go anywhere. A captive audience, as it were.

"You swear to God you aren't rogue?"

"I don't believe in God, but I swear to the true immortals and the wrath of the Tribunal I'm innocent of whatever charges they have against me."

"You mean you don't even know what you're being accused of?"

"No. I just know I'm being framed for something huge, because no one is willing to help me. I figured they would have to tell you, if they'd convinced you to take the contract."

"Sig didn't give me a choice in taking the contract. I left, and he kidnapped me to bring me home so I'd complete it."

He let out a long sigh. "You have to help me."

"How am I supposed to help you?"

"You need to find out what it is I'm being accused of and prove I didn't do it."

"Would you like me to solve the mystery of the JFK assassination while I'm at it? Or perhaps you'd like me to waltz up to the Tribunal and say 'Well, he says he didn't do it, so let's brainstorm a new solution.'" I crossed my arms over my chest.

"Juan Carlos will eat the still-beating half-breed heart out of my chest before he tells me what you're accused of or believes me when I say you're innocent."

"What about Daria?"

"Daria follows the rules. She'd never break the council rule about guarding the accusation."

"Then you need to convince Sig. He's their leader, and he already has a weak spot for you."

I ignored his comment. "You risked your life coming here. Why?"

He rolled off me, allowing me to sit up, and rose to his feet. "I had to believe our history meant something. That you wouldn't immediately assume I was guilty."

"That was a big risk."

"Are you saying it hasn't paid off?"

When I got up we were standing face-to-face at the end of my bed. He looked down at me, worry deepening the lines around his eyes and mouth. How could I say no after everything we'd been through and all the times he'd saved my life in the past?

"If I'm wrong about this, they'll kill me," I confessed. No sense in sugarcoating it, the reality of our situation was ugly. "And then they'll kill you."

"If I'm wrong about you, I'm already dead." With cunning vampire speed, he dipped his head and kissed me. It sucked the breath out of my lungs and left my head spinning. Out of instinct I moved my hand to his neck so I could hold my balance, and then found myself kissing him back. The embrace was a whirlwind, and the cool electricity of the kiss swam all the way into my toes and sparked throughout my whole body. His lips were cold, but not in an unpleasant way. It felt like a kiss in the winter, one where you could see your breath when it was over.

He pulled away first, and I didn't fight him. I staggered a little, surprised by the intensity of the incident. Holden and I had always had a weird chemistry. We ignored it in the past, all but once, but now with the dreams and this unexpected kiss, it was hard not to think about it.

"My life is in your hands, you know." He touched my cheek, one cool hand against the flushed warmth of my skin. "I need to trust you."

"I—"

He was out of the room, and the sound of the front door clicking closed echoed through the darkness. I flopped backwards onto the bed and let out a whoosh of air.

Welcome home, indeed.

Chapter Thirteen

"You're on your own on this one, McQueen."

I was sitting in the office of Francis Keats, my business partner, mentor and one badass assassin. We were facing each other across a large oak desk in an unassuming study, neither of us suiting the role we filled. Keaty looked nothing like an assassin, which was one of the most genius things about him. He could have been a doctor or an accountant.

His dark blond hair was cut short and styled with precision. His shirt and pants were tailored, but generic enough to not say anything about his income or status, and his face was as unreadable as always.

I, on the other hand, was dressed as low-key as possible in my tank and shorts. My hair, as predicted, was a mess of curls down past my shoulders with no hope of being brushed smooth. I was biting my fingernail and tapping my shoe against the edge of his desk. He remained composed, but I knew him well enough to know I was driving him crazy.

"You have to help me, Keaty." I was repeating Holden's words from last night.

"I don't *have* to do anything, Secret. You know that perfectly well." He leaned back in his leather desk chair, lacing his fingers together across his stomach. The expression on his face told me nothing. This was the man who'd saved my life when I first came to the city. The man who had trained me to be the topnotch vampire killer I was today. And here he was, telling me he wouldn't help me in my hour of need.

"But—"

"No."

"I—"

His face broke from its meticulous calm, setting into a deep frown, his brow furrowing and all the fake friendliness seeping from his eyes. For an instant he appeared every ounce the killer he could be, and although he was a hundred percent human, right then I was genuinely afraid of him.

I stopped arguing.

If parents knew how to give that look, teenagers would never act out.

"The only time I'll help a vampire is if it involves killing another vampire. So if you want to let me kill Chancery for you, then by all means I'll help you. I will not, however, dedicate time and resources to help you prove he's innocent of some unknown vampire crime I don't give a rat's ass about."

Well, he didn't beat around the bush.

"I can't kill someone who is innocent, Keaty. It would be immoral."

"He's a vampire," he said, as if this made it okay.

"So am I."

"It's not the same." For all of his bravado and posturing, Keaty had one hell of a soft spot for me. He, who hated monsters in all shapes and forms, had made a huge exception when he allowed me into his life. Not only was I part monster, I was *all* monster. He—and Mercedes, who knew only of the werewolf half—seemed able to rationalize their way around this fact by focusing on how much they liked me as a person.

I decided not to fight Keaty on this point. He knew all too well what I was, and I found our relationship worked better when we didn't discuss it. He only brought it up when it benefitted us in some way.

Francis Keats, ever the pragmatist.

"I can't do this alone."

"Then kill him and be done with it."

I sighed loudly and picked up a large rock with no discernable purpose off his desk. I tossed it back and forth between my hands until he held his hand out, palm up, and waited. I dropped the rock into it, and he put it on the table behind him.

"The displaced soul of a Cheyenne shaman is trapped in that stone. I don't think he likes to be bounced around like a hacky sack."

I continued to tap my foot on the desk, and finally he relented.

"I can't help you *personally*, because I can't afford to burn my rather rickety bridge to the Tribunal. I need to stay in their good graces, you understand?"

I did, but I didn't want to admit it.

"I do, however, know of some people who might be able to steer you in the right direction. As much as it pains me."

He turned and unlocked the top drawer of a file cabinet behind him, then pulled out a small address book. From inside, he withdrew a business card and handed it to me. It was black, except for a small silver inscription which read *Bramley*.

"Bramley?" I flipped the card over, and then back, but it told me nothing else. I didn't know if Bramley was a person, a place or some kind of password. The font was Banknote Gothic, which told me nothing else about the mystery word except that it was pretentious.

Keaty leaned back in his chair again, looking every bit like the cat who'd gotten the cream.

"On 96th and 1st you will find an unassuming little hole-in-the-wall Irish pub. It has no sign, and it is not the most welcoming place." Sounded like a few werewolf and vampire locales I knew of, enchanted to make them unappealing to the human population. Keaty nodded to the card in my hand. "If you have that, you'll get past the man at the door." His lips tweaked into a smile.

"And after that?"

He sniggered a little, the amused sound out of place coming from Keaty.

"Just tell them your name."

"And how are a bunch of antisocial Irishmen going to help me?" I slipped the card into the front pocket of the ivory-colored linen shorts I was wearing.

"Let's put it this way, McQueen—if you and I are the Yankees of demon hunting, the folks at Bramley are the farm league."

My lip curled in disgust. "Wannabe vampire slayers?"

"I'd turn down the snobbery a few levels. In case you missed the memo, your favored status within the Tribunal hasn't exactly made you popular with the monsters who want to stay hidden. And working with me makes it pretty damned unlikely anyone with any information on your warden—"

"Sentry. He would be a sentry now." I remembered what Holden had told me about his power shift, and couldn't stop myself from correcting my partner.

Keaty didn't amend himself, he just looked annoyed by my interruption. "The bad guys can't trust you, Secret. You're too well connected and have too high a profile. The people at Bramley, they can still talk to your average, low-rung vamp or half-demon. If anyone knows anything, it will be them. Ask for Jameson."

"Well, it *is* an Irish bar." I smirked.

"The man, not the whiskey."

"Obviously, Keaty, geez." I rose from my chair, and he mirrored the motion, less out of chivalry than a killer instinct to stay on the same level as someone who could pose a threat to him. I was flattered and offended all at the same time.

I was wearing a sheer black top with the shorts, and a short-sleeved black jacket to hide my shoulder holster. After the last two days I had no intention of going anywhere without being armed, so my trusty SIG 9mm was sticking with me. For all the good guns seemed to do me. If I could avoid being knocked unconscious or shot, I could make use of one.

I was also sporting a brand-new accessory—a pretty, three-finger ring made of a heavy-duty alloy. It was a feminine take on brass knuckles. It also wasn't real silver or I would have no skin left on my fingers.

After my ineffectual smackdown on Holden the previous evening, I wanted more bang for my buck. Leary Fallon, the owner of the gun shop on 8th where I special ordered my silver bullets, was more than happy to sell me something that fit the bill. It even had little diamonds set in it to give it the illusion of a ring set.

"Just see what they know. If anyone can help you, it's Jameson," Keaty said, getting the final word.

I stepped out onto West 80th and was greeted by a wall of hot air and the putrid reek of summer garbage festering on the street corners. East 96th and 1st was on the complete opposite side of the city from where I was, and since I couldn't take the subway, I was left with few options—a cab or walking.

It wasn't that New York had a *no monster hybrid* policy for the transit system. The problem was I had difficulty controlling myself in small spaces. It was worse still in small spaces cramped with bodies. That spelled trouble for my self-restraint.

The last thing I needed was my fangs popping out on the A train during the evening commuter rush. I'd taken the subway a few times and the results were always the same—me, dizzy and anxious, desperate to get away from the crush of warm human bodies before the monsters in me decided to stop acting in opposition and finally worked together to create one hell of a memorable massacre.

I'd had my fair share of drama in the subways before. Not to mention, I hadn't eaten in over a day, which was foolish at the best of times and given my emotional turmoil would be a recipe for disaster.

Thanks, but no thanks. I'd rather be one of the good guys and stick to walking. A cab would have been nice, especially one with functional air conditioning, but we'd have to skirt Central Park and double back. Walking across the Park would save me time.

Not to mention money.

I hadn't checked my bank account since I'd been home, but I was fairly certain four months of rent, plus the overdue utility bills and my shiny new fisticuff bling, meant the five grand I'd earned for bringing in Alexandre Peyton would be almost gone. If you think your life doesn't have a price, you're wrong. Almost losing mine didn't even pay for the cost of living in a city like New York for six months. It was a sad statement on my existence.

I didn't exactly make a consistent income from the Tribunal. Keaty paid me biweekly, but since I'd been gone for three months, I understood why those checks hadn't kept coming.

I trotted down the steps of Keaty's brownstone, heading east towards the park. Ah, the glamorous life of a vampire hunter. I guess the plus side of it was I didn't have to worry about buying groceries.

I ensured the safety on my gun was off before entering the park. It was still early in the evening—couples and families continued to wander around the better-lit paths—but I planned on taking a more direct route, and one never knows what can be found in the darker woods of Central Park after nightfall.

Chapter Fourteen

I emerged no worse for the wear on East 83rd about twenty minutes later. I was grateful but a little disappointed by my uneventful walk. I was wound up, and I wasn't sure if I needed a good lay or a good fight to get my head right.

Probably both.

As I moved northeast through the nighttime streets of New York, I thought about the last day and a half. I'd woken up in bed with Sig, made love to Desmond, made out with Lucas and beat up—then kissed—Holden.

It was a little too much for me to deal with. I felt dirty just taking a mental inventory.

I used to think I was a one-man woman. Then, after a particularly disastrous blind date orchestrated by Mercedes with one of her fellow cops, I almost accepted being a no-man woman. A few months ago that had to be reassessed when Fate forced me to become a two-man woman. But there was no effing way I could be a four-man woman.

Even metaphysics couldn't keep that from being whorey.

Before I knew it I had arrived outside of a small brick building in a row of pathetic-looking small brick buildings. The garbage had been collected recently, so the lingering smell in the air was that of sweat and hot concrete.

Hot town, summer in the city.

"Can I help you, miss?"

It took me a moment to process the question because of the man asking it. He stood about three and a half feet tall, wearing all black, with a thicket of dark red hair. He was broad and had the semi-flattened nose of a boxer, which was incongruous with the explosion of freckles over his entire face. That same face told me he was all business, but his voice was what surprised me the most.

When this tiny, spritely man spoke, he had the voice of a chain-smoking, three-hundred-pound African-American blues singer. It was deep, hoarse and commanding.

I squinted at him, trying to tell whether his appearance was a masking charm for his true form. I didn't have the gift of magic-sight, sadly.

"Fae?" I questioned out loud, as if that would narrow things down.

Asking someone if they were fae wasn't an insult, but it was about as useful as asking a person if they were human. The fae were so varied and abundant I doubted anyone knew the full extent of their kind.

I'd only ever met a full-blooded fae in Calliope's realm. As a half-fairy/half-god, her fairy side was considered fae. No one would ever use the word out loud to describe her, as she would take it as a grave insult, considering her other half was—after all—a god. Fairies were counted as the highest level of the fae—magical, beautiful and immortal. The lowest levels of the fae were creatures like trolls or gnomes, but I'd never seen or heard mention of such things, so perhaps they weren't even real. I *had* met an ogre once.

The man who owned my choice gun store was mid-level half-fae, a land-bound merman with allure capabilities similar to a siren, which explained why his shitty-looking shop did such good business. And why I kept going back. Not to mention being the reason he never asked me what I wanted silver bullets for. Keeping things within the paranormal community had its benefits.

The guy in front of me looked, for all the world, like a leprechaun. But, standing in front of an Irish pub, with all that red hair? Wouldn't that be too clichéd?

"Maybe," he half-answered my query. "What's it to you, Blondie?" The deep voice was incredibly off-putting.

I fumbled in my front pocket and held the card out to show him. He looked from the card, to me, then back. He grumbled something under his breath which sounded Gaelic, then stepped away from the door. He thrust the card back into my hand as I passed, but didn't say another word to me.

"What the hell was that?" I asked myself once inside.

"That was Fagan." I was startled by the arrival of a large human man standing in the interior entrance of the pub.

This man was the exact opposite of Fagan. He was six feet tall and almost as broad as the doorframe. He had silver-gray hair, slicked back into a short ponytail, and his face showed signs of a hard and violent life. One scar bisected his cheek in an ugly, pale, six-inch gash. He looked to be about fifty but had one of those faces that could be ten years older or younger than it actually was.

"Fagan is a brownie. A hob." At first I thought the man might be tossing out insults, until I realized he was telling me what type of fae Fagan was. "They make the best doormen. Reliable, persistent, and I literally pay him in milk and honey." He chuckled.

"Guess that means if I follow him home later he won't take me to a pot of gold?"

"No. But he would take you to a great dim sum place. Dynamite pot stickers." He moved his bulk out of the door to let me in. The room was poorly lit and sparsely populated. It looked like every other Irish, English or Scottish pub I'd ever seen. There were scarred wood tables, Guinness paraphernalia, and various football trophies and scarves adorning the walls. It felt warm inside and smelled of good ale and the best whiskey.

There were enough hushed conversations taking place I couldn't focus on any one specific line of dialogue, and it came as a relief to not feel like I was intruding.

"Who gave you the card?" the big man asked. "I've never seen you before, so someone must have sent you to us," he explained, to soften his original, abrupt question.

I was still holding the card in my hand where Fagan had placed it.

"Keats," I said.

"Ah, the famous Mr. Keats. Did he consider himself above whatever problem you brought him?" The man smirked, and I kept my face impassive, but I was insulted on Keaty's behalf. We were partners, after all. "Poltergeist, is it? Or a dream demon, perhaps?"

"I'm looking for Jameson," I replied.

The condescending look disappeared from his face, and he fixed me with a hard, assessing stare.

"Well, you've found him." I had assumed as much, based on the authoritative manner he had adopted from the offset. "And who might you be, little lady?"

Keaty had said I should tell them my name, so I figured I might as well start there. "I'm Secret McQueen," I announced, building my slight frame up as tall as I could. I'm not much to look at, size-wise, but big surprises come in little packages.

Silence fell over the room like a sudden onset of fog. Behind the bar someone dropped a glass and the sound echoed outwards in a crystalline ripple. Every pair of eyes in the room fixed on me, and I tried not to let it make me nervous, but I was itching to go for my gun.

The silence held for longer than was comfortable. I guess my reputation extended beyond the vampire community.

The large man, now confirmed to be Jameson, cleared his throat, and on cue the patrons of the bar resumed their normal activities.

"My apologies, Miss McQueen—"

"Secret, please." I loathed the formality of Miss McQueen, and those who commonly used it were not the type of people I liked to correct, so whenever I had the opportunity to avoid the title, I did.

"Secret." He smiled. "What brings you to Bramley?"

"I need help with something and was hoping you or one of your associates might have some information."

He indicated a table in the back of the room, where two other patrons were already seated. He was giving us a little privacy to further discuss my situation.

I took a chair with its back against the wall so I could see the room and the entrance. Any assassin worth their salt knows you never leave your back exposed.

Jameson took the chair across from mine, clearly trusting that no one in the room meant him harm. I wish I could have felt so sure in any room. Beside Jameson was a young, somber-looking Japanese girl. I would have liked to call her pretty, with her straight black hair and flawless complexion, but her face was so rigid and tense it was difficult to judge her real level of beauty.

Beside me but out of reach was a man who appeared to be about my same age. He was of the ethnic minority I'd only ever seen in New York, which was the unique blending of Latino and African-American. He had strong features—pillowy, full lips and a jaw that looked carved out of marble. Beneath the white T-shirt he wore it was obvious he was well built and had the kind of large biceps that made me want to know what a hug from him would feel like.

His skin was a soft, honeyed brown, and his black hair had been cut so close to his scalp it was impossible to tell if it had once been curly. His eyes weren't brown, but rather an unexpected shade of gray, and his gaze was locked on my forehead. He looked as serious as the Japanese girl, but on him the expression was less practiced. Though his build and appearance would pigeonhole him as a thug, I suspected he was naturally prone to a cheerful disposition. His eyes gave him away, because they were too warm and lacked the deadened glaze of a true killer.

I liked to think mine still had a little glimmer of life to them too.

"This is Noriko." Jameson indicated the girl, who nodded tightly, never lowering her gaze. "And that's Nolan."

Nolan smiled and moved to offer me his hand before catching a disapproving glare from Jameson and resuming his stoic pose.

"Pleasure to meet you," he said in spite of himself. "We hear lots 'bout you 'round here."

Jameson sighed dramatically, and Nolan recognized his mistake. It was also my introduction to Nolan's unique voice, which was low and smooth. He seemed unable to attach the letter A to the beginning of words and had a classic Brooklyn accent that warmed my heart.

"What kind of information are you looking for?" Jameson asked.

"I've been contracted to eliminate a rogue threat by the name of Holden Chancery." I watched them for any flicker of recognition and got nothing.

"And?"

"I believe Mr. Chancery's contract is...unjust. In order to prove it, I need to find out what he's been accused of."

Another long silence, this one isolated to our table, hung in the air. It was Nolan, not Jameson, who finally spoke up.

"You mean you want to help *save* the vampire?"

"Yes."

"But, you're like some big-shot vampire slayer, ya? The biggest, baddest, 'ccording to word on the street."

"I'm not disagreeing with that."

"Then I don't get it."

Jameson must have been just as curious, because he hadn't stopped Nolan from talking.

"This vampire is a friend. I trust when he says he's innocent. He's always had my back." I hoped they could appreciate that.

Noriko stared at me with an expression so cold I got a chill.

"I came to you people because I thought you might want to save a life, rather than running around trying to take them," I finished.

"We *do* save lives, Miss McQueen," Jameson said, back to formal titles. "Every vampire we kill is a dozen lives we've saved."

I formed my mouth into a thin line, and I narrowed my eyes at him. "You're a fool if you think killing one vampire will save lives. The vampires you kill, the ones you can catch, they're babies. Probably less than fifty years old and untrained in avoiding maniac vampire-slayer wannabes. If you ever met a true rogue, it would rip you and everyone in this bar to pieces in seconds. The true rogues are older than this city." This was, of course, not true. Most rogues were middle-aged by vampire standards. One or two hundred years old and hell-bent on some sort of destructive agenda. They would still murder a group of mediocre slayers, though. The older vampire rogues, the ones who didn't care about anything but bloodshed, they were the really scary ones. Vampires who didn't care for the laws that kept their existence a secret, and only cared about the feed.

I'd known a few of them in my time, and those rogues even made me fearful for my life. When all you care about is death, you have little else to lose. Those vampires were the scariest. I doubted anyone in this room had ever met a vampire more than thirty years dead.

I rubbed the bridge of my nose and fought off the looming headache a few minutes longer. I was crankier than usual, thanks to my hunger, and being irritated wasn't helping. There was no avoiding it; I'd need to stop at Calliope's before I went home. I needed blood.

"I'm sorry. I know you think what you do is noble, and in theory it is. But there are vampires who mean no harm to humans."

"Every vampire means harm to humans," Nolan said, and pain flashed over his face. There was a story there, and I wanted to know it.

"Look, my mother was almost killed by a vampire, I *get* it," I replied. This was, for all intents and purposes, true. What I didn't mention was the vampire in question had been my formerly human father, and thanks to the vampire blood he fed her, I became the freak show I was today. My confession seemed to soothe Nolan's frustration.

"If they almost killed someone you love, how could you work for them?" he asked.

I didn't bother explaining how often I wished my father had finished the job, or how there was *no* love between Mercy McQueen and me. My personal history didn't belong here because no one would ever be able to deal with the complexities of it all. I barely could.

"The vampire council exists to protect humanity, whether or not you want to believe it. They police vampires and make sure humanity never learns the truth about the existence of vampires in the world. That keeps human collateral to a minimum."

"Human collateral?" Nolan looked disgusted. My word choice was poor at best, but I'd been with the monsters too long. Even I sometimes saw death that way.

"I'm a killer, Nolan," I admitted. "I'm not the most...delicate person to explain this."

Jameson drummed his fingers on the table, returning my attention to the rest of the group.

"Given our clear ineptitude at vampire hunting, how would you propose we help you?" He was clearly offended, but I suspected it was more because I'd drawn awareness to the truth rather than spoken a lie. He must have lost others to more experienced rogues and had probably earned his nasty scar in a similar fashion. If Jameson had survived a fight with a true rogue, I owed him more respect than I had been giving him, and I decided to operate henceforth as if he had earned it.

"I'm too well-known," I admitted. "I don't have the same access to information you do. I thought one of you might have heard of something, some reason why a vampire warden would be declared a rogue."

"As you pointed out," Jameson said, "we don't pay much attention to the distinction between rogue and non-rogue vampires." The disdain was still evident in his voice, but he was talking to me, which was a good enough sign for me to press on.

"You must keep an ear to the ground, though. Vampires are easier to kill once they're removed from the council's immediate protection. I'm guessing the ones you guys most commonly see are young vampires attempting to live alone for the first time. If Holden had been exiled from the council, there must have been some kind of a buzz about it."

"At Havana the other—" Nolan was interrupted by both Noriko and Jameson cursing for him to be silent, but it was too late.

"Havana? You let your people go to the vampire bar?" I was shocked.

"Not into the bar, no." Jameson sighed. "Everyone here is human except for Fagan and a few other half-fae. It would be far too risky to send them in. They would be under the thrall before they passed the coat check."

Smart man. He was a better leader than I'd expected.

"But we do often send people out to patrol nearby in case a vampire should go out alone and attempt to feed."

Jesus. I could only imagine some vampire, with his enthralled feed for the night, no intention of taking any lives, brought to the final death by the Scooby Gang here. It made me a little sad. These people needed proper training and real knowledge about vampires. I didn't say anything, because I didn't want to add to the damage caused by my previous outburst, but under the surface I was seething.

"I was patrolling the other night," Nolan explained. He apparently had already done the damage by telling me about their presence outside Havana, because neither Noriko nor Jameson stopped him this time. "I didn't find no solo vamps, but I heard two of them talking. They were saying something 'bout a 'half-breed lover'? I didn't know what that meant." He shrugged. "But they said something like 'he never was good at keeping secrets.'"

That stung. I'd always known Holden dealt with a lot of flack for being my warden, primarily because I was a difficult charge to keep in line, but more so because the other vampires didn't trust me. He suffered for being my friend. The secrets the vampires mentioned were just a singular Secret.

I tried to look unmoved by his words, but I couldn't mask the pain in my eyes, so I lowered them. Thank goodness no one at the table was a werewolf, because I didn't want any of them to mistake the action for submissiveness. They'd have walked all over me after that, deserved or not.

"I appreciate your time," I said, when the tone of my voice wasn't at risk of giving me away.

Without a doubt in my mind, I now believed Holden had been framed because of me. I'd gone from being unsure of whether or not I could trust him, to feeling guilty for his current situation. It wasn't to say that whatever he was accused of was related to me directly, because there was little they could pin on him there. No, he was on the run now because other vampires *believed* he was guilty, thanks to his relationship with me.

I rose from the table, as did Jameson and Nolan. Only Noriko remained seated, her dark eyes never looking away from my face. She hadn't missed the pain. I extended a hand to Jameson, as both a farewell and a peace offering.

"I'm sorry," I continued. "For not being more supportive of the work you do." I wanted to lecture them on the differences between types of vampires a little more, but some people will never see a vampire as anything other than evil. Maybe they were the smart ones.

"I don't know if we were of any help." His voice had lost its former edge. We had reached an understanding, it seemed. He looked me in the eyes, and his handshake was firm and dry. Jameson saw me as an equal. While I would have rather he viewed me as his superior, at least in this field, I would accept equality. A twenty-two-year-old girl wasn't going to get anything better from a fifty-something man, and I was lucky to get that.

Once I dropped his hand, I did something I bet none of them expected. I turned to Nolan, and instead of shaking his hand, I pulled him in for a hug. The purpose was twofold, but I was counting on them only understanding half of it.

As expected, Nolan didn't fight the hug. He let me embrace him and pushed the gesture further by placing a hand on my lower back, as Lucas was so fond of doing, and pulling me closer. I *had* wanted to know what a hug in those arms felt like, and found my answer. It was solid and comforting, and though I was testing him, I couldn't help but enjoy it a little.

The point, as Jameson and Noriko would understand it, was that I'd proven how ineffectual Nolan was as a fighter. He hadn't resisted my invasion into his space. He didn't try to go for my gun to disarm me, and he'd willingly allowed me into his defensive zone. Foolish boy.

But my purpose was more sinister than they could have anticipated. While I was close to him, I nuzzled my face as close to his neck as I could, given how tall he was, and I took a big whiff. With so many different smells clouding the air in the bar I wanted to be certain I could recognize Nolan's specific scent again. That he had let me get so close to his neck only proved how unprepared he was for the work he was doing.

Nolan, the would-be vampire slayer, had let a hungry half-vampire press herself right up to his jugular. Another hour or two without eating and the temptation would have proven too much for me. As it was, breathing in the luscious, musky smell of him, my fangs extended with anticipation. I clamped my mouth shut and stepped back. Patting Nolan on the cheek, I gave him a sad, tight smile, and shared a look with Jameson to be sure he understood what I'd just shown him.

His white, sweat-dappled face assured me the point had been made.

I didn't say anything else, because I couldn't risk flashing fang at them. Once they were exposed, I needed to feed. If I was in better control, I could calm myself down enough to retract them, but I wasn't going to get that lucky tonight. The monster was out, and it called for blood.

Instead, I nodded curtly to everyone and took my exit. They let me leave without further comment.

In the alley, I was once again alone with Fagan, who had relaxed his doorman attitude a little now that he knew I wasn't a potential threat to Bramley.

"Get what you needed?" he asked me, his deep voice filling the dark alley.

I looked up at the night sky, admiring the low, three-quarter moon. "Not yet," I confessed, keeping my lips tight and gritting my teeth together. "But I have a plan."

Chapter Fifteen

The twenty-four-hour Starbucks on the corner of West 52nd and 8th was hardly spectacular to look at. Like several other New York outposts of the chain, the exterior was painted brown to give the white letters a little extra pop. If you made it through the doors and onto the other side, the back interior wall had a long mirror along the top half, allowing the light from the two windowed walls to reflect farther into the room. There was a row of banquette seating for several two-person tables. These tables were almost always occupied by one person and a laptop, the new New York power couple.

I walked through the doors at least once a week, but I almost never made it inside.

This particular Starbucks was special for one reason—it served as a gateway to a separate reality from the human world. The realm on the other side of the door was only accessible to someone of the paranormal persuasion who was in genuine need. However, it was forbidden for werewolves or wereanimals of any kind to enter.

Because time functioned differently there, wereanimals couldn't count on their control to work as it should. Without the ebb and flow of the moon, they might shift unexpectedly, which would be disastrous. A werewolf who shifts against its will is not only angry, it is a force with which there is no reckoning.

My wolf had been so repressed by the calming influence of my vampire blood, I didn't shift even at the height of the full moon. So Calliope, mistress of the alternative reality gatehouse, made a unique exception for me.

I stepped through the door of the Starbucks, and for one heart-pounding second I feared I might not cross over. My need was genuine, though. My gums were throbbing with the pain of extended fangs, and my jaw hurt from keeping my mouth clamped shut. If I didn't end up in Calliope's waiting room, everyone in the Starbucks would be in trouble.

Thankfully, the world got hazy and dark, and when it refocused, the room I was in looked nothing like a coffee shop. I'd never been happier to see Calliope's oddly decorated waiting room than I was right then. The last time I'd been in the immortal's home, I'd been so close to death at least a few people didn't believe I was going to pull through.

The memory of the defeated look on Desmond's face made my chest tighten. He hadn't been able to be with me when I healed, and I doubted that had helped our situation.

The mansion was one of a kind. It didn't abide by the laws of physics. It could expand in size depending on the need, so it could have as many or as few rooms as the moment demanded. It could also be day and night simultaneously, so the sun might be shining in windows upstairs, while the courtyard outside could be bathed in moonlight. Calliope's was the only place I'd ever seen the sun, as artificial as it was. The mansion was an augmented reality, and even though you couldn't trust any of your senses, there was something comforting about it.

This room in particular invited a long stay. Large, high-backed armchairs and a couple of couches lined one wall. On the adjacent side, a fire was lit, which helped the small number of wall-mounted lamps illuminate the room. Persian rugs were scattered in a haphazard fashion across the floor, most in deep jewel tones, and the whole room was adorned with paintings of Calliope.

It wasn't that she was vain, but rather she was proud. She had been a muse for many men in a variety of her human forms, and she appreciated the art they had created in her honor. Calliope was only a half-god, but all deities loved a good offering.

I'd been in the room many, many times, and the number of occupants varied every time. Today it was empty. Sometimes it housed other paranormals in need, and sometimes there were dazed-looking teen boys who had recently donated some blood or aura energy to feed Calliope's cravings. Those boys always left well paid and a little lacking in the memory department.

We all have our odd proclivities.

The large doors opened at the end of the room, bathing the whole space in warm light, and Calliope drifted in.

The woman herself would have looked familiar to anyone. One of Calliope's forms on Earth had been that of Marilyn Monroe. She had taken the body of poor Norma Jean and transformed her into one of the most recognized sex symbols in the world. Then she'd gotten bored, as immortals often do, and left Norma Jean and Marilyn in an aura of mystery and eternal fame.

Sometimes she was attended by an enormous white tiger, whose origin and purpose I had never questioned. Tonight she was alone. She was leaner now than she'd been in her Marilyn years, and her hair was its natural shade of raven-wing black. Her wardrobe varied between goddess chic and twenty-something casual. Tonight she was wearing a knee-length peacock-print dress, with a low neck and back and a bouncy hemline. Her hair was braided and hung down her back in a thick rope.

"Secret!" Her voice was childlike, sweet and bubbly, and didn't hint at the power that lurked within. She danced across the room and wrapped me into an embrace before I could stop her. Typically I didn't like people getting too close to me, but Calliope wasn't people, and she didn't intend me any harm.

Calliope was a trusted friend of the vampire council. They would send her newborn vampires who were still unable to control themselves within the human population. She weaned them with bagged blood and helped them learn to keep their fangs to themselves, or at least to willing victims.

A vampire needed to be able to feed without killing before the council would trust them out in the world, and that was where Calliope came in. Her help meant the council got to keep its secrets and new vampires got to avoid meeting me alone in the dark.

I hugged Calliope back and relaxed. I'd never met a pure-blood fairy, so I didn't know if they had a scent I would recognize or if the god part of her cancelled out anything I might be able to pick up on. Calliope always smelled like nothing.

She placed a hand on either side of my face and looked me in the eyes. She was still smiling, but her gaze told me she was judging my condition. "Let's see."

I opened my mouth, and she clucked her tongue at me. "Left it too long, I see."

"Almost," I admitted.

"Come on, then." She took my hand and led me out of the room.

In a bedroom I had started to view as mine, Calliope sat me down on the sun-dappled window seat and leaned in close to get a good look at my eyes.

"Secret, why do you push yourself like this?"

"I was busy, and—"

"There are no excuses." She sat on the bed and fixed me with a stern look. The Oracle, in spite of how youthful she looked, had always been something of a mother figure to me. To see the look of disappointment in her eyes made my heart sink.

"I'm sorry."

"You could have lost control." She leaned closer to me and placed the back of her hand against my cheek. "The risks are too high for you to be so foolish."

I bit my tongue. She was being a little harsh. I knew I'd left feeding for far too long, but nothing had happened. Her reaction was a bit dramatic.

"I don't understand why you're making such a big deal out of this. I'm here now, aren't I?"

Calliope dropped her hand and sat back. I could tell she wasn't happy. "You are closed to me."

I had no idea what she meant, but I didn't like the sound of it. She opened a small fridge hidden inside the nightstand and threw a bag of blood to me.

Then she continued. "Your whole mind is focused on the need to consume. It's drowning out your spirit." She cocked her head to the side and watched me as I bit open the bag and began to feed. "Your future is lost."

I choked on the blood. "Lost *how*?"

"There is much I need to tell you, especially about your warden. But your path is no longer clear. Without your spirit intact, I know nothing. I can't see what your future holds."

She stood up and touched my hair, shaking her head sadly, then turned and left the room.

She didn't come back.

I exited the Starbucks an hour later, my cheeks rosy and a conspicuous Styrofoam container clutched in my hands. Having eaten, I no longer felt the need to kill every human in a twenty-foot radius. The contents of the container meant I wouldn't need to worry about getting *that* bad for another week.

I was nearly home, which was only a three-block walk from the Starbucks, when my phone rang. It had been awhile since I'd been on the receiving end of a call, and the sound of Tom Petty's "Free Fallin'" coming from my jacket pocket startled me. I fumbled for my phone, precariously balancing the cooler on my hip as I flipped the cell open to talk.

"Hello?"

"Can we talk?" It was Lucas.

Now that I was in front of my building, I paused and said nothing.

"Secret?" I could tell by his tone he was trying to be patient, but I knew I sometimes made this difficult. I wedged the phone between my shoulder and ear, listening to him breathe while I tried to find my keys. I wished he were breathing next to me.

"What is there to say?" I asked, unlocking my entrance door and stepping into the small landing. I leaned against the wall, not ready to be alone in my apartment with his voice in my ear.

"I don't regret what I did to bring you home, and I won't apologize for doing it."

Well, we were off to a good start. My sharp intake of breath must have let him know I wasn't pleased with his statement.

"Good*bye*, Lucas." I wasn't actually prepared to hang up yet; I just wanted him to know I wasn't impressed. He took advantage of the pause that followed my false farewell.

"Listen to me." His tone was even, but it was an order. I didn't want to yield to his power as king, but I *was* half wolf, and that part of me found it impossible not to listen. "I *am* sorry you were hurt, and I'm sorry I couldn't tell you what the vampire had planned, but that's because I didn't know. And I *couldn't* tell you anything, because you didn't tell me a damn thing about where you'd gone."

"Okay."

"Okay, what?"

"Okay, I should have told you where I was going."

"You never should have left in the first place."

I sighed angrily and kicked my front door. Not enough to damage it, because I was sure I didn't have enough in my bank account to pay for a new one. "You don't get to decide that, Lucas."

"You didn't give me an opportunity to talk you out of it."

"You couldn't have."

"Could Desmond have done it?"

And there it was. The two of them could pretend all they wanted that they were okay with sharing me, but I'd known it bothered Lucas more than he had let on, and now he had all but admitted I was right. It must have cut deep that even though he was the king, it was his second-in-command who had gotten me into bed first. And second. And third.

"No," I answered truthfully.

Another long pause.

"I left because of what happened. I left because I was worried you *and* Desmond would never be able to look at me the same after you found out what I was. I mean, I drank your blood, Lucas. Isn't that sort of a relationship deal breaker?"

"God*dammit*, Secret. This isn't time to be glib."

I wanted to ask if there was ever an appropriate time for me to be glib, because it seemed like all the times I did it weren't the right ones. I unlocked my front door after a long struggle with the key and let myself in to the dark apartment. We both breathed at each other over the phone and said nothing.

"I thought you would hate me," I admitted, putting the container of donor blood bags in the fridge. "And I wanted to avoid knowing that as long as I could."

"I don't hate you," he replied, his voice almost a whisper.

"Dominick says you needed me back so you could assert your authority better. He says I'm the pack protector now."

"Yes, but that's not why I needed you back."

I made a mental note to ask him more about my new position within the pack later, because this didn't seem like the appropriate time to change the subject. "Why, then?"

He sucked in a breath, and I could hear him pacing back and forth over a hardwood floor. It sounded like he was in his bedroom suite at the hotel. He'd come in from the country, and being so close to the full moon, with an unsteady pack on his hands, meant he'd come for only one reason. Me.

I sat on one of the two small stools in my puny little kitchen and let my head rest against the wall behind me. Neither of us spoke for a long time. "Tell me why, Lucas."

"I needed you back because..." He searched for the right words, which I already knew, but had to hear him say.

"Say it," I whispered.

"Because I love you."

After what felt like an eternity, I said, "I forgive you." Then I hung up.

Chapter Sixteen

Try as I might, I couldn't relax after my conversation with Lucas. I attempted to watch TV, but I couldn't focus on what people were saying in the cheery 1960s romantic comedy I had on. I tried to fall asleep early, but I was too amped up from the blood. When I willingly picked up Rio and scratched her behind the ears, I knew I had to leave the apartment.

The purring kitten protested with little mewls as I tied up my running shoes, but I ignored her. I dug my iPod out of the bedside dresser and was thrilled to see it had maintained a little battery life since I'd been gone. Enough for a run, anyway.

Back in Central Park for the second time that night, this time with only an hour or so until sunrise, I turned my iPod on and began to run. My running music of choice was a mix of Nina Simone and Bob Seger, which wouldn't make sense to most, but the slower pace of the music kept me from running too fast. If I ran at the speed I was capable of, it might draw unnecessary attention.

Not that anyone was outside right then to witness it, but it was always best to keep up my illusions whenever I could. If you got too sloppy, it could spell trouble later on when it really mattered. Bob began to sing "Night Moves", and I let my feet fall into step with the music as I headed towards the Ramble. Being in the deeper woods reminded me of Elmwood and made my wolf half feel relaxed.

The music took me away from my thoughts, and running on the twisty hills and unpaved paths of the Ramble meant I had to pay attention to something other than the churning worry in my gut. The night was still hot, but it no longer smothered me, and every so often I would round a bend and feel the reward of a slight breeze over my cheeks.

After about ten minutes, and in the middle of Nina Simone's "Feelin' Good", I heard a sound, like the crack of weight on dry wood, that made me stop dead. I ripped the headphones out of my ears and stood, not breathing, in the middle of a low path with rock faces rising above me and the moon reflecting off the surface of the pond to my right.

I was so still I could have heard anything, from a rabbit moving in the brush, to the swishing feet of the swans in the water. A pair of joggers came down the path towards me, their feet slapping pavement in perfect unison. They nodded to me as they passed, and I turned to watch them until they were gone. The sound of their shoes was nothing like the noise that had made me stop, but I was prepared to admit my music might have distorted my perception. I pivoted back to the path.

Where I walked directly into Sig.

I kept from screaming, but just barely, and only because I recognized him. Even so, he'd doubtlessly noticed the change in my heartbeat and could probably smell the fear I was feeling.

"Nice night for a run," he said.

I could have killed him.

Sig couldn't have looked more pleased with himself. He was wearing a long-sleeved black shirt and well-tailored black slacks. The slacks made me wonder what happened to the brown leather pants he used to favor so much. He had his hands placed in his front pockets and was barefoot as usual.

I often marveled at how Sig moved around the city without bothering to put on shoes and never seemed to be any worse for it. Vampires couldn't fly, but he must have had some uncanny gift to keep from stepping on glass. It made me wonder if he left the comfort of the Tribunal all that often, or if coming to see me was more unusual than I had previously considered.

He rocked back on his heels and smiled his sly smile at me. The Tribunal leader was up to something.

"If you're here to kidnap me, I've had my quota for this month, thanks."

"Nonsense, Secret. If I wanted you to come with me, you'd come."

I wasn't sure what he meant by that, but it terrified me. I didn't want to believe I'd be powerless against him, but if I was the betting sort, I'd put my money on Sig being absolutely right.

My iPod switched over to Seger's "Turn the Page", but the sound was coming from farther away since my headphones were draped over my shoulders.

"Walk with me," he instructed.

The stubborn part of me that wanted to show him how independent I was insisted I stay rooted to the spot. But this wasn't a time for playing games with an old and very scary master vampire. Sig had never done anything to me to warrant my constant fear of him, but a vampire didn't live for twenty centuries without being a little cutthroat. Sig's greatest power was in convincing people he meant them no harm.

In his presence, that gift poured over me, and I relaxed against my better judgment.

Of course he won't hurt you, the voice in my head told me.

I knew better, but I also believed if he meant to harm me tonight, I wouldn't have gotten his initial warning sound. He would have just come to me in the darkness and ended it all. That I was certain he could kill me so easily should have been reason alone to not follow him.

Instead I jogged to catch up to where he'd gotten on the path.

"How is your task coming along?" he inquired, as though he was any normal boss and I was working on any old project.

I shrugged. "Working on it."

"Do you think, perhaps, it might have been wise to do something about it when he was in your apartment last night?"

I stopped walking, and Sig took another step or two before he stopped as well. Flabbergasted, I couldn't understand how he knew or how he could be so calm about it. He tilted his head to the side, an invitation to continue walking. I looked back up to the rock face and tried to see if there was a trap waiting for me.

"You're quite safe. For tonight." He extended an arm, inviting me to move closer.

I did, and he put his arm around me, pulling me tight against his side and holding me close enough I knew it wasn't a purely friendly gesture. We walked in silence because all the noises of the woods had quieted in his presence. Everything hidden in the dark was withdrawing, and I wished I could do the same.

"He didn't do it," I insisted.

"Mmm." His hand squeezed my shoulder and it hurt. "Did young Mr. Chancery tell you that?"

"He didn't have to."

"So you no longer want to know what he's done, because you are so certain he is innocent?"

It wasn't what I said, but I didn't feel up to correcting him. "Something like that."

"You've been to see the Oracle tonight." It wasn't a question.

"Yes," I confirmed anyway.

"And did she tell you anything about Holden?" For the briefest flicker his voice sounded hopeful, and it all became clear. I halted again, and this time he was forced to stop along with me or risk knocking me over.

Sig couldn't ask Calliope about Holden's guilt or innocence, because he was banned from Calliope's realm. Some time during the Renaissance they had been an item, and he'd broken her heart. The thing they say about hell having no fury like a woman scorned? You can amplify it a thousandfold for an immortal. Calliope was still mad, and to my knowledge the only time he'd been permitted in her reality, she had forced him to stay outside and had only let him get that far because he'd come to see me.

My eyes searched his, hoping for some further evidence of the hope I'd heard in his voice. Something in his face had to tell me I wasn't jumping to insane conclusions. He looked curious but little else.

It only then dawned on me. "You think he's innocent too."

"What did the Oracle tell you?" He wasn't denying it, and that was close enough to an admission to satisfy me.

"Calliope couldn't tell me anything." I could tell he didn't believe me because disappointment knit his brows together. I explained why Calliope hadn't been able to read anything off me that night. "I was too far gone for her to see my path. She had to feed me."

I wished I'd thought to visit Calliope as soon as I got home. Had I known how linked Holden's path was to my own, I might have realized she could give me some of the answers I craved.

"Stupid girl," he seethed.

Sig and I stared at each other, a breeze rustling the charged air between us. He grabbed my other arm so suddenly I didn't see his hand move. I knew vampires were fast, but this was unlike anything I'd experienced before. There was no blur of motion, nothing to indicate he'd moved at all. It was as though his hand had always been on my arm.

My heart tripped a little as he bent his head and lowered it to my neck. I was trembling, but just as he'd warned, I did nothing to stop him. He was so tall he had to stoop down to reach me. His lips brushed the skin of my neck against the rattle of my trapped pulse, and goose bumps rose all over my body.

He was doing exactly what I'd done to Nolan, by demonstrating how unprepared I was. The shock of it was enough to shake me into action.

I closed my eyes and called up my vampire half. Between being freshly fed and engaging my werewolf with the run, the vampire part of me had been content to rest dormant, but now I was reaching deep inside myself to pull it out of its restful state. It wasn't happy.

I hauled back and punched Sig. My new knuckledusters did an admirable job of making a solid crunch against his jaw, and at least this time the sound wasn't made by my bones. He barely flinched, but he did straighten up and release my arms. My fangs were extended, this time for a fight, not the feed. I snarled at him, and in return, he smiled. Maybe I couldn't hurt a master vampire in hand-to-hand combat, but at least I could still surprise him.

He started walking again, touching his jaw as he spoke. "Something about the accusation of Holden never sat right."

I stood trembling in the middle of the path, a trickle of cold sweat sliding from the back of my neck all the way down my spine. It had been a test. One I gathered I had passed. What if I hadn't resisted? Would he have actually bitten me?

Looking at him as his lithe, tall form disappeared down the trail, I wondered what I was to Sig. Ingrid referred to me as his pet. Calliope seemed to imagine something different, but she never voiced what that was to me. I had just seen the disapproval on her face when he'd come to see me. I'd never been able to understand why he showed so much interest in me.

This time I didn't run to catch up with him. He was walking slow enough my regular pace was suitable, and I was soon in step behind him. I was thankful he didn't try to make me walk next to him again. That much contact rendered me at his mercy apparently, and I didn't want to be at the mercy of Sigvard, Finnish vampire and destroyer of immortal hearts.

Once I was close again, he continued. "Holden is a meticulous record keeper, I don't know if you know that about him." He didn't wait for me to answer. "He has dozens of journals, and he has a keen mind for detail. They go back decades, these books he has, but they seem to have increased in number in the last five or six years."

The emphasis on the time wasn't lost on me. Holden had been assigned the unwelcome task of becoming my warden six years ago.

Sig continued. "See, Holden has records of everything. He wrote about meeting you for the first time. I believe his phrasing was 'irritating teenager hell-bent on her own destruction, won't live out the year'." His muted Scandinavian accent dropped away in a perfect imitation of Holden. It was so spot on I was too stupefied to even reply to the insult. Besides, when Holden met me, I *had* been a stupid, foolhardy sixteen-year-old. His description was almost polite.

"So, Holden wrote a lot. What does that prove?"

Sig shot me a warning look over his shoulder. So this was going to be a monologue, not a discussion. I could handle that, couldn't I?

"Funny thing about those journals is that he stopped sharing them with the council about two years ago. Funnier still, most of Holden's current problems can be traced back about that far." He paused and looked at me meaningfully.

I still didn't understand. Nor did I think any of what he mentioned was very funny. So Holden had journals, and he kept them a secret. Big deal. If I had a diary, I wouldn't want Sig to read it either.

Then something occurred to me. "Wait, I know you can't tell me *what* he's accused of, but if it's something specific, there must be a date involved. Can you tell me *when* it happened?" My heart skipped a beat. If Sig believed Holden was innocent, then maybe there was a way to get his help without ignoring the rules of the Tribunal.

He smiled and put his hands back in his pockets.

"Dates." He looked up at the dark night sky and rocked back on his heels. Then he turned to leave, speaking as he walked. "Dates can be so fleeting. I can say things like August 14, 2009. Or December 6, 2008." I stopped breathing when he said the latter. My birthday? "I don't know if dates will help you. I just know something didn't sit right about the warrant."

Sig vanished into the darkness, leaving me alone and cold against the heat of the summer night. He had told me something important; I just wished it wasn't shrouded in so much mystery.

Why couldn't vampires ever say what they meant?

Chapter Seventeen

When I awoke the next night, there was a voicemail from Lucas waiting on my cell phone. It was short and to the point. "I'll be at Two Moon Grill at ten, and I hope you'll meet me there." After I'd listened to it for the twelfth time, I stopped arguing the multitude of reasons I couldn't go—I had to find who was framing Holden, after all—and settled on one very good reason I should go. I had a werewolf king who was in love with me.

Problem was, I had been neglecting a major part of my warden assignment, and if I didn't want Sig sending Brigit to live with me again, I was going to have to check in on my charge. The last thing I needed was more attention being drawn to me because I wasn't doing my job for the council, and at least this job I was still somewhat willing to do.

That was how I found myself seated at the foot of a king-sized bed, in a cozy, furnished apartment in Chelsea. How the council had found an apartment in Chelsea that could hold a king-sized bed was beyond my comprehension, but Brigit seemed blissfully unaware of how lucky she was.

I'd arrived at the apartment about ten minutes earlier, and the entire time I hadn't gotten a word in edgewise.

"...says there's this amazing place off of Delancey that does these incredible Thai massages. And then, when I was at that other place? You know, the one where they have all the trees in the windows?" I had no clue what she was talking about.

"Anyway, someone else told me there's a busboy there who will let you..."

I stopped listening, because I was entirely certain I didn't want to know what said busboy would let a buxom young vampire do to him. Brigit was speaking to me from the depths of her closet, and every so often her voice would muffle as she tried on whatever it was she was finding in there.

Climbing off the foot of the bed, I took time to survey the apartment, curious as to what kind of arrangements Sig had managed to make for her on such short notice.

The living room and kitchen were classic New York—cramped and hot. The kitchen was smaller than mine, with barely two feet of counter space between the two-element stove and the ancient fridge. There wasn't room for a table, though I doubted Brigit would notice, considering all of her food was stacked in individual bags inside the fridge. The kitchen had no upper cupboards, but there were hooks on the wall where pots and pans had once hung. While the paint on the lower cupboards had probably once been white, years of smoke from a previous tenant had left them an unpleasant yellow-brown. The floor was the type of tile that had been popular in kitchens throughout the late seventies. That is to say hideous brown linoleum.

The living room had no personality, per se, with the singular exception of the beaded curtain covering the hall closet which was a take on the famous Japanese painting of a big blue wave. I ran my hand over the wooden beads and enjoyed the clicking rattle they made as they tapped against each other.

There was a single loveseat in the room, and it looked too large for the space. Against the wall leading to the kitchen was one empty bookshelf, and next to the front door was an old, antenna-operated television. I didn't think analog worked in the city anymore, but trust a vampire decorator to be out of the loop on that. At least someone had gotten her a DVD player, and by the looks of it, the first few seasons of *Gilmore Girls*.

The afghan on the back of the loveseat was a nice touch too.

I stopped playing with the beaded curtain and gave the afghan another, harder look. It was a bit *too* nice of a touch, and certainly not something anyone rushing to find a home for a newborn vampire would have thought to add.

I walked over to the couch and snatched the blanket up, sniffing it more carefully. It smelled like old hand lotion, age and the faintest hint of the chemical people used for perms. I dropped the blanket in disgust.

This apartment had belonged to someone else. Recently.

I stalked back into the bedroom, which now seemed more incongruous with the rest of the apartment, with its bright white walls and giant bed. I made an angry mental note to ask Sig if they had at least waited for the old lady who once lived here to die before the council annexed her rent-controlled abode.

"...just gave me all these clothes, which is so cool! I mean, I'd rather have gotten them myself, because seriously who's ever heard of Miss...Mees...Missoni?" She tossed a burgundy sweater out into the room, where it landed on a pile of other discarded clothes.

For someone who had lived the New York party-girl lifestyle when she was alive, Brigit Stewart was blithely unaware of a majority of the fashionable labels most girls her age would kill for. I was willing to bet she had only borrowed my twelve-hundred-dollar shoes because she thought they were pretty.

I pouted to recall those very same shoes would never be the same again after their adventure in Lucas's pool.

What does it say about me that I can be distracted from wondering about the demise of a nice afghan-knitting little old lady by the thought of shoes? Probably that I'm a bad person.

"*Aha.*" The triumphant cry from within the bowels of her closet drew my attention back to the mission at hand.

I had called Brigit after getting Lucas's message and insisted I needed her help preparing for my date tonight. I figured this way I could check on her, see how she was adjusting to being alone, and I could also find an outfit. I may have a lot of shoes, but I have very little to wear them with. And nothing in my closet screamed *date with royalty.* On my last date with Lucas I'd felt woefully underdressed.

Not that it mattered, because the whole outfit ended up getting covered in blood anyway.

What I needed for tonight was twofold. I wanted an outfit appropriate for a night out with Lucas, but I needed it to carry on with me for the latter part of the night, which would involve a little lying, troublemaking and general no-goodery.

Plus, my only date-worthy dress had been left at a dry cleaners over a year ago to get bloodstains out, and I hadn't made it a priority to get it back. Wearing a dress you'd killed someone in was probably bad luck for any date anyway. Especially when the man you would be with might be able to smell the old blood on you.

I have a lot of problems with getting blood on me in my line of work.

"Found one!" the closet doors declared.

I needed to start learning to dress myself for fancy occasions. Getting help from vampires made me feel a little pitiful sometimes.

Brigit re-emerged from the closet, holding something I wouldn't have imagined any vampire in their right mind choosing, but coming from Brigit it made perfect sense. It was a sweet-looking candy-pink strapless dress, which appeared to have pockets in the skirt. I hated myself for admitting it, but I found the dress charming in spite of how very *pink* it was.

She held it out to me like a proud cat showing off a dead sparrow.

"Like it?"

"Amazingly enough." I took it out of her hands and held it against me so I could assess it in the full-length mirror hanging on her bedroom wall. She clapped delightedly, then collapsed backwards onto the giant pile of clothes behind her. "Thanks, Brigit."

"Anytime. Put it on!"

I stripped down, almost embarrassed by my day-to-day uniform of jeans and a V-neck T-shirt, and slipped the dress over my head, thankful one of the many physical traits Brigit and I shared was our dress size. I was also glad whoever had put this dress in the closet for her had considerably underestimated her chest size.

The dress was even better on me than it had been on the hanger. The rose undertones of the fabric provoked the illusion of color in my cheeks, and it somehow managed to make the blonde of my hair look less yellow and more gold. If I'd thought I could wear that dress to do all of my work from then on, I would have.

But there was always the blood to consider.

"Lucas is going to *die*," Brigit said cheerfully.

"God, I hope not," was my all-too-honest reply.

At ten to ten I was standing outside of the Two Moon Grill on Madison, feeling like a high-school girl waiting for her prom date. At least that's what I imagined the feeling was equal to considering I'd never been to high school or a prom.

As much as I had wanted to go all-out glam for my date, I had learned a few lessons in my tenure as a vampire-slaying bounty hunter. My heels, pretty as they were, were easy to slip off, and inside the ridiculously huge purse I was carrying I had a pair of flats and a handgun.

I had places to be after my date with Lucas, and I didn't think my plans for the night were going to wait for me to go home and get a gun.

I hiked the purse straps higher on my shoulder and stuffed my hands in the front pockets of the dress. From this point forward I was only ever going to own dresses with pockets. I was way too fidgety when I was nervous, and having pockets at least allowed me a place to steady my idle hands. A breeze drifted past me, and with it came the wolf king.

I tasted Lucas before I saw him. The sudden sweetness of cinnamon was almost overwhelming, and my whole mouth filled with the spicy and aromatic swell of it. After the taste came his arms, strong and a little warmer than the air. Werewolves are always hot, any time of year, and I found it comforting. My own skin maintained a happy medium between hot werewolf blood and cold vampire blood, so I just felt normal. It was one of the only parts of my life that was—at least on the surface—human.

He rubbed his cheek against the side of my head, his beard snagging against my hair. I heard a rumble in his chest, a contented sigh as he pulled me closer into the familiarity and safety of his embrace. Though my anger was now a distant memory, I felt like I was supposed to still be mad at him. But it was difficult to be mad at a handsome, strong man who just one night earlier confessed his love to me.

Nevertheless, I insisted, "Hey, I'm still mad at you."

"Mmm," he murmured, snuggling me tighter. Over the sweetness of cinnamon, there was a scent that was entirely Lucas. All werewolves smelled like peat and evergreen, but with Lucas the musk was uniquely his and so intoxicating it was in another universe from all other wolves. The fragrance was dangerous and promising, and it made me want to bury my nose in the crook of his neck, nip at the sensitive skin, and...

My eyes were suddenly wide open. I worried that if my train of thought followed the path it had started, I would be back into a shared mind-space with Holden. With Desmond, the task at hand had been consuming enough he hadn't noticed what was going on. I didn't know if Lucas would be able to overlook my sudden catatonia as I went into a shared dream with the vampire.

Lucas had once shared a dream with me, and I had never asked how he'd been able to do it. I had been too grateful for the part it played in saving my life. Now I was beginning to wonder if I was easy to violate on the subconscious plane, or if I just opened myself up to people I was close to without realizing it.

One more question to answer, one more mystery to solve.

But nothing could be more important than finding a way to save Holden from condemnation and death at my hand. I was a tool of the Tribunal, and I could only keep them from forcing me to do their bidding for so long. I didn't think anyone, even Sig, could convince Juan Carlos not to kill me if I refused to finish this job.

Juan Carlos was looking for any excuse, and I wasn't about to deliver one to him on a silver platter.

Tonight, when the vampires came out to play, I would try to find some answers. But for right now I was here with my wolf king, and I wanted to hear what he had to say for himself. I extricated myself from his arms, sad to be out of them, and turned to face him at last.

The beard was still so foreign to his face, it felt like I was looking at his evil twin.

I reached up and ran my hand over his cheek, letting the short hairs tickle the palm of my hand. As an experiment, I scratched the beard on his cheek as if it were fur, and he grinned at me.

"It makes you look old," I said.

His grin faded and his hand caught mine at the wrist, then lowered it from his face. I flinched, realizing too late I'd insulted him, which hadn't been my intention. I was just unsettled by the maturity it lent to a face I remembered being full of candid, youthful sweetness.

A lot had changed since I'd left.

He held my wrist a little longer, then twined his big fingers with mine so our hands were palm to palm. "Let's go eat."

Two Moon Grill, according to *The New York Times*, was the premiere restaurant in the city for a good steak. A year ago it had been STK. The year before it had been a place called Red. Considering a blue-rare steak was about the only thing I could eat aside from blood that was of any nutritional benefit to me, I was in a unique position to think of myself as a bit of a steak snob.

I ignored the array of steak sauces brought to our table and eschewed the offer of any kind of side dish. The waiter gave Lucas an imploring look when I asked for it bloody rare, like he hoped the man at the table might persuade me to let them cook the steak until it was at least *warm*.

Lucas offered him no help, but smiled politely and ordered a bottle of Chilean Pinot Noir to go with our cold twenty-two-ounce porterhouses.

Once the waiter was gone, we stared at each other awkwardly across the huge butcher-block table. This restaurant wasn't the most romantic atmosphere for a date, but it was dark and it was quiet without being silent, so I couldn't complain too much.

While the restaurant might not have been silent, the space between Lucas and I filled with anxiousness and avoidance. After the silence moved from comfortable to smothering, I felt the need to break it before it broke us.

"Did you ever stop to think maybe I was planning to come back on my own?" I hadn't meant for the first thing out of my mouth to sound so accusatory, but when it came to good date conversation, I was out of practice.

Lucas wove his fingers together and pressed both palms flat on the table. He breathed deeply through his nose, like an athlete preparing to execute a difficult maneuver.

"I thought about it, yes," he began, his focus fixed on his thumbnails, where they dragged across the rough wood of the table. "I thought about it for one month. And then another." The lines his nails drew out got longer and longer, the two hands now separated from each other by a wide berth. Subtle. "Then, after the third month, I started to see things a little differently."

The waiter returned, keeping him from saying more and giving me time to feel ashamed of myself. Our wine was presented, and Lucas did the big show of smelling and sampling it, then giving our waiter approval to serve it.

The wine smelled heavenly—rich and dark, with the hidden promise of blackberry tartness. I took a small sip, but not much more. I wanted to have a level head for this conversation, and I was one heck of a cheap drunk.

Lucas continued as if we'd never been interrupted.

"By the time your vampire came to see me, I was certain you had no intention of coming home without some...convincing."

What had felt like a knot of shame in my gut unraveled. I had thought Lucas and I could talk this out without any of the anger I'd experienced before, but I was sorely mistaken. It roared to life, carried by the instincts of my inner wolf, who was not really the forgive-and-forget type.

"So, you thought having two strangers kidnap me and stick me in a car trunk would be the best way to *convince* me?" My voice rose above the sounds of the ambient jazz quartet hidden in one corner. Lucas looked me in the eyes, and there was a quiet warning in his expression.

I placed my fisted hands in my lap and refused to avert my eyes. I wouldn't be cowed by a withering stare. I wasn't his wolf. But I didn't speak again.

"You need to know what you left behind."

I think of anything he could have said, this frightened me the most. After hearing Dominick's assessment of the damage I'd done, I wasn't sure I was ready to hear it directly from the wolf's mouth. It would be difficult to be high and mighty if Lucas did something stupid, like confess how much my leaving had hurt him. I turned away.

"Okay," I acquiesced.

"Secret, look at me." His tone was gentle rather than demanding.

I raised my gaze slowly, afraid he might have become a Gorgon and I would be turned to stone by looking at him. I feared his pain much more than his indignation. Of course, when I faced him, all that greeted me were his pale, glimmering blue eyes. His former annoyance had faded, and he was once again my Lucas.

He reached his hands out to me, and I placed my own in them. His palms were so much larger than mine he could have enclosed my whole hand in his. His skin was rougher than I remembered, and I wondered if that was new or if I'd forgotten little pieces of him over the spring.

"Even though you killed Marcus," he said, "there was still a level of uncertainty in the pack because of what he had done by bringing that many rogues out and by finding a Southern pack princess to be his mate." By this he meant my mother. "And by almost killing *my* mate..."

I almost protested. Lucas may have announced his intentions to court me, but I had not been formally acknowledged as his mate. Call me old-fashioned, but if I'm going to be mated to a billionaire, I sort of want a ring.

Or at least to be *asked*.

He carried on without seeming to notice his *faux pas*. He had also avoided mentioning Marcus's partnership with a certain nasty Cajun vampire. I wondered if he hoped we could avoid discussing vampires altogether.

"The entire foundation of my leadership came into question. Others in the pack, especially the older families in the small towns, started to ask themselves if I was fit to rule. Or if I was too young to be king." He squeezed my hands a little too hard.

I'd never asked Lucas about his father's death. Everyone, at least everyone in public, knew about his sudden and tragic death at the age of fifty-eight from an undiagnosed pancreatic tumor. Since my romance with Lucas had been quick, dramatic and lacking in time for most of the small details of our pasts, I had not had the chance to ask if that was a cover story.

It seemed far more likely Jeremiah Rain had died defending his pack from an enemy, either one from outside or within. But now wasn't the time to ask. Another question for another day. I knew Lucas resented the doubt his age cast over his ability to lead his people. I wasn't part of his pack, but nothing would ever make me doubt his loyalty to his wolves. I marveled at how anyone who knew him could hesitate to trust his leadership.

"I didn't help things, did I?" I asked.

He smiled, but it wasn't a happy smile. "Dominick told you about the special designation for those who save the king by killing a usurper, right?"

"Pack protector."

For the first time that evening I realized I hadn't seen the blond bodyguard once. Either I was being trusted again, or he was hiding somewhere and I hadn't thought to look.

"He was less than clear about what the implications of being a pack protector were, though," I admitted as I looked around the room, seeing no sign of him.

Lucas's thumb rubbed small, soothing circles onto my palm, and some of my anxiety melted away. I stopped looking for Dominick.

"Pack protector is a title for anyone who puts their own life at risk to protect the king or the sanctity of the pack. Basically, anyone who places the pack above themselves. It is a sacred position, and one of great respect. To be the king's mate *and* pack protector proves your loyalty to the pack beyond reproach."

"Oh." My palm went cold in his hand.

"To be the pack protector and then vanish when the pack is at its weakest shows you had no respect for the position. It's considered an unforgivable insult."

"*Oh,*" I said again. A lump was growing in my gut, and while it was not as familiar as it should have been, I knew what it was. Guilt.

"By leaving, you did more than hurt me personally. You helped add doubt to the already restless minds of those who were the least certain of me." Though his tone was matter-of-fact, I heard the sharpened edge to his words.

I had suspected he might have issues to deal with after I left, and I'd had three months to battle the guilt of what my absence might have meant to him. But having him lay it all out on the table did something I couldn't have expected. It sort of pissed me off. Sure, I'd made things harder for him, I wasn't denying that, but if he was the king, wasn't it sort of his job to deal with difficult situations?

"Lucas..." I took a breath to calm myself, resisting the urge to say something I couldn't take back. I had to remember that I'd never really been a part of anything bigger than myself. Before becoming a warden, I hadn't been a member of the vampire council, but rather was their pawn. I hadn't considered myself to be a part of Lucas's pack, so of course I wouldn't have considered how my individual actions could have impacted the group. Maybe it was foolish of me, but if you've never been responsible for anyone but yourself, a lone wolf, it's hard to wrap your head around a pack mentality.

"I know you had your reasons. I know you were freaked out by what happened in that basement..."

That was the understatement of the decade. I'd forced my new boyfriend to accept I was part vampire so I could feed off him in order to not die. Afterwards, I hadn't been sure if I'd ever see him or Desmond again.

"I ran." I pulled my hands away from him. "I didn't know how to face you. I didn't know if you'd want to see me after what happened. So I ran."

"Shouldn't that have been for me to decide?"

"Shouldn't coming home have been for *me* to decide?" I retorted. Even though I wasn't really angry, I found it frustrating he couldn't see outside the box.

He huffed. "The vampire would have brought you back anyway. At least with Jackson there, I knew you'd be safe."

I flashed to my graceless, bloody exit from the car trunk. "I guess we were both wrong," I said.

Our steaks came then, and we watched each other in chilly silence. Neither of us moved to eat once the waiter left. I wasn't hungry anymore. Instead I sipped my wine with less reserve than before.

"I meant what I said yesterday," he offered. I don't know if he was trying to make peace between us or to change the subject, but I found myself more annoyed than flattered that he would bring it up right then.

I swished the wine around in my glass and watched the translucent fingers of it claw down the inside walls of the bowl.

"Secret." He was trying to keep the anger out of his voice, but minute traces of it clung regardless.

I could only imagine how frustrating it must be for Lucas to be soul-bonded to such a single-minded and stubborn woman as myself. I was willing to bet he asked himself often if it was worth the effort to be with me to please the Fates. I bet he wondered if I was a test. I couldn't blame him. But all the same, he wasn't exactly the prize he seemed to be.

Who knew even supernaturally selected relationships would be so complicated?

"Say it, then," I instructed tartly, swallowing the rest of my wine. It tasted like cinnamon and made me cringe.

"Now?"

"No time like the present." My eyes narrowed, and I spun the stem of the wineglass back and forth between my finger and thumb.

Lucas's lips pursed. "You know something?" He pushed his untouched plate away from him. "I knew you were royalty the moment we met. I knew we were destined to be together the first time I saw your face. I *love* you, Secret, I do. I love every fiber of your fucked-up DNA. I love your insecurity and your stubbornness." He was gripping the corners of the table, and there was an edge to his voice that both frightened and aroused me. He continued, "But until this moment, I never thought you'd be so willing to act like the spoiled little princess you could have been."

It had been a perfectly suitable declaration up until the end.

I put my empty glass down, then folded my napkin and placed it next to my plate.

"All right. Well, Lucas Rain, how's this? I *could* love you." I pushed my chair back an inch, and his cheeks flushed. "But right now, acting like a pompous douchebag who thinks being king gives him the right to treat me like something he owns? It doesn't make me *like* you very much."

Before he could counter, I grabbed my purse and left the table, leaving a tongue-tied wolf king in my wake.

Chapter Eighteen

It was ten forty by the time I was back out on Madison. I doubted Lucas was planning to follow me, hobbled by ego as he was, so I stopped outside the entrance and traded my heels for a pair of flats.

The rest of my night would not be as dramatic as dinner had been, but I was willing to bet it would be a bit more active.

Now four inches shorter, I headed south towards Gramercy, home of the vampire bar Havana. Leave it to the vampires of Manhattan to place their den of inequity a stone's throw from some of the wealthiest, most famous people in New York.

I briefly wondered if anyone with fangs had a key to Gramercy Park but knew how silly and obvious the answer was. Of course they would. I wouldn't be surprised to discover someone with fangs had keys to the Oval Office.

The night was bright and warm, without any of the hazy burden of too-hot air. The city lit up the sky overhead, creating a constant state of artificial twilight. In summer the darkness never seemed able to reach its full potential.

I crossed the street in front of the Flatiron Building, weaving in between a gaggle of camera-wielding tourists who were snapping pictures of the landmark skyscraper.

I pushed my dinner disaster out of my mind. The last time I'd told someone I loved him it had been my former live-in boyfriend, Gabriel Holbrook. Three weeks after I'd said it,

Gabriel had moved out. Now I'd almost said it again, then proceeded to call my boyfriend a pompous douchebag.

Maybe I really was meant to be single.

All I knew right then was that compartmentalization was a wonderful thing for the professional assassin.

Havana was a stone's throw away from Gramercy Park. It was down a long alley between two tall brick apartment buildings. I doubted the denizens of those door-manned manors knew what was happening betwixt and between their towers of solitude.

Vampires loved doing their nasty business where they were most likely to be caught, but in such a manner they knew they wouldn't be. Sort of like a constant state of having sex in public, only they rarely had their pants down while doing it.

I stood across the street from the alley, with my back to the gated park, thinking about my plan and waiting for the next essential piece of it to appear.

While I waited I focused on my hunger. Not eating dinner at Two Moon Grill was proving to be one of the smartest things I'd done all night. By fixating on my empty stomach, I was able to coax the vampire part of me to come out of dormancy and roar to the surface.

I was getting better at distinguishing between the two monsters inside me and manipulating the one I needed most at any given time. But manipulation wasn't the same thing as control, and I had to be sure I didn't let either of my monsters become the master instead of the puppet.

Letting my vampire and werewolf halves come out to play meant I was constantly risking whatever remained of my humanity. I was always on the precipice, one inch away from the abyss.

But tonight I couldn't be worried about risks. Tonight what I needed to be was a vampire. I needed to smell like one, look like one and pass for one.

And there was one more thing I needed, which I caught a whiff of on the faint breeze. I followed it down the block, still within sight of the alley. I crept up slow and soundless until I was within inches of my prey.

I leaned in from behind so my lips were almost flush with his ear, and then I let myself be known.

"Hello," I purred.

Nolan, the good-natured, unpracticed vampire hunter from Bramley, had just let a vampire sneak up on him. He yelped and turned to face me, stumbling off the bench he'd been sitting on.

"S-S-Secret?" he stammered.

"Calm down." I climbed over the back of the bench, plopping my purse in the center, and sat on the backrest instead of the seat he'd formerly occupied. It gave me a good vantage point to look down at him where he sat on the sidewalk. "I won't bite," I added, then leered wolfishly. I clasped my hands together and rested them on my knees. "I won't bite," I repeated. "But you're a block away from a giant clusterfuck of vampires who wouldn't think twice about it. And if *I* can sneak up on you, so can they."

He brushed some gravel off his palms and sucked up his cheeks in a familiar, defensive posture. "I just wasn't—"

"You weren't paying attention. And that will get you killed with a rogue." I looked him over. His jeans were faded and so worn they appeared about as thin as a cotton shirt. His T-shirt was a size too small, which worked well for his well-muscled chest and arms, but I didn't think that was the reason for the size. Nolan smelled of something unmistakable and sad. Desperation. He was trying too hard to prove himself my equal, and I wondered why it was so important for him to be accepted as a vampire slayer.

"Nolan," I said. "Have you ever actually confronted a vampire? Face-to-face, I mean?"

He stood, rubbing his scuffed hands on his jeans, and tried to make himself look bigger than he was by puffing up his chest and straightening to his full six-foot frame. I found it more endearing than menacing. There was a reason vampires didn't tell scary stories about Nolan to their newborns. There were no cautionary tales for baby vamps about the Jamesons and Norikos and Nolans of the world.

Me, on the other hand, they all knew my name.

"I'll take that as a no," I concluded when he didn't say anything.

I hopped off the bench to stand next to him, where I was dwarfed by his height but still somehow the tougher of the two of us. I placed a hand on each of my hips and stared up at him. He glanced at my face but wouldn't meet my eyes. After a moment he couldn't even look at my forehead and turned his head away, slumping as he did.

"What kind of weapon do you have?" I held out one of my hands.

He acted indignant, but after I sighed and crooked my fingers he stopped fighting me and mumbled, "Uh." He pulled something out of his back pocket and handed it to me.

I laughed out loud. "No. Seriously."

He flinched and put his empty hands back into his pockets, blushing. I gawked at the sharpened wooden stake he'd given me and tasted bile rising in my throat. What was he going to do with a stake? Start a teeny fire and burn the vampire to death? That would only work if the rogue in question was too busy laughing his ass off to think about killing the boy.

My fist tightened around the stake, and then with a whoosh I chucked it over the fence and into the park beyond.

"Hey!" Nolan protested.

"Trust me, Nolan, you're better off with nothing than with that. When we're done here, if you still want to do this, I want you to go see Leary Fallon on 8th. Tell him I sent you. He'll get you something *useful*. Don't ever bring a stake to the hunt again."

I brushed my hands on my dress, offended by what I'd just touched.

"What do you mean *when we're done here*?" he asked nervously, trying to hide the tremor in his voice. His Brooklyn accent seemed to thicken in relation to how frightened he was.

"You really want to be a vampire hunter, Nolan?"

"Yes." This time he spoke with total confidence. If Nolan made it through the night, I wanted to hear his story, his whole story.

"All right then." I grabbed him by the arm and dragged him towards the alley. "Time for lesson one."

"W-w-which is?" He was so surprised I'd been able to move him, he wasn't even fighting me. He would be putty if someone got the thrall on him.

"We meet a real vampire."

We passed under a streetlight, and he got his first good look at my face.

"Secret? What's wrong with your eyes? They're..." His voice was cold with fear.

My eyes were solid black, of course. I had the vampire hunger to thank for that. Pretty soon I wouldn't be able to stop from flashing fang, but I was hoping to save that for a more opportune moment.

"You'll see," I promised, as we came to a stop in front of the entrance to Havana. "You'll see."

Chapter Nineteen

Havana was like no other club I'd ever been to. This was my first foray into the interior of the establishment, and I was amazed by how different it was from what I'd expected. It was dimly lit, but not the moody darkness of a human bar. Even if the lights had been lowered it would have been more for ambience than anything else, because dark or light, the vampires there could see perfectly.

The music was kept at midlevel volume rather than blaring obnoxiously. It helped create an illusion of privacy.

Nolan and I entered into a small antechamber where a spiral staircase set into the floor promised to lead us onward. The walls were a deep, rich green color and the floor was polished black hardwood. Heavy brocade curtains were draped over doorframes and windows to protect the secrets that lay beyond.

Between us and the staircase a slender girl sat in a high-backed armchair. She had her legs crossed at the knee, and her fingers were tented in front of her smirking lips. Her hair was white blonde and cut short in an asymmetrical pixie style that complemented her angular facial features. She reminded me of Sig, if he were a waifish, arresting girl.

She wore a simple black minidress, which accented the ten miles of leg she was showing off. Her sky-high purple pumps made me both jealous of her and self-conscious of my own height and footwear.

The gatekeeper couldn't have been more than sixteen when she died, but she wore her power like a tailored suit. She didn't give off a vibe of old age some vamps did, but she felt important to me, and I knew I should give her my respect, if not for my sake, then for Nolan's.

I relaxed my grip on the boy's arm and skated my hands over his too-tight shirt, my fingernails dragging over his chest. Then, catching a fistful of the T-shirt material, I yanked him towards me. I couldn't tell him what I was doing, so I hoped he'd be smart enough to play along. We moved to stand in front of the girl, and the tremor of Nolan's throbbing heart pulsed against my chest.

The girl hadn't moved an inch, not to take a breath or bat an eyelash. She was sizing us both up, and the twist of a smile on her lips didn't falter for a moment. When she began to speak, I knew immediately the power of this girl was not to be trifled with.

"You've brought a beautiful toy to us, assassin." Her voice was a honey-smooth drawl, and judging by the tension that eased out of Nolan, she was one of the few vampires in the world who could enthrall with voice alone.

My lip curled. Of course she would know who I was. My own heartbeat was the one thing I couldn't hide, and this girl was smart enough to put the pieces together. But it didn't hinder my plan.

"If you know me, then you also know I am a warden now," I replied.

She crossed, then uncrossed her legs elegantly, but her gaze never left my face. The smile remained, but there was a coolness in her expression.

"Yes, I suppose you are." Her accent was Southern, but not the same way *Grandmere*'s was. I would stake money on Georgia for this one. The ladylike poise, tweaked for modernity, was another hint at a belle's upbringing. So was the forced politeness.

Maybe it was the voice, but in spite of her obvious disdain for me, I sort of found myself liking her. Tough nuts are endearing to me.

"Very well, *warden*. What can Havana offer you tonight?" Her head tilted to the side, big green eyes boring into me. "You look a little...hungry."

I'd never heard the word sound so erotic before. Feeding was a high for most vampires, but I'd never experienced it that way, at least not until my dream with Holden. I had fed to kill, fed to eat and fed to live, but never fed for lust. The way the gatekeeper said it made it sound like there was no other way.

My hand tightened on Nolan's shirt. "This one is mine."

She frowned a little. "There is much to see and try here. Are you certain you don't want to share?"

"He is mine," I repeated.

"Greedy." But there was a twitch of amusement. "You really are Sig's."

This startled me, but I said nothing about it. "May we pass?"

"Is someone stopping you?" She and I watched each other warily for a moment, and then Nolan and I skirted around her and towards the staircase, followed by her last words, "Have fun, warden. Play nice."

When we were almost at the bottom of the iron staircase, Nolan had his first meltdown. I was impressed he'd held it until then, so I let him have it.

"Whatswrongwithyoureyes? Whatsawarden? Whydidshe letyouin? And what the *fuck* do you mean, I'm *yours*?" He had the common sense not to raise his voice above a tense whisper.

I grabbed him by the chin, and we stopped our descent.

"What I'm about to tell you does *not* leave this building, do you understand?" His eyes grew wide with fear, but he nodded. "I don't just work for Keats. I report directly to the vampire council."

His pulse quickened even as color began to drain from his face. He tried to pull away, but I was stronger. That seemed to scare him as much, if not more, than my proclamation.

"I am still the same vampire-slaying, demon-hunting girl you had so much respect for back at the bar. I'm just not a vigilante."

"But you're one of 'em," he choked out.

"I will *never* be one of them. That much you can be certain of." There was a hint of regret in my voice, but I doubted he would be able to contextualize it. I dropped my hand away from his face. "I told them you're mine because under council law it means no other vampire can touch you. It means you're protected."

"Is it permanent?"

I wasn't expecting that, as far as questions went. "Unless another vampire petitions me for you, you will always be mine. At least in the eyes of the council." Honesty. It felt nice to not lie to him.

He nodded tightly and began to descend on his own. "I guess if I have to belong to someone, it may as well be a tight little blonde."

At the bottom of the stairs we passed through a heavy curtain and into the darkened grand ballroom. The ceiling swelled thirty feet up, with old tin-roof tiles polished to reflect the candle-lit sconces, which were the only light in the room. Red beads were draped on the walls and over other objects, giving the illusion of bejeweled blood splashes.

Individual chambers lined the walls, each three steps off the main floor, with curtains to give privacy to those who dwelled within. Somewhere inside one of those booths was someone with the answers I needed.

"Stay close, and for the love of God, whatever happens, just go with it." I placed a hand on the back of his neck, which looked quite peculiar given how much taller he was, but I needed to show everyone he belonged to me.

There were about thirty vampires in the room, and perhaps forty humans. It was impossible to tell if the breathers were daytime servants or enthralled evening snacks. Telling the vampires from the humans was easy enough, though.

What surprised me was that the girl behind the bar was not among the former.

I steered Nolan up to the long black bar that had all the fixings of a normal, human bar, but would be serving something a little bloodier as well. The girl turned her attention to us. She appeared to be a few years older than me, but if I was guessing her age from her eyes, I'd say she was decades older than her body claimed. Her skin was a flawless brown color, like rich chocolate. Her hair was cut short, but instead of making her look boyish, it showed off her incredible face. She had big round eyes with sleepy lids, and a full mouth that wasn't smiling.

She looked at my hand on Nolan's neck, then ignored him and focused on me. This girl understood the system. Nolan was chattel and I was the master.

"What can I get you?" she asked. Her nod was curt, and she stared right in between my eyes like Nolan had when we'd first met. Smart, this one.

"AB."

"Pos or Neg?"

Nolan choked back a noise that might have screwed us totally. Instead it sounded like a burp.

"Surprise me."

"And for your pet?" She inspected Nolan admiringly, then turned back to me. He *was* easy on the eyes.

"I—" he began, before I squeezed his neck and he quieted.

"He'll have a Coke. And can I leave him here for a second?"

She glanced at him again as she filled a martini glass with a dark red liquid and handed it to me. I couldn't tell where she'd poured it from, but when I felt that it was warm, I decided

I was better off not knowing. She cracked open a can of Coke and placed it on the bar, along with a glass of ice and a cocktail napkin.

"He gonna be trouble?" Her head tipped to the side, and she stared at him like he couldn't hear her. I had to wonder what kind of a state people were usually in when they came here.

I sipped the blood out of the martini glass and waited for Nolan to look at me. We stared at each other for what felt like an eternity until he nodded and sat on the stool nearest to us.

"No," he told her. "No trouble."

The bartender seemed surprised to hear him speak but left it alone.

"I'm looking for someone," I confided to the girl.

"What kind of someone?" She leaned her hip against the prep counter behind the bar and crossed her arms over her chest. She had a lot of spirit for a human working in a vampire bar.

"Someone who knows things." This was where my plan got a little hazy. I hadn't expected to get so far without resorting to bloodshed. Since I wasn't sure who I was here for or what I needed to ask them, I didn't know how to be more specific.

But vampires love their vagaries, and the bartender was no stranger to this. Speaking to some vampires was like playing a frustrating version of charades, and this girl played the game like a pro. She pointed to a lone booth at the end of the room whose curtains were drawn.

I thanked her, placed a twenty on the bar and rubbed Nolan's shoulder as I passed. "I'm coming back," I promised.

I hoped I wasn't lying to him.

Chapter Twenty

There was no way to knock and no guard to announce me, so I cleared my throat loudly as I parted the curtains and stepped into the booth. I was so taken aback by what I saw I almost tripped and fell backwards down the steps.

A spectacular-looking redhead, her hair straight instead of the halo of curls I remembered it being last, was nestled up to an equally striking brunette. The picture they painted was so intimate it made me blush.

"G-Genevieve?" I stammered.

The redhead opened her big violet eyes and grinned at me a little lasciviously. "Well, well, well. Look what the cat dragged in," she purred.

Genevieve Renard was the absolute last person I would have expected to find in the booth. She was a were-ocelot. Their queen, in fact, and no one would doubt her royal claim if they looked at her. Genevieve was just about the most beautiful woman I had ever seen.

But that was before I'd seen the woman she was with.

Righting herself from the embrace of the feline queen, the other woman glanced up at me, her eyes the sleek black of a vampire longing to feed. Her hair was so dark it was the color of charcoal, and her skin had probably been its current shade of ivory when she was human. Her features were dainty, and everything from her makeup to her clothes screamed sophistication. *She* was the one I was here for.

"Secret," Genevieve cooed. "Do you know Rebecca?"

I shook my head, still not quite able to form words.

Even with both of them fully clothed, I felt like I was interrupting something very personal. And judging by the miffed expression on Rebecca's face, I wasn't wrong. Genevieve pressed against the vampire, brushing her nose up Rebecca's neck and nibbling playfully at her ear.

"Say hello," the ocelot queen instructed. I didn't know which one of us she was speaking to, but it couldn't hurt to assume it was me.

"Hello," I said to Rebecca.

"*Bonjour*," the vampire replied, her French accent evident in every syllable.

I was always intrigued by vampires with accents. Some, like Rebecca here and the Southern belle upstairs, maintained the accents they'd had in their human lives. Others, like Holden, seemed more suited to adapt to the new world they lived in. Though he'd been born in England, he'd been in America for over a hundred years, and I rarely heard him say anything that hinted at his history. It must have been a decision for them, to adapt or to keep that part of their human life.

Rebecca had clearly decided to stay French.

"I'll leave you two," Genevieve said, placing a kiss on the vampire's mouth before rising to her feet. As usual, she wore sky-high heels. Her dress was simple and red and shouted *dangerous curves ahead*. She stood next to me and kissed each of my cheeks, then pouted a little. "Trouble in paradise?"

"*What?*" I gaped at her.

"You smelled like dessert last time I was with you, love. Now you smell like stale candy." She patted my face fondly.

"I'm fine."

"Don't let those wolves bowl you over, Secret. You're the prize, not the property." She grasped the curtain and moved to step out, but I grabbed her wrist to stop her.

"What are you doing here, Genevieve?"

She smiled at me and held both hands in the air, her fingers dancing like the light in her eyes. "Fingers in pies, Miss McQueen. Fingers in pies." She winked at her paramour and then was gone, leaving me alone with the mysterious French vampire.

I sipped my drink again, gulping in spite of myself, and stood in the doorway, waiting for Rebecca to speak.

"Well then, *belle, asseyez-vous.*" She nodded to the plush couch that wrapped in a U shape around the entirety of the booth.

I sat a little farther away than I normally might, but she was still black-eyed and I'd forced her playmate to leave for the night. I was playing it safe. I finished off my drink and placed the empty glass on the small table, its film of blood glinting in the candlelight. I stared at the glass so I didn't have to look at her.

"I may have all night, *Mademoiselle* McQueen, but I'd prefer we pretend I do not and let us get on with it, shall we?"

"Are you with the council?" I asked.

"*Oui.* I am a council elder." She inspected her manicure and radiated perfect vampiric boredom.

"Then you know about Holden Chancery's warrant."

She smiled, although I wasn't sure I liked it, given the context. "Oh you clever little girl. Did Sig send you?"

"No." My voice wavered slightly. He hadn't, really. I'd decided to come here when I left Bramley, before my run-in with Sig in Central Park. But I was beginning to wonder how much of what I was doing was my idea and what was suggestions from others being put in to action.

For my entire adult life I'd been doing the bidding of others. My whole life in this city I'd been the puppet on the end of Sig's strings, and I was only now becoming truly aware of that.

Rebecca kept smiling, running her fingers over the back of the couch behind her. "Of course not. *Non.* That would be against the rules, wouldn't it? Sig would be smarter than to send his beloved pet to her death."

Okay, seriously, did *everyone* know about Sig's peculiar attachment to me? What did it mean that the entire council believed I was Sig's pet?

"Ask me your questions," she urged.

"Do you know what Holden is accused of?"

"*Oui,*" Rebecca answered without hesitation. I was stunned into muteness. It couldn't be this easy, could it?

"Can you tell me?"

"I don't see why not. The warrant is issued. It cannot be undone now, and I am not bound to keep it a secret like the Tribunal is." She kicked her shoes off, and each fell to the floor with a hollow thud, then tucked her feet under herself. Outside, music was humming, but I couldn't have told you what was playing if you paid me a million dollars. I was sitting forward on the edge of my seat, staring at her expectantly.

"What did he do?"

"Holden Chancery stands accused of being a traitor to the council."

"But that's crazy. Holden has devoted his life to the council."

"Certainly. But did we not also ignore his right for advancement? Did we not give him reasons to loathe us, all because of—"

"Me."

"*Oui.*" She was watching me for a reaction, and I was doing my best not to give her one. Everything she was telling me was something I'd thought already. I knew Holden's supposed betrayal could be traced back to me. I couldn't let the guilt overwhelm me, because it was more important I prove Holden's innocence than focus on the part I'd played to make him look guilty.

"You know he didn't do it, don't you?"

"Does it matter now?" She wasn't denying it.

"It matters to me. It matters to Holden."

"Is that because Holden matters to you?" Rebecca seemed genuinely curious.

"Yes." I let my face show nothing.

"How interesting."

"Tell me." I was barely touching my seat, I had shuffled so far forward. She sat up, mirroring my stance, and looked me right in the eyes. Her smile flashed fang.

"Your warden could not have done what they say he has done."

"What do they say he did?"

"In our council, a council you now count yourself a member of, there are some who need to be protected. Their safety is a priority to us all, because they know secrets or are keepers of power we cannot allow to be risked."

I nodded, but I was still a few mental steps behind her.

"The council, we have something akin to your human world's witness protection. Only ours has always worked. Until recently."

"What changed?"

"Failure...is death."

"They were killed?"

"Not all, *non*. But two elders this year were, and another three last year. These were old vampires, well protected, who believed the council would protect them above all else. Protect them even from ourselves. And we failed them."

"And Holden is supposed to have killed them?"

"*Apparently.*" But her tone told me she didn't believe it for a second.

"Why don't you think he did it?"

"I know he did not because he would never have had access to their locations. He was not powerful enough or trusted enough to be given those details. We would have been fools indeed to give the locations of our protected elders to the warden responsible for our council's assassin."

"Bounty hunter," I said, but felt stupid for it because both of us knew what my real job was.

"Your title is irrelevant, Secret. You are paid handsomely and your prey does not come back alive. You are feared, but not respected. And because of that, Holden was not respected. You made an easy target of a good man."

I choked back the swell of guilt threatening to eat me alive.

"Holden was always loyal to the council," I defended.

"And what a great lot of good his loyalty got him in the end."

I left the booth feeling flustered and burdened, with enough time to see Nolan disappearing up the staircase with a slight, blonde vampire. Just my luck. I strode across the floor, giving the bartender an accusatory glare on my way. She shrugged, but on her face I could see smug satisfaction wrestling with uncertain worry. That look told me everything. She was glad Nolan was away from me, his keeper, but she was worried he was out of the frying pan and into the fire.

There was no sign of them in the hallway, so I took the stairs two at a time back up to the main foyer. The gatekeeper was gone. I ran into the alley and was slapped by a wave of hot air. I breathed in through my nose, hoping to get Nolan's scent while it was still fresh.

A sound at the mouth of the alley drew my attention, and I followed it, running down to the street and skidding to a halt under a streetlight. Nolan was backed against the brick wall, a blonde vampire latched on to his neck. At his sides his hands hung limp, and his eyelids were open so I could see the whites of his eyes from where they had rolled back into his head.

A thin trail of blood ran down his neck, but he looked for all the world like he was having the most pleasurable experience of his life.

"That's enough," I whispered.

For a moment no one reacted, and I might as well have been speaking to the night sky. I took the extra two steps towards the pair, grabbed a fistful of long blonde hair and hissed into her ear.

"Brigit. *Enough.*"

My protégée released her victim, and after the longest two-second pause of my life, Nolan's eyes rolled back forward and he let out a raspy sigh.

"Whha?" He looked from me to Brigit, then back. Brigit was smiling sweetly, in spite of the smear of his blood across her cheek. I was less than pleased.

"Do you see now?" I asked him. "Do you see how thin the line between life and death is when it comes to vampires?"

He gaped at the blood on Brigit's face, then his hand shot to his neck and the pieces of the puzzle came together. His big body sagged, and he slid down the wall, slumping to a defeated puddle on the sidewalk. I let go of Brigit and went to stand in front of him, crouching down and placing one hand on either of his knees.

"Nolan?"

He looked up at me, tears streaking down his hot-chocolate-colored cheeks. I squeezed his knees protectively.

"I would never have let her hurt you."

He nodded.

"But I can't make that promise for any of the others. You are mine in the eyes of the council, but do you see how easy it is for someone to get to you?"

Nolan put his head in his hands and lowered them to his knees, rocking himself back and forth. He made a low sobbing noise over and over. His reaction told me that this experience wasn't new to him. Brigit and I had thrown him into the dark, frightening corners of a memory we knew nothing about, and in turn had done more harm than good. I'd set out to teach him a lesson, not to break him. I wanted his story, but not like this.

I grabbed his face in my hands and made him look at me. His mind was especially fragile, and I had just fed. I was hoping with my vampire so close to the surface that what I was about to try wouldn't be an abject failure.

"You are fine," I said sternly. "You had a fright, but everything is fine."

His breathing began to steady and his tears slowed. Brigit was watching us with interest, but I didn't think she needed any lessons on the thrall. She'd succeeded in getting him here without an issue.

"You're fine," I repeated. "The past is gone. You're fine."

With a final, shuddering sigh, Nolan blinked several times and then he was himself again, awakening from a bad dream. I stood up. Looking at Brigit, I pointed at her face and then wiped my own so she would know to get rid of the blood.

I helped Nolan to his feet and gave him a guarded smile.

"How're you feeling?" Testing the water.

"Fi—" His eyes got wide, and he grabbed me by the torso. We tumbled to the ground with him landing heavily on top of me one instant before the blade of a sword swung through what had been my head, colliding with the brick wall instead.

The clang of metal against rock echoed through the empty street, shouting the fatal promise of violence into the night. And Death was calling my name.

Chapter Twenty-One

Sparks rained down onto the sidewalk from where metal had struck brick. Time passed in slow motion, and the electric pinpricks of fire that fell from the wall singed my arm hairs. Nolan's breathing came short and fast, and the crush of his ribs dug in to mine with each gasp. He had his hands on my face, and his mouth was asking *are you okay* but there was no sound. All I could hear was the ringing vibration from the blade of the sword and the thump of Nolan's heartbeat.

I rolled Nolan over so I was on top of him and balled my hands in his shirt so I could drag him with me. The sword fell with great force, twanging again, screaming its rage at being denied the kill for a second time. I got to my feet, pulling Nolan up with me, and stood between him and our assailant, although I suspected I was the target.

Flesh wounds were less fatal for me than for him.

I turned to face the attacker at the same moment Brigit launched in to action. I'd been on the receiving end of an attack from Brigit in all her vampire glory, and let me tell you the girl packs a hell of a wallop when she wants to. She had jumped on our attacker from behind, grabbing a handful of hair, and was making great strides to go for a neck bite.

Watching a vampire attack with intent to kill is something that should be on the Discovery Channel. Forget Shark Week. A vampire going for the bite is such a cunning example of predatory guile it makes a crocodile's death roll look like children playing leap frog.

Brigit meant business, but our attacker was apparently no fool when it came to vampire attacks. During the attempt to keep Brigit's fangs off, I saw who had come after us with such vigor. Nolan recognized her too.

"Noriko?" His surprise was genuine. He tried to move past me to help her, but I put my arm out to stop him.

The girl who had seemed so withdrawn and terse at Bramley was standing in the street wearing an all black spandex catsuit and carrying a pretty dangerous-looking katana. I'd have been impressed, but the one I had at home made hers look mail order.

Problem was, I didn't have my sword with me and Noriko did. She was also armed with the obvious intent to use hers for something more permanent than teaching me a lesson. Why the hell did the girl want me dead? Sure, I could have been a little more pleasant at the bar, and yeah, I'd put Nolan in harm's way tonight, but she couldn't have known about that.

Could she?

"What the fuck?" I queried eloquently.

Noriko let out an enraged shriek, still attempting to rid herself of the hungry fledgling vampire on her back.

"Bri, get off," I commanded.

The vampire, her eyes oily black, snarled at me with her canines elongated. Two could play that game, and I was geared up enough for it. My own fangs descended and I growled right back at her, my still-human eyes flashing a warning. Brigit hesitated, and that was all it took for Noriko to throw the blonde off her.

Brigit thumped to the sidewalk but quickly regained her footing. She did not relaunch her attack on Noriko, but watched the sword-wielding vampire hunter cautiously, waiting for any indication an attack should be resumed. Noriko was panting, and her eyes looked wild with anger rather than fear. She still had the sword pointed at me.

I stepped in front of Nolan again. God help me, but I felt responsible for the kid and I didn't want to see him turned into a human shish kebab if this all went south. This time he didn't try to skirt around me, he just kept close enough I could feel the rise and fall of his chest at my back. Knowing he was alive made me feel stronger somehow.

"What's the meaning of this?" I asked. This time I was a little more rational.

Her sword hand hadn't once trembled or shaken. She obviously knew how to use the weapon well enough to swing it, even if she hadn't landed any hits. I was still amazed Nolan had managed to move us in time. There might not be a killer instinct in him, but I now knew for sure there was a survivor's speed.

"Step away from the boy," she demanded.

"Put down the sword." As far as counteroffers went, I thought I was being fair.

"I know what you are."

That gave me pause. My eyes had returned to normal, and at the moment my fangs were withdrawn. There was no way for Noriko to know all of what I was, but I was willing to play along.

"So?"

"*So?*" Her voice welled with astonishment, but I knew fake surprise when I heard it. "You think you had everyone fooled."

"Fooled how?" I gave her a quizzical look. "I don't know what you think I am, Noriko, but I assure you I've never tried to fool anyone."

"You're a monster."

"We're all monsters here." I inclined my head towards my former roommate, who bared her fangs for good measure. My gaze darted to Noriko's sword. "You aren't so innocent."

She kept looking around the street, then back to Nolan before glancing away again. After a beat, she advanced a step with her sword raised, anger turning her eyes the flat color of a nighttime ocean. Nolan and I shuffled back a step in response. Brigit didn't move, but she was coiled like a spring and at any instant she might launch. I was going to do my best to not give her an opportunity.

I raised my hands, palms out and up in a gesture of peace but not surrender.

"Put down the sword," I repeated.

"No."

I hadn't expected her to agree, but it would have been nice. "Noriko, no one has to die here tonight."

She snorted.

I continued as if I hadn't heard her. "But, you should know, if it comes down to it, the person who dies won't be me."

"You're already dead."

Oh. So she knew I was a vampire. That narrowed things down a bit. At least now her attack made more sense.

"No. I have a beating heart. I breathe." I took Nolan's hand without looking at him and placed it on my neck. "Tell her, Nolan."

His fingers were cold and sweaty; I could feel them shake against my skin. "Sh-she has a pulse," he confirmed.

"You enthralled him." Something about her tone bothered me. She didn't sound worried or even terribly interested in what was happening. Her body, too, showed none of the nervous energy I would expect from someone in her position. She was *faking* it. If she'd been afraid, I would have smelled it on her. The act was good, so good I'd almost believed it, and good enough I was playing along, but it was total bullshit.

Nolan didn't move his hand, insisting, "No she didn't."

Fact of the matter was, I had. My mind was still reeling from how well my experiment earlier had worked and that

Nolan wasn't still catatonic on the sidewalk. But this wasn't the time to discuss that.

"What do you want from me?" I asked her.

Silence swam across the street, and for the first time Noriko looked right at me. Her expression was hard and cold, and no part of her showed any fear. All pretense dropped when she realized I was on to her. She lowered the sword and her entire stature changed.

Gone was the wary, fight-ready stance. She cocked her hip to the side and leaned against her sword like a Victorian dandy with a walking stick. A look of contempt with a hint of humor colored her face. This was the real Noriko.

"Well aren't you smart?" she remarked.

"I'm rarely accused of that."

She twirled the sword against the sidewalk so with each turn the shiny blade caught the streetlight and flashed it in my eyes. She stared at me without flinching. Brigit had relaxed slightly, but she was still waiting for me to give the word. Nolan's hand had tightened almost painfully on my neck. I could smell his fear, and I wanted to lick it.

"She was right about you. She told me this wouldn't be easy, that you wouldn't go like a fool. Can't say I didn't try." The smirk grew, held, and then was gone. "Come on, Nolan." She stepped off the sidewalk and into the empty street, turning to look at the boy. I should have tried harder to think of him as a man, but the fear radiating off him made it impossible.

He held firm to me and implored, "Secret?"

"Mmm?" My mind was overwhelmed, spinning in wild circles, trying to make sense of what Noriko had said. *She* who?

Nolan was standing beside me, staring at me. Brigit was snarling low and menacing at Noriko, but the petite Asian ignored the petite blonde.

"She won't hurt you," I said, watching Noriko, making sure she understood the promise of my words. "Will she?"

"Of course not."

I didn't see the harm. Wherever Nolan lived, whatever his life before tonight had been, it was shared in part with Noriko and no harm had befallen him yet. Her quarrel tonight had been with me, but I still couldn't figure out why she would attempt to kill me.

Nolan followed Noriko out onto the street, but his gaze was all for me as they walked away. Brigit came to stand next to me, and we watched the pair retreat into the night. She licked her lips, hoping for any forgotten traces of blood and finding none.

"Who was she talking about?" Brigit asked.

"Beats the hell out of me."

During our westward walk to Chelsea, I scolded Brigit voraciously about the etiquette of eating the unwilling.

"I told you to spook him, I didn't tell you to feed off him!"

"But I *did* spook him," she protested.

"You almost broke him."

Brigit shrugged, and I found it disconcerting how easily she had adapted to the vampire mentality. Maybe there was something in the blood that made it easy to ignore the well-being of humans, or maybe it was something specific to her maker's line. That I shared a dark and bloody history with Brigit's sire wasn't a secret. He'd turned her into a vampire to goad me into fighting him, which I didn't view as fair play.

At the time Brigit had been inconsolable about the loss of her mortality. Now, only a few short months later, she had begun to conform to the vampire way of life. She was still new, and as such was still receiving her blood primarily from Calliope like I did. But in spite of her overzealousness tonight, she had proven she might be ready to feed on live humans.

We parted ways for the night, but not without a few more curses on my part about her toeing the line too closely. If I was going to be her warden, I wanted to be just as irritating and pushy with her as Holden had been with me.

Holden.

I continued to walk north to Hell's Kitchen, the night air as warm as a lover's breath whispering dirty little secrets to me in the swell of each breeze. I closed my eyes, willing myself to fall into the dreamlike state where he could find me. I walked without seeing, guided by memory. He did not come to me in a dream.

I opened my eyes when I felt him physically.

"You look awfully silly walking around with your eyes closed, you know?"

I smiled at him, somehow unsurprised he'd found me.

"How long have you been following me?"

"I like to stay close," he replied vaguely.

"Were you at Havana?"

He smiled but shook his head. "I want to keep an eye on you, Secret, but not to my own downfall. If I went anywhere near Havana, they'd have found me."

I nodded, and we kept walking. I wondered about this ability he had to appear and disappear at a moment's notice from my side, and how Sig seemed capable of the exact same thing. If the two of them had the same vampiric homing device on me, how was it they hadn't accidentally crossed paths with each other this whole time?

My theory that Sig had no desire whatsoever to catch Holden gained a little momentum with that thought. Surely if a two-thousand-year-old vampire could find me in Central Park without a problem and my two-hundred-year-old warden could find me south of Hell's Kitchen, one must be able to find the other.

"If Sig wanted to, he could find you, couldn't he?" I asked out loud.

"Possibly."

"But he can find *me* as easily as you can."

Holden stopped walking, and I was forced to do the same if we were to continue our conversation. He asked, "How many times has Sig come to you?"

"This week?"

"He's come to you enough you need to ask that question?"

"Twice, I guess. Why?"

"And he always knows where you are?"

"Well, to be fair, one time he hired someone to have me where he wanted me. But yesterday he found me in the park."

"Secret, I need you to be honest. Have you given him your blood?"

I recalled how close Sig had been to biting my neck the night before, and how willingly I would have given in if he had. My cheeks flushed. "No."

"*Honestly.*" His tone was accusatory.

"I said no," I replied hotly. "And what does that have to do with it anyway? I've never let you feed off me, either, but you have no trouble finding me."

"That's because of our bond," he said, referring to the warden-ward bond he'd recently revealed to me. "You shouldn't have the same bond with Sig. Not unless he's marked you somehow."

I didn't like the sound of that. "What do you mean *marked*?"

His shoulders sagged slightly. Between Holden and Lucas, I was getting tired of the men in my life pointing out how ignorant I was about things. Lucas had a valid reason to be irritated, because I'd spent my first twenty-odd years ignoring the werewolf part of my life. Holden, however, had only himself and his council to blame. The vampires kept me in the dark about a great deal of the inner workings of their world, so my ignorance was entirely their fault. So for him to be giving me the shoulder sag of disappointment pushed my buttons, and not for the better.

I scowled. "Either tell me, or bugger off. I've had my fill of vampire crap for the night, thanks. And I'd like to point out you're to blame for most of it." I felt the unfairness of my statement, considering how much of his situation I was responsible for.

"What happened at Havana?" he asked.

"Don't think I don't see how you're ignoring me."

"Secret."

We were walking down a quiet residential street somewhere between the good and bad of the city's areas. It was the kind of place where you could still get mugged at night, but people would pretend to be surprised by it. Two boys in oversize sweatshirts and low caps swaggered past us, but Holden and I both ignored them. Had I been walking alone dressed as I was, I'd probably have had to deal with them in some fashion, but with Holden beside me they seemed content to walk past.

I didn't know what it was about Holden that made thugs stay away from him. He was good looking, well dressed, and almost always on his own. Yet somehow they recognized the predator in him and avoided crossing his path. Maybe vampires gave off a pheromone that told others to fuck off, unless eating was involved. I wish I had a screw-off pheromone. It would have saved me a lot of hassle some nights in the city.

"Okay," I acquiesced. "I spoke to a council elder named Rebecca."

He sucked in a breath through his teeth.

"I take it you know her."

"Yes."

"Pretty well?"

"You could say that."

"I *did*." I was trying to get him to give me more to go on. I wanted whatever story was lurking behind his comment, but Holden was too savvy for my attempt.

"What did Rebecca have to say?"

"She doesn't seem to think you're guilty."

"Well that's something, I suppose."

We were passing West 48th Street on 8th Avenue, so we were almost back to my block. Night had moved past its apex and was cooling with each passing moment. The sky had lost all the yellow tones of its former self and was now a deep, rich blue.

I was so tired of this night.

"Holden, Sig told me something about you last night." I waited a beat, but he didn't reply so I continued. "He told me about your journals?"

By phrasing it as a question, I left it open for him to decide how much of the blanks to fill in. To be honest, what Sig had told me about Holden's journals left me with more questions than answers, so anything Holden himself could clarify might offer me some help.

"My journals."

"Yeah. He said you were meticulous. And then he said something about certain dates. One of them was December sixth."

"Your birthday?"

My cheeks flushed with a warm glow. Sure, my birthday had meaning to me, but dates rarely meant anything to vampires. That Holden remembered the day was my birthday flattered me more than I cared to admit.

"I don't know what he—" I was thinking out loud as I started to walk ahead, but Holden stopped me.

"Secret." He grabbed my arm and pulled me close to him. We were pressed face-to-face, he had one hand looped around my waist and the other held my arm. Breath whooshed out from my lips as my lungs compressed against his chest. My eyes were reflected in his, and for a brief, sweet second all we did was look at each other. My heart thrummed.

When I thought about the kiss we'd shared in my apartment, my stupid knees buckled a little. His hold on my waist was firm, and I righted myself before I fell. I wished I was still wearing heels so I could have blamed them.

"What did Rebecca tell you?" His lips were caressing my ear, but the intimacy of our embrace didn't match the words coming out of his mouth.

"Wuh?" At the best of times I am ineloquent. I am especially challenged when in the arms of a beautiful man. Maybe I was human after all.

His voice was a low whisper, so low I understood now the meaning of our unusual position. He was holding me in a lover's embrace, his lips brushing my neck, his fingers trailing a dangerous path down my spine. To anyone passing by, we were a couple in love. But that wasn't his motivation.

No. Holden was masking our conversation from any potential eavesdroppers. By holding me this close he could speak lower than any human ears could hear. So low even paranormal hearing wouldn't pick up on it. He was barely uttering the words. It was as if the movement of his lips alone told me what he was saying.

If anyone was following us, they would have no idea what we were talking about.

"She told me what you've been accused of."

His hand spasmed on my back, and all pretense of breathing left his body. "What?"

"There are claims you're responsible for the death of several protected council elders."

"Well." He pulled his head back from my ear and looked at my face. "We knew it had to be something serious. I didn't think it would be something so...impressive."

"She doesn't think you did it. Neither does Sig."

His eyes widened, and I watched as something lit up within them. The brightness of a realization dawning. Where his hand was holding my arm I felt a sudden pain, but I didn't interrupt his thoughts.

"Of course," he said.

"Share with the class?"

He released my arm and cupped my chin with his cool palm. "I need to get something. But once I bring it to you, I think everything will be clear." He kissed my lips delicately, with such aching softness I almost thought it was the summer breeze.

When I opened my eyes again he was gone, and I stood alone on the sidewalk.

The rest of the walk home passed in a daze. I moved by Calliope's Starbucks without the slightest inclination to stop. I just dragged myself the rest of the way back to my apartment.

And that's when shit got weird.

Chapter Twenty-Two

Waiting for me in the foyer of my apartment was a wolf roughly the size of an Irish wolfhound.

On steroids.

I was so taken aback by the presence of the animal, I tripped backwards over something and smacked my head against the exterior door. My vision swam and pain dazzled the space around me with pinpoints of brightness. Dazed, I slumped to the ground.

When I reached for my fallen purse to grab my gun, I saw what I'd tripped over. A large duffel bag was near the entrance, and next to it a pair of navy, men's Vans slip-on shoes—the object I'd taken a backwards tumble on. Beneath the wolf's feet was a pair of jeans and a well-worn navy blue New York Yankees T-shirt. None of the clothing was ripped, and there was no blood or any signs of struggle.

The wolf sat back on its haunches and fixed its gray eyes on me, with its large ears upright and alert. Its huge jaws gaped open, flashing a daunting set of teeth, and the wolf actually grinned at me with its big tongue dangling out the corner of its mouth. As if it were nothing more than a house pet.

As the panic started to melt away from me, my hand wandered to the back of my head to feel the goose egg growing there. I'd hit the door pretty hard and was still feeling woozy. That must have been why I thought I *knew* the animal sitting less than five feet away from me.

I licked my dry lips and tasted citrus. The reality of it hit me harder than the door, and my gun slipped from my fingers.

"Desmond?"

Not only did I know the wolf, I knew him carnally. I should have recognized it was him. The violet-gray eyes, the deep black coat. He came closer and licked my face. When I didn't flinch away, he pushed his nose under my arm and whined. I took the hint and used his stability to push myself back up to my feet.

He padded over to my door and scratched at it. I was still too perplexed to ask questions. It wasn't like he could answer them in his current form, so I unlocked the door and held it open for him while he walked into the apartment, sniffing around until he vanished into my bedroom.

Rio hissed and Desmond growled in response. The white demon bolted out of my room and took up residence under the loveseat. When Desmond didn't come back, I grabbed the bag from the hallway, along with his discarded clothing, and tossed them inside my front door, then locked the door and latched the deadbolt.

From my bedroom I heard the most disturbing array of noises. At first it was just a racket of popping I couldn't put a name to, but by the time I realized it was the sound of joints bursting out of their sockets, it had already changed. The wolf made a low, rumbly growl, followed by the resonance of cracking bone and tearing flesh.

My blood ran cold, and though the last thing in the world I wanted to do was see with my eyes what I was hearing, I couldn't stand there and ignore it. I walked to the door of my bedroom with the apprehension of a horror-movie heroine.

The transformation was already almost done, but what remained was gruesome. Desmond was curled into a fetal position on the ground, with the skin of his fingers split open, long claws retracting back into the exposed bones of his hands. Under the now-hairless surface of his skin I could see bones shifting, altering their position and configuration, and with each adjustment came the unnatural *crack-pop* noise I'd heard earlier. Watching the bones of his face move was hardest. The canine snout broke itself down, elongating his jaw and flattening his cheeks before he was restored to his lovely, human face.

His mouth opened but the fangs of a wolf were still there. For a moment he looked like a vampire, and then the fangs retracted, blunted, and it was over. He was left naked and panting on my bedroom floor, covered in a sheen of sweat, his eyelids clamped shut against the pain.

I unzipped my dress, letting it fall to the floor. I stepped out of the satiny puddle and sank to all fours, crawling to where he was, then I lay down behind him so my front melted against the slick surface of his back. He released a shuddering sigh when I wrapped my arms and legs around him, and for a long while we just lay quiet on the floor, until his breathing returned to normal and he was my Desmond again.

"You mind telling me what the hell that was all about?" We were sitting together on the loveseat in my living room, me with my legs draped over his lap, he with a cup of tea in his hand. I wasn't even sure the tea was still good. I'd bought it over a year ago for Mercedes, but she was over so rarely it sat in my cupboard unopened. It was hard to take Desmond seriously as a big, scary werewolf, with a steaming mug of Peppermint Princess tea held to his lips.

We hadn't bothered to put on clothes. Being naked didn't bother me, and it wasn't like Desmond hadn't seen it before. Getting dressed seemed like more effort than he had in him, and he claimed the skin-to-skin contact was helping him regain his strength. There was some truth to that, but based on the placement of his free hand on my upper thigh he had other healing in mind. That of the sexual variety.

"It was my fault, really. It's so close to the full moon and I'm not with the pack like I should be. It shuts down my control. When you didn't come home after your dinner with Lucas, I started to worry. After a few more hours, I guess it overwhelmed me. Heightened emotion makes it easier to take on the change if you're not careful. Especially this time of the month."

It was the first time I'd ever heard a man blame his fragile emotional state on his *time of the month*. I couldn't help myself, I snickered. Insensitive? Probably. But I'd had a little too much seriousness for one night.

Rio, no longer afraid of Desmond, was perched on the arm of the loveseat, watching us with mindful boredom. She seemed annoyed by my outburst. Desmond was equally unimpressed.

"Sorry," I said unapologetically.

"I should be used to it by now." He put his empty mug on the back of the couch, resting it against the wall, and ran his now-free hand over my bare arm. We were wrapped in a lightweight blanket, and all of a sudden even the thin weave was too hot.

"What are you doing here, Desmond?" My voice was little more than a quiver because his other hand had started to move upwards as well.

"Oh, yeah. About that." His thumb traced my lower lip, and my eyes closed. I took the digit into my mouth, exploring the rough surface with my tongue. I didn't think anything he said next could matter.

Boy was I wrong.

As he shifted his weight to move closer to me, he spoke against my lips. "I'm moving in."

I was wrapped in the blanket, up and off the couch, having pushed him away from me, and was standing next to my fireplace before he had a chance to complete the sentence. It should have made the situation funny, somehow, that Desmond was left naked on my couch, still in the midst of making his move.

I wasn't laughing.

"Jesus, how did you move that fast?" he asked.

"You're going to want to be answering questions rather than asking them." I hugged the blanket closer to me as he righted himself on the couch and looked for all the world like he couldn't be less uncomfortable. In fact, he already seemed right at home with his arms outstretched across the back of my loveseat.

"Well, then. Ask a question."

"What do you mean you're *moving in*?" The pitch of my voice bordered on hysterical. It felt like arguing with Lucas all over again. If I thought vampires were frustrating, I had a thing or two to learn about how annoying werewolves could be.

"I don't see how that can be misunderstood." He pointed at the bag by the front door. "You and I will be cohabitating."

"No." I shook my head firmly and stamped my foot in frustration. "*Hell* no."

"Secret..."

I was fed up. I threw the blanket at him and stormed into my bedroom, but it was impossible to properly express my irritation when my carpet wouldn't allow me to slam my door and I was stomping around butt naked.

Desmond stood outside my half-closed bedroom door, and I slumped into my armchair so I didn't have to face him. He had the good sense not to come in, but that didn't mean he went away.

"Even if I say no, you're staying, aren't you?" I didn't want to sound so defeated, but I already knew this battle was lost. When the wolves got it in their mind that something was going to happen, there was no arguing. They were a lot like the Tribunal in that sense. I hated how little control over some aspects of my life I had. I'd expected more respect from Desmond.

"Trust me, I wish this had happened differently. I wish you'd asked. I wish it had been my choice."

Of course. Of course this had Lucas's name written all over it.

"He thinks I'm going to leave again."

"He says it's because he worries your work with the council puts you at risk. But, it's more than that." He measured the look on my face and answered my question with, "Yes. He thinks you're a flight risk."

I turned and looked at him over my shoulder. His face was impassive, and trying to read his eyes was like trying to find a right angle in a Pollock painting.

"And what do you think?"

His cheek was against the frame of the door. "Lucas wants—"

"I don't care what Lucas wants right now. I asked what you thought."

Desmond's jaw tightened. This was hard for him. He was being torn between the duty he was bound to do for his king and yielding to my will.

"You won't leave again."

"Why not?" I was all the way around in the chair now, watching him.

"Because it would kill me."

The frankness of his words cut me right to the core. I got up and pushed the door back open, standing in front of him and looking up at his eyes. There was a thin film of emotion shining there, threatening to cheat him of his masculine posturing.

"So you're moving in?"

"Yes."

"And Lucas ordered you to do this?"

"He didn't have to break fingers or anything, but it's by his decree. Officially I'm your bodyguard. The Queen's Guard, if we're being titular about it."

"Queen's Guard," I repeated, taking one of his hands in mine so our fingers twined together. "That sounds serious."

"Very serious." He pushed my hair off my shoulder and stepped across the threshold of the room so only a sliver of summer-hot air separated us. He trailed his fingers down my arm so slowly I thought they might be beaded sweat. I shivered.

"You'll have to stay close to me."

"Yes." He dipped his head and kissed the space where my neck met my collarbone. Once, a vampire had bitten through that same bone, and though it had long since healed I still felt a cold chill whenever anyone touched me there. A visceral reminder of how close I could come to death.

No one was untouchable.

I took his hand and placed it on the small of my back as we moved together towards my bed. The hard, muscular curve of his pelvis pressed against my stomach.

"Desmond?"

He was kissing his way down my chest, his lips dangerously close to my left nipple and the point of no return. I grabbed a fistful of his hair and forced him to stop.

"Did Lucas ask you to move in before or after our dinner?" I didn't know why, but a lot rested on his answer. Perhaps all my hopes for saving my relationship with the wolf king. It seemed like a funny thing to worry about at the moment, but then again, when was a good time to worry about it? If Lucas had asked before, it meant nothing I said at dinner factored in at all and he'd never intended to trust me. If he'd made his request after our fight, I could understand why he'd worry about me bolting.

"After," Desmond mumbled, taking no time to think up a lie.

It was the answer I'd needed to hear. I released his head, and immediately his mouth latched in to place and my eyes fluttered shut. There would be no more questions tonight.

Chapter Twenty-Three

It was snowing.

I walked down the sloped paths of the Ramble barefoot and in step with Sig, and felt each cool flake melt beneath my warm soles. I was wearing a thin cotton slip for pajamas, but in spite of the chill in the air I wasn't bothered by the cold.

We came to a footbridge overlooking the lake. The reflection of sleeping giants glittered over the still surface, not yet frozen over, and huge feathery flakes of snow dropped like precious gems in the light.

I was dreaming.

"I was in bed," I said to Sig.

"You still are."

"It's cold."

"It's winter."

I took the words at face value. It was winter here, of that there was no doubt. I asked something more pressing instead. "Why don't you *ever* wear shoes?" I sounded petulant.

Sig smirked and looked down at our equally naked feet.

"I've learned to watch my step."

The night was still, as though my imagination could remember only fragments of what winter was and couldn't quite conjure up the rest. Sig handed me a wrapped, rectangular package tied with a silver ribbon. He hadn't been carrying it before.

"What's this?"

"Happy birthday, Secret."

I awoke, sucking back words not meant to be spoken out loud. In the dark confines of my room I was able to register that everything still looked the same and I was back in the real world. All was as it had been, with one exception.

Across my chest, a masculine arm was laying and a broad hand was possessively cupping one of my breasts. Even at rest, Desmond was staking claims. He was sleeping on his stomach, his other arm tucked under him and his face angled towards me. A fresh crop of stubble had shown itself during our rest, giving him a darker appearance than usual.

What caught me most off guard, though, was how peaceful he looked. His lips were parted, and he had given himself over to sleep. Shifting while away from the pack, twice in one night, must have taken a toll on him. Otherwise he never would have slept through the whole day with me.

I rolled over and placed my hand on his backside, giving him a playful squeeze. I'd have done something a little more provocative, but the wily man was sleeping downwards, so he wasn't providing me the necessary access.

He groaned, still half asleep, but a smile played on his lips.

"You can't want more already."

"Rent is due," I teased.

His eyes opened and his face lit up with a grin. "Is that how this works, then?" Lightning quick, he jerked me against him for a languid, sweetly familiar kiss.

A girl could get used to waking up this way.

I moved to wrap my leg over him, but instead I kicked something hard at the end of the bed. Startled, I broke away from him mid-kiss and reached down to collect the offending object. Funny, the size and weight of it felt precisely like the thing Sig had given me in my dream.

I flicked on the bedside lamp, wanting to see the finer details of it better than I could in the dark. It was a book, old and worn looking, but not smelling of must or decay. I thumbed through the stiff, cream-colored pages while Desmond watched me with passive interest.

When I passed a page in the middle, a sheaf of white paper fell out. I recognized the handwriting, and in fact, the whole book was filled with the familiar scrawl. Every page was written in Holden's strong, demanding hand. I picked up the note, which appeared to be recently written and was addressed to me.

Secret,

You will be awake soon enough. It did not seem necessary to wake you or the wolf, as time for explanations grows short.

Be sure Sig reads this. I believe you will understand the relevance.

Yours,
Holden

I handed the letter to Desmond so he wouldn't think I was hiding anything from him, and opened the book to the page where the letter had been.

December 7, 2008

Any hopes I have of advancing beyond the position of warden were dealt a blow this past evening. Ever diligent in her mission to infuriate and exhaust my patience, the young Miss McQueen may now be legitimately planning to be my undoing. In the four years I have been entrusted with her guardianship, I have never seen such reckless abandon used by a ward of the council.

She would think me remiss if I did not begin by stating for the record, yesterday was her birthday. For those of us who have long since put to rest our Lives Before, the idea of a birthday, let alone the idea of celebrating one, has died along with the memories of who we once were. It is, admittedly, difficult for me sometimes to recognize that Secret still maintains many human attachments, owing to her unusual heritage. Apparently, by her approximation, the desire to celebrate her twentieth year of living required some sort of festivities.

I scanned the pages, trying to see if Holden would come to a point where he wasn't bitching about my foolish human traits, and how silly it was for a twenty-year-old girl to want to celebrate her birthday. Having a bicentennial gave him the right to be dismissive of my own life milestones, it seemed. Better yet, I doubted he would even understand why reading this would irritate me.

Skipping ahead, I found the part of the entry that finally hit home.

Upon our exit from the theatre, Secret caught the scent of blood. I don't know how I missed it, whether it was the crush of smells from the theatre patrons, or my own foolishness, letting my guard down in public, but regardless of the reasons, she smelled it before I did. Enough of it she refused to brush it off as a passing incident. We followed the smell to a vacant storefront, and in the basement discovered...

But I didn't need to read more to know what we'd discovered. I remembered it perfectly. I remembered Holden agreeing to take me to see *The Lion King* on Broadway for my birthday, and how he'd actually enjoyed himself no matter how hard he'd tried to fake a grumpy scowl. I remembered smelling the blood and going down the rusted metal ladder into that basement, which was colder than the streets outside, the walls slick with melting ice.

And the cots.

Threadbare mattresses on crumbling old military frames. Six on each side of the room, and each one had a body on it. I remember them as bodies, because even though they were alive it was hard to think of them as people. They were hollowed-out husks of their former selves, with slack mouths, gaunt skin and eyes wide and dry with a frozen look of horror.

The air had reeked of human discard and the sticky-sweet smell of blood.

That was the night I had hunted down and killed my first rogues without sanction of the council. I had found them and done things to them no warrant would have ever allowed for. If I'd thought they could be made to live on, forever wincing in remembrance of that night and frightened of their own shadows, I would have found a way.

Death had been too kind. It had been a kindness I'd been forced to visit on those twelve empty shells.

I gagged.

Desmond sat straight up, surprised by the sudden reaction. I did it again and he moved to help me, but I placed a hand on his chest to stop him.

"What is it?"

I closed the book and wiped a stray, unwelcome tear off my cheek. I didn't remember it happening on my birthday. Somehow, I'd disconnected the two things in my head so my birthday wouldn't be tainted by the horrible deaths of a dozen people. But I had all the important points in front of me now, and all I had to do was draw a line.

If Holden stood accused of killing a protected elder on that date, I could prove he didn't do it. He'd been violating a different set of laws that night, by helping me dismember a sect of rogues and bury the skeletons from their closet.

I pushed the book away from me, letting it fall with a thump onto my carpeted floor.

"Get dressed," I whispered. "We need to go."

I left Desmond behind, still struggling to get his left shoe on, and was halfway down the block when he caught up with me. I stopped walking and did an about-face, nearly colliding with him.

"Wha—?" He looked confused.

I had dressed in such a hurry I was wearing my shorts from earlier in the week and the discarded Yankees shirt Desmond had left at my front door. This had forced him to grab the first shirt he could find in his duffel bag, so fresh there were still fold marks in the white cotton tee. The button on his jeans was undone, and his hair stuck up to one side in fond remembrance of the pillow we had just left.

I brushed past him, digging through my purse. "Hold," I said as I handed him my gun, which he took but held uncomfortably. I knew Desmond could handle a weapon because he'd taken mine from me in the past. I think it was the idea I was carrying a 9mm pistol in my purse that made it so off-putting for him.

I found what I was looking for and hauled the keys out of my purse. With one push of the key fob, a pair of headlights blinked at us, and my car announced itself with a chirpy honk. I'd almost forgotten I had the stupid thing.

"Is that—?"

"I'm borrowing it."

We looked at each other, and he handed the gun back to me. I checked the safety, then slid it into the back of my pants, letting the looseness of the shirt hide it perfectly.

"Lucas would look pretty goofy in a yellow convertible," he said, moving around to the passenger side. Farther down the block I could see his vintage Dodge Challenger sitting forlorn in the night.

184

I doubted I'd ever get used to being able to drive places in the city. New York was a town ruled by pedestrian law. Drivers ranked below cyclists in the hierarchy of the streets.

I got into the driver's seat and the car purred to life.

Then again, there was nothing not to love about that sound.

Twenty minutes later we were pulling up to the Plaza Hotel, and I was loathing New York streets and cursing myself for not walking. I handed the keys off to the eager valet, while Desmond clambered out the other side, having survived the diatribe of my sailor's tongue the whole way here.

At the front desk a stout woman with water-colored eyes and a painfully tight bun of mouse-brown hair stared at the pair of us. Her expression was like a visual sigh.

"Yes?" she deigned to address us. She would have gotten along swimmingly with Melvin over at Rain Hotel. We had skipped right over the *Welcome to the Plaza, how may I assist you today?* and directly into the condescending glares.

"Residential elevators, please." I knew I was in the right place, although I'd never had to make this particular visit in the past.

"Residential…" She looked perplexed by my question.

"I need to get to someone's apartment."

"No one—"

"I don't have time for this," I grumbled.

Desmond gently pushed me aside, then leaned against the counter with casual grace. He smiled at the lady in a way that would probably feed her fantasies for months to come. She blushed and he hadn't even spoken yet.

"Beverley," he crooned, glancing at her nametag. "Can I call you that?"

"Yes." Her gaze darted over to me. I didn't have people skills. Not the same way the men in my life seemed to. Women generally didn't like me, and I was fine with that under normal circumstances.

"Beverley, my friend and I are trying to visit someone. We understand the need for residents here to maintain their privacy." He winked at her conspiratorially, and she fell for it hook, line and sinker. "But if you could point us in the direction of residential access, we'll be on our way."

"Take the elevator to twenty-six. Take the third door to the left. There's a second elevator there, and it goes directly to the resident floor of your choice. They're labeled." Desmond might as well have enthralled her, the answer was so precise.

How was his question different than mine? Sure, it was more eloquently phrased, and he was flirting instead of yelling at her, but still.

In the elevator I pouted a little, but he beamed at me with I-told-you-so variety pride.

"What are we doing here, anyway?" he asked.

"We're here to see a woman about a vampire."

"And she lives at the Plaza?"

"I know." I shifted my gaze to him. "How can you trust someone who lives in a hotel, right?"

Chapter Twenty-Four

Sig's daytime servant, Ingrid, was no fan of mine.

There should be some sort of support group for people who disliked me. Ingrid wouldn't be leading the meetings, but she'd still sit in a metal folding chair with her Styrofoam coffee cup and say, "Hello, my name is Ingrid, and I hate Secret."

Nevertheless, when I arrived at the front door of her personal apartment with a werewolf in tow, she didn't think twice about letting me in.

For a seven-hundred-year-old milkmaid from Germany, Ingrid had held up well. She was human, but the bond she shared with Sig meant she'd inherited his longevity. As long as Sig lived on, so would Ingrid. She had traded a life in service to him for immortality, and it didn't seem to bother her in the slightest.

She had been in her late teens when she'd met Sig, and retained the youthful roundness of her face and figure. Her cheeks had a ruddy, flushed complexion from hours spent in the sun with no fear of cancer, and her blonde hair looked especially flaxen this season. I hated her for her daytime privilege.

"Secret," she acknowledged, stepping away from the front door. "Won't you please come in."

The gesture, while unnecessary, was flattering. Full vampires couldn't enter a human residence without invitation.

Since I was not a full-blooded vampire, the rule didn't seem to apply to me, but I appreciated that she offered it.

"Wolf," she said in the tone of someone speaking to a pet rather than a person.

"Desmond," he corrected, and extended a hand to her. They'd met once, but the circumstances hadn't been ideal for introductions.

Ingrid looked at him like he'd performed a particularly humorous trick, and then rewarded him by shaking his hand. "Ingrid."

"Now that we're done playing *name that paranormal creature,* can we get on with it? I don't think you want us here all night." And I wondered why Ingrid disliked me.

"Surely not." Her smile remained bemused as she continued to look Desmond over. "But Sig did tell me to expect you, and therefore I will do my utmost to make you feel welcome."

We followed her through the small foyer and into a sunken living room with huge picture windows overlooking Central Park. She had no balcony, but the view was worth the sacrifice. The city gleamed like an unbroken promise, beautiful and safe.

For the first time I noticed how casual Ingrid appeared tonight. Her hair was tied back in a messy fishtail plait, and she wore a pair of skinny black jeans and a long black tank top. If Audrey Hepburn had a perpetually cranky German cousin, Ingrid would be it.

She indicated the sectional sofa, which wrapped around three sides of the sunk-in area. On the fourth side was a large flat-screen television and a fancy stereo which was playing Mozart's *"Eine kleine Nachtmusik"* through hidden speakers all over the apartment. That Ingrid predated the original performance of the symphony was not lost on me.

"Sig told you we were coming?" I sat on the sofa, and Desmond found a comfortable place next to me. He was perfectly at ease in the room, having been raised in the opulence of life with the Rain family. I, on the other hand, would never be comfortable surrounded by such obvious displays of wealth. You couldn't grow up in a town like Elmwood and make a smooth adjustment to things like driving BMWs or having an original Rothko hanging in the dining room.

"He knew you'd sort things out eventually." She sat opposite us and smiled. "What have you brought me?"

I pulled the journal from my purse, opened it to the correct page and held it out to her. She read it, saying nothing, then closed the book, placed it next to her on the couch and waited for me to continue.

"If I understand Sig, and what he told me the other night, then one of the protected vampires was killed on December sixth of that year."

Her smile thinned, and she brushed her hand over the cover of the book. "Perhaps."

"Then Holden couldn't have done it. He was with me."

"And the Tribunal will take the word of a half-breed, why?" She wasn't attacking me, I realized, she was testing me. I was prepared to answer this question; I just hadn't expected her to be the one to ask it.

"The death of the three rogues I killed is on record. I had to stand before the Tribunal to account for the unsanctioned assassinations. Holden's account was given the same night as mine." My eyes flared defiantly. *Take that.*

"It is as Sig feared." Ingrid picked up the book, then rose from the couch and took it into another room. I don't know what she did with it, but when she returned, the journal was gone.

"Sig knew Holden was innocent."

"He did not believe a warden in Holden's position would be capable of the charges in question."

"So why agree to the warrant?"

Ingrid looked at Desmond, then back at me, debating whether or not to continue while he was still present. She seemed to make up her mind and carried on. "Sig believes there is a betrayer in the council. He is quite certain it is someone in a position of tremendous power. An elder."

"Someone who would know about those under protection."

"Yes. Even I know nothing of their names or whereabouts. There are few who are trusted with such knowledge. Only a fool would believe Holden Chancery would be given such a treasured gift. But Sig agreed to the warrant because Holden was an easy target. Others in the council would be quick to mistrust him because—"

"Because he was my warden."

"His attachment to you..." She treaded lightly, knowing anything she said about Holden could apply to her master as well. "It put him in a regrettable position, especially with such a low rank. You are, at times, viewed as a corrupting influence, Secret."

If I didn't know better, I might think she was complimenting me.

"Who knew the names of the vampires who were killed?"

"The Tribunal, of course. And a few select elders. But something else should be mentioned."

"Yes?"

"Several of the kills were, according to Sig, perpetrated a great distance away. In order for vampires to travel any great distance, they must have help."

"Daytime help," I concluded.

"Yes."

"Ingrid." I shuffled forward on my seat. "Did you drive Sig when he came to collect me?"

She smirked. "No. That was a short drive. He could do it without me. I wouldn't have minded to see your face when he showed up, though."

I shook the thought off. "So we're looking for a vampire who knows how unpopular I can be and is old enough and powerful enough for a daytime servant?"

"Yes."

"Narrows it down a little, doesn't it?"

"Well, it eliminates some possibilities, yes."

"It narrows them all down, Ingrid. I *know* who is responsible." If a little light bulb could have gone off over my head at that moment, it would have.

Who hated me enough to create a perfect situation for killing me? If Holden took the blame and I was assigned his warrant, then I was being set up to fail. They must have known I wouldn't go through with it, and the expectation would then be that my life would be forfeit for my failure.

And if that person was the one responsible for killing those other vampires, it would be a win-win for him. Pass off responsibility for his own murders and be rid of an annoying half-breed thorn in his side all at the same time.

I was a fool for not seeing it sooner.

"It's Juan Carlos."

Chapter Twenty-Five

Never in all my years of knowing her had I ever heard Ingrid laugh like she did then.

Dismissive chuckles, sure. Loaded trills, showing a little too much enjoyment at my suffering? Absolutely. But this was something new. Her face lit up, mouth fell open, and she all-out belly laughed like what I'd said was either the funniest or most ridiculously stupid thing she'd ever heard.

I was placing my meager funds on the latter.

Desmond was enchanted by her mirth. I saw him smile, and the corners of his lips twitched with the urge to laugh along with her. I was less appreciative of the laughter and was sitting on the edge of the couch, trying to kill Ingrid with my stare.

When she stopped laughing, she wiped away a tear from the corner of each eye and took a swallow of air.

"Oh, Secret. I'm sorry." She was smiling, and the amusement hadn't left her face. She looked positively youthful with her usual scowl dissipated. "I don't mean it to seem like I'm insulting your assessment. Quite the contrary. Juan Carlos would seem like the perfect candidate, I don't disagree. Especially given his dislike of you."

"Thanks."

Ingrid shrugged one shoulder, dismissing my grumblings. "The problem is, he doesn't fit the profile you already established." She held one palm out flat, offering me something invisible. "We know the vampire responsible must have a daytime servant, yes?"

"Yes."

She held out her other empty palm. "Juan Carlos does not."

Well, that put a damper on my accusation. "Are you sure? Could he have one and no one knows?" Ingrid was shaking her head through every word. "Not even a Renfield?"

"No." The period at the end of the sentence was so matter-of-fact it wouldn't allow for argument. That was that. She could sense my disappointment. "I'm no friend of Juan Carlos, believe me. I wish he were guilty on many levels. But he chides Sig and Daria for having daytime servants. He calls us their *daylight wives*." Her lip curled.

"Man, I'd love to hear what he calls me behind my back."

"Half-breed wh—"

Desmond choked on a laugh, and I raised my hand to stop Ingrid before she could finish. "Rhetorical."

In the silence that fell, a tinny, muffled version of "Free Fallin'" did its best to make things that much more awkward. Tom Petty sang while I scrambled for my purse and tried to find my cell phone.

I quieted the ringer with a sheepish smile and looked at Desmond, who seemed a little surprised by the ring tone choice. Ingrid appeared to have never heard the song before. I didn't recognize the number on the caller ID screen.

"Sorry," I said, and stepped out of the living room to answer the call. "Hello?"

"McQueen?" It was a gruff, unfamiliar male voice, strained with worry. In the background I heard someone shout, followed by the sound of something smashing. "It's Jameson."

The voice matched up in my head with a visual of the burly vampire hunter from Bramley. Judging by the ruckus in the background, it would seem like he had found himself in a bit of a bind.

"What's wrong?"

"We stumbled on a nest. We thought it was only one vamp, but we got here and it was a fucking ambush." Another holler and more breaking glass. "Noriko vanished, and someone's got Nolan." There was a long pause and I strained to make out any sounds, thinking the line had gone dead.

All I needed to hear was that Nolan was in trouble to decide I would go. I don't know what it was about the kid, but I wanted to keep him safe from the big bads going bump in the night. He deserved better than my life.

But he'd have to live if that was going to be possible.

"Jameson?"

"We need help." There was a crackle of static on the line.

"Where are you?" More silence. "Jameson, where are you?"

I heard a low breath inhale, followed by the kind of laughter that sends chills into every corner of your body. A voice, neither male nor female, barely human, clucked into the phone. "Jameson can't come out to play," it said. "But if you'd like to join him…" It let the open invitation linger.

Son of a bitch. My mind was arranging fractured memories of a vampire who had twice very nearly been the death of me. The voice on the other end of the phone did not belong to Alexandre Peyton, but the coldness of the laugh and the demonic pleasure it took in evoking terror was the same.

Vampires like this were the reason I had a job. Demented nutjobs who were so scarily confident in themselves they believed they were really unkillable.

"I'd rather play with *you*," I said, my hand reaching instinctively to my back to make sure my gun was still there.

The vampire didn't know what to do with that. There was a pause filled with nothing but the eerie clucking and the sound of an oft-unused tongue sucking air at the back of a throat, learning how to work again. Finally it spoke. "Play with us."

"I will."

"We are where the fun has gone to die."

I shivered. "Care to vague that up a bit for me?"

It clucked loudly, annoyed. "Where the midway lights no longer shine and the carnival games are no longer played."

That narrowed things down for me. I had a pretty solid idea of where the voice meant. The abandoned amusement park near Rhinebeck, about two hours north of the city. I'd been reading about the plans to convert it into a garden park or any number of other ridiculous things, but much like all abandoned property, no conclusions were easy to reach.

I, for one, wished every abandoned property would be torn the hell down. They create perfect dwellings for vampires, and I was not too fond of walking into dark, spooky places with lots of good hiding spots.

I sighed. "Leave the good prizes until I get there."

In the living room, I was a little surprised to find they hadn't sat in silence waiting for my return. Desmond was leaning forward on the sofa, talking animatedly about Roman architecture, and Ingrid was defending him to the death about the merits of the Gothic style.

Capturing Desmond's attention, I nodded towards the door. "I'm sorry to leave so soon, Ingrid, but something has come up. Please see that Sig gets Holden's journal."

Desmond met me at the entrance and politely shook Ingrid's hand a second time. "Pleasure to meet you, Ingrid."

"You as well." She smiled at him, then turned her focus to me. "Holden won't be safe until we can prove someone else was responsible. Sig will believe the evidence, but in order to have the council respect his annulment of the warrant, someone else will need to stand accused."

"So, even though I found you evidence to clear him..."

"You still need to find out who actually did it."

I had been worried about that since she'd taken the book. "Can't I blame Juan Carlos and call it a day?"

"Would that you could, Secret." She held the door open and let us out. Before she closed the door, she offered me a business card made of the same stiff material as the warrants Sig issued me. On it was her first name and a 212 area code number.

Leave it to Ingrid to score a 212. She'd probably had it since seven-digit dialing still existed in Manhattan. In the living room, Mozart played on. Ingrid existed simultaneously in several centuries and seemed to feel comfortable that way.

"What's this for?" I asked.

"For whatever you need." She rested her head against the half-open door. "I've been told I am responsible for ensuring your needs are met." She didn't explain any further, but she didn't need to.

Sig had told her she had to do anything I asked.

"Just get him the book," I said, and slipped the card into my pocket, along with my phone. I hoped I wouldn't ever have cause to use it.

Chapter Twenty-Six

"I'm dropping you off at the apartment," I told Desmond once the valet had returned with my car. He began to protest, which I knew he would. "There's something I need you to do for me, and I don't have time to argue about it. Please."

Mollified, he climbed into the passenger seat, and while we drove he waited patiently for me to give him his assignment. I chose to stay silent until we were almost back at the apartment before I continued.

"You need to call Lucas. He needs to ask Jackson who the man was who helped him kidnap me. Then you need to find that man and tell him if he doesn't pay reparation to me, I will find a goddess to make sure the rule of three comes to bite his witch ass with a vengeance."

"What. The. *Hell*?"

"Just trust me."

He opened the car door and looked over at me. "Do you actually know a goddess?"

"Half-goddess."

He got out and walked around the car to my side, leaning against the window and fixing me with a hard look. "Look. I appreciate that this time you aren't sneaking out and leaving me passed out on your living room floor, I really do. But, if I ask you where you're going, will you tell me?"

"Yes."

"Where are you going?"

"To save three sad-sack vampire slayers from the scariest-sounding vampire I've ever had the displeasure of speaking to. At an amusement park. In Rhinebeck." There was more to it, but I didn't have time to explain my gut feeling about the vampire on the phone being linked to the dead elders. I wasn't sure why, but something inside me told me the two things were connected.

Desmond straightened. "My life would be so much simpler if I thought you'd made that up."

"Your life would have been a lot simpler if you'd decided to date Kellen Rain instead of me."

He frowned, but I couldn't tell if it was because he was surprised I knew about Kellen's former love for him, or if he'd been oblivious to it. I regretted saying it, like so many things I'd said recently, and grabbed his hand before he could leave. "Desmond?"

"Yes?" He looked down at me again, his face barely concealing the concern.

"I'll be fine."

His tight smile didn't reach all the way to his eyes. "I know you think so."

"But if I'm not..." *Oh hell, let's just throw all caution to the wind.* Honesty was a contagious disease. Once you started telling people the truth, it was hard to stop. "If not, I want you to know—"

"Say it when you come back, Secret."

"But..."

He squeezed my hand, brought it to his lips and dusted my knuckle with a kiss. "I need to call a wolf about a witch. And you have a heck of a drive ahead."

"Clearly you've never driven on the highway with a vampire." I revved the engine for good measure, which brought a smile to his lips, but it was a smile I'd seen before. Without taking more time than necessary to dwell on Desmond's sad smiles, I pulled away from the curb and into the dark.

It felt like I was going back to Lucas's estate. The drive north from the city with its tree-lined highways and alien appearance reminded me of the trip to his mansion. Instinct told me I should take the detour, go out of my way and get the pack. What was so great about being pack protector if I couldn't get the pack to help me when I needed it?

But the moon was dangerously close to full, and judging by what had happened with Desmond the previous night, the wolves weren't at their most stable. The last thing I needed was a bunch of moon-drunk werewolves going nuts, exploding out of their skin and ruining all my chances of saving Nolan.

As I drove, I thought more about the connections between my investigation into Holden's innocence and the arrival of the vampire slayers into my life.

It couldn't be coincidence that Noriko had found Nolan and me outside of Havana the same night I discovered the truth about Holden, and now everything coming together with a nest of rogue vampires out in the middle of nowhere. There was no way it was a fluke. I didn't know how Jameson and Noriko were involved, whether their intent was pure or not, or if they were being played to get to me. Noriko had attacked me at Havana because she believed I was a vampire and endangering Nolan. But there was more to it than that.

Like, how had she known to find me there?

Something wasn't adding up. Once all the dots were connected in some messy Rorschach disaster and all the t's dotted and i's crossed, things might not look much clearer but someone would be found guilty and someone would be dead. I was hoping both would apply to the same someone, and dead wouldn't apply to me. But my job didn't come with a long-term health insurance plan.

Eventually I'd come up on the losing end of a fight. My close encounter with Peyton in the spring had proven that.

So I was without the pack, without Holden, and hanging on to a wing and a prayer, so to speak. If Desmond couldn't get Jackson to help him contact the witch, I was screwed. If the witch didn't understand what I needed, I was screwed. Not since the Clinton administration had anyone been as hypothetically screwed as I was.

I pulled onto an old road in bad need of repair. Why anyone had built an amusement park near Rhinebeck was beyond my comprehension. Rhinebeck felt like *Connecticut: the Sequel,* with its rambling farm-style houses that were well overpriced for the average farmer, quaint antique shops and old country charm. It was where middle-aged city-goers came to stay at a bed-and-breakfast and watch the leaves change color in the fall. No one wanted to come to Rhinebeck to ride a Ferris wheel and eat corn dogs and stale popcorn, at least not all the time. The Dutchess County Fairgrounds were a popular August attraction, but someone had thought having an amusement park three seasons out of the year was a brilliant plan.

When New Yorkers crave a taste of their youth, they go to Coney Island, not Rhinebeck.

The Rhinebeck Amusement Park closed eighteen months after it opened, and that had been three years ago. Most of the rides were auctioned off to traveling amusement shows or placed in storage for use at the Dutchess County Fair each year. It was a huge story in the papers for an entire summer.

What remained was a ghost town.

It had been featured the previous fall in a photo spread for *Vogue*—models in Alexander McQueen and Gucci draped over rusting metal bumper-car pavilions and in doors of haunted houses. Patrick Demarchelier had done the photography and it had all been *trés chic.*

I drove the BMW under an unlit neon archway, which had once announced *Amusement* in bold pink and orange letters, but no one was laughing now. The parking lot was unkempt and sprawled long and dark in every direction. The pavement had begun to crack from disrepair, and grass cropped up through the crevices.

A ten-foot-tall chain-link fence wrapped around the entirety of the blackened park, and beyond it were the handful of reminders of what had been before. The husk of the Ferris wheel, which no longer had its passenger buckets, was an eerie iron wheel against the purple blue of the night sky.

The haunted house sat off the midway a few paces, recessed from the fun and looming with sinister promise. My money was on it for the nest's home base. Vampires love clichés, and nothing was more clichéd than a haunted house. It was a beautiful mockup of an old Victorian home, and it reminded me a great deal of the Addams family mansion. Which was probably intentional.

I parked the car next to an early nineties red Jeep Cherokee that had seen better days. This had to be Jameson's car because there were no other signs of life in the parking lot. When I shut the engine off and killed the headlights, I took a moment to adjust to the quiet and let myself drink in the scenery.

Outside the car the silence felt heavier somehow.

I'd expected the sounds of screaming, or fighting, or any indication I'd come to the right place. There was only the sound of wind whistling through torn canopies and the constant smacking of a screen door beating against a wall. I took a sniff of the air and got back a big whiff of fear.

Fear, blood and vampires.

I was *definitely* in the right place.

The front gate was still chained and padlocked, so no one had gotten in that way. I tugged at the lock once to be sure, but it didn't budge. I didn't want to waste any time looking for a secondary entrance or checking for holes in the fence. Not when my path in was right in front of me. I hooked my fingers through the chain links and got a foot up on the locked chain, using it for leverage. I scrambled up the few necessary feet, then swung my legs over the top of the fence, getting snagged in the thigh by a loose bit of metal, which cut deep enough to make me bleed.

I dropped to the ground, landing in a crouch, then stood to investigate the wound. A thin beaded line of blood had sprung up, but it wasn't serious. It would heal quickly, and in the meantime I had just announced myself to any hungry vampires who hadn't heard me pull up.

Checking my gun, I flicked off the safety and chose to keep the weapon out and ready rather than tucked into my pants. The steel frame glinted merrily in the moonlight. Loaded with fifteen silver rounds, the gun was pretty pleased with itself. I hoped it knew something I didn't, because I didn't have any extra clips.

To my left the old bumper-car area was now reduced to a fenced-in concrete pad with broken glass on the ground from the bulbs that had once lit the overhead rafters. To the right was an aisle of abandoned concession carts promising popcorn, lemonade, hot dogs and cotton candy. The signs had begun to fade over years of dormancy, and the air lacked the cheerful smell of any carnival foods. Behind the bumper cars was the Ferris wheel, and beyond it all was my destination.

I crossed the midway cautiously. No one had come for me yet, and it made me wonder what they were waiting for. And if there was no noise, was I too late to save anyone? No, if there was fear in the air, then there must still be a little hope. I held the gun out but downward, ready to raise it at any moment. My heartbeat thumped along steadily, my pulse not yet above average.

The thumping of the screen door grew louder as I approached the path leading to the haunted house. On the front porch the old door swung open, then smacked closed, swung open and smacked closed, over and over in a steady rhythm. A little too steady, actually, considering the wind had all but died since I'd hopped the fence.

Yet there it was, smacking and squealing at me, doing its best to lend the night a more frightful atmosphere than necessary. In one of the upstairs windows a blue light flickered on for a fraction of a second, illuminating a figure. My finger tensed on the trigger as I took aim, but when the light flickered a second time it showed the figure to be nothing more than a dummy dressed up like a villainous hag.

I lowered my weapon and stood in awe of the house. Dense fog had begun to roll out from beneath the front door, but the smell of it was faintly chalky. Smoke-machine haze.

"*Okaaaaay,*" I whispered.

Either this place was haunted by one seriously unoriginal ghost, or the power had been restored to this building. No sooner had the thought crossed my mind when a deafening pop echoed through the air, the sound of a breaker being thrown, and the whole park came back to life.

Neon lights, most broken or faded, lit up as best they could, and to my right, in the distance, a carousel I hadn't noticed before began to move in slow rotations. The still-life horses looked macabre with their open-mouthed whinnies and wild eyes. The air filled with the sounds of music and the irritating bells and whistles of midway din.

A chill cut through me and my heartbeat quickened a pace.

This was all wrong.

I took a step towards the house, where flashes of green-and-blue light were now intensifying and the fog had grown thick, spilling down the front steps. The soundtrack of the haunted house was playing full volume, filling the night with manufactured screams and the noises of moaning ghosts and ghouls.

If anyone called for help, I wouldn't be able to tell. The suddenness of the lights and sounds had thrown my senses off balance. I couldn't tell if the movement from the shadows was a trick of the light or if someone was actually there. I didn't want to be outside and exposed anymore.

I reached the front of the house and was about to pull the door open when a hissing crackle over the park's loudspeakers froze me on the spot, my hand still extended.

First it was just white noise, but that was replaced by the sound of someone singing the tune from a jack-in-the-box. The slow, creepy way the voice sang each note made me draw my hand back from the door and step away from the house so I could get a better look at the midway. In between notes the voice began to laugh. It started as hiccup-like bursts of giggling, interrupting the song and giving the tune a markedly demented quality.

Then it broke down into a maniacal cackle that had nothing to do with amusement and would have given a supervillain the willies.

I held tight to my gun, wishing I had something to shoot at.

The singing resumed, but the song was coming to an end. Once the final note had been sung, the jack-in-the-box should have popped out. But there was only silence and white noise. My heart was pounding.

"*Boo*," came the voice I'd heard on the phone.

Only it wasn't over the speakers, it was right in my ear. I choked back a scream and spun around to fire, but before I could, the power shut off again.

Chapter Twenty-Seven

In a moment of shock, before I could readjust to the dark, a hand darted out and grabbed me by the throat. It was a large, rough palm that seemed capable of wrapping itself all the way around my neck. My fangs were out—the fight instinct had kicked in almost the second the voice sounded in my ear—but fangs are only useful if I can bite something.

I aimed my gun, but by the time I sank the barrel into something fleshy and pulled the trigger, the sound of the bullet was an empty echo, having missed its intended target. I had been dropped to the ground. Scrambling to my feet, I aimed back to where my attacker once stood. There was no one there.

Panting, I did a scan of the area, but there appeared to be no one else present. I couldn't hear or smell anyone near me. It was almost like whoever attacked me had vanished into thin air. And why hadn't I heard or smelled him before he came up behind me?

On cue, the laughter burst through the silence, right next to my ear. When I pivoted to shoot, the sound was suddenly ten yards away. I lowered my gun and let my gaze travel the midway. With the lights shut off, I got a better sense of what was there and knew none of the shadows were stirring.

The laughter erupted again, loud and foreboding over the speakers, and a moment later from inside the house.

Vampires can move fast, but I've never seen a vampire go that many places that quickly. I'd assumed it was a vampire because of the inhuman quality of its voice over the phone. Now I no longer knew what kind of monster I was dealing with.

Deciding it wasn't a vampire should have made me happy, but it only managed to make the situation worse because I didn't know what I was up against. And Jameson had said they'd followed vampires here. If that was true—and I had no reason to believe it wasn't, considering what I'd smelled when I got here—then I still had a nest of vampires to deal with on top of whatever this freak show was.

And Jameson, Nolan and Noriko still needed my help.

"*Hey*," I shouted, interrupting the rapid-fire laughter bouncing all over the park. It was giving me a serious case of the heebie-jeebies, but I was here to do a job. "You wanted me to come play? *Well here I am.*"

The park was dead silent. It was so quiet, in fact, I could hear the *thump-thump-thump* of my own heart trying to free itself from my rib cage. Some assassin I was, letting a little light and noise scare me like this. It was sort of pathetic that I—

It appeared in front of me, without any sounds or flashes of smoke to announce it. It just sort of...materialized. I yelped and stumbled backwards, but managed to keep my footing. Now that I had a good look at it, I wished it had stayed in the dark.

The creature had gray skin with a pallor of green beneath it—the skin of a long-rotting corpse. The rest of its face was so monstrous it was hard to believe what I was seeing was real. The cheeks were gaunt, the skin sunk so deep into the crevices it rested right against the bone. Its eyes were hollow, and one socket was completely empty, revealing a hole so black staring into it threatened to suck you in. The other eye was still there, loose and milky white, unseeing but all seeing. Even with no pupil I could tell it was fixed right on me.

Its arms were skeletal at best. One ended in a bony claw of a hand, while the other still maintained a fleshy glove of skin, which would have been the one I'd felt around my neck. The thought of that hand touching me made bile rise in the back of my throat.

The creature opened its mouth and a rattling hiss passed where its lips should have been, but now only the strained, peeling tissue of dwindling muscle remained. A tongue appeared, shockingly pink and wet in the dead mouth of the corpse head. It wet its lips, and its white eyeball twitched.

I retched.

The tongue moved, independent of any real purpose, just flicking around like a small pink fish. Then the creature sighed a rattling breath and released the high, miserable laugh I'd been hearing. To witness it up close chilled me to my core. I raised my weapon, and it watched me take aim at its head, laughing all the while.

"You came to play. Stay to play." It cackled, wheezy laughter bubbling through its dry lungs.

"I. Don't. Want. To. Play. With. You." I spat out each word through a clenched jaw.

"We don't understand *want*," it said, its eyeball moving freely, looking at everything or at nothing. "You will play." This time there was no laughter, only cold demand.

The monster and I stared at each other for what seemed like a long time but must have only been seconds. It kept sucking in breaths that I could hear seeping out through the holes in its decaying body.

"Okay," I said. "We'll play."

It grinned, and as it did, a chunk of gaunt cheek sloughed away, exposing bare jaws and two rows of age-yellowed teeth. The grin didn't flicker. And that was when I saw the fangs, exactly where they were on every vampire I'd ever met.

I didn't have time to think about what it meant.

"Tag." The word came out as I pulled the trigger. Its eye widened, and then the whole messy patchwork of its head exploded in a fine mist of bone and skin. "You're it."

So I'd been right and wrong. It wasn't a vampire, not anymore, but it had been once. And now it was nothing. But in the time between life and death what had become of it? What could turn a vampire into a ghost? And what kind of ghost could be killed by bullets?

This night kept getting stranger and stranger.

I jogged up the steps to the house, not letting anything else distract me from my purpose. I kicked open the inner door and had my weapon at the ready if anything was waiting for me inside, but the main floor of the house was empty.

The power had been shut down again, and the last remnants of the smoke-machine haze were fading away, leaving only a low-lying gloom over the floors that kept the bottom half of the room invisible.

In front of me was a large oak-banister staircase leading to the second floor. The room on the left had been converted into storage and was filled with boxes and various parts of the park's former life. To the right, a room bathed in moonlight appeared to contain only a shiny black coffin on a pedestal. More leftovers from the house's former life. Behind it, a mummy dummy rested at an angle against the empty bookshelves, arms pointed outward in preparation to grab an unsuspecting passerby.

I sniffed the air, but the dry smell of the fog was overwhelming. If anyone was in here with me, I couldn't tell, so I was effectively fighting blind. I took a few tentative steps forward, and when I didn't trip over anything, I moved with more confidence towards the stairs. Following the staircase to the second floor, I did a sweep.

The house's layout had been designed for tours rather than living, so the second floor was a maze of rooms and attractions. I stood stupefied, looking at what was laid out before me. There was a crumbling drywall framework, which I could see through to more walls beyond. I felt like a mouse in a laboratory maze. I stepped through the first doorway, ducking under the broken wall into a high-ceilinged room lined with mirrors.

"Fuuuuuuuck."

About a hundred of me swore along in unison. Adjusting my shooting grip, I pressed my back to the closest wall and scooted along, shadowed by my consortium of doppelgangers as we searched for the right exit into the next room of this house of horrors.

Up here, away from the smoke machine, the smell of blood was strong, but there was a stale quality to it. Not long aged, it also wasn't brand new. I didn't know if that was a good thing or a bad thing, but I chose to hope it was the former.

I followed the mirrored walls, bumping into adjacent mirrors several times. As I moved, I avoided looking at my own alarmed expression. It was hard to pretend you weren't afraid when thirty-six horrified reflections of you were staring back.

A black square with no reflection on it appeared, and I gratefully stepped through into the space waiting beyond. Into a graveyard.

At first I thought I was mistaken. The ground underfoot was real dirt, and there were a dozen graves laid out before me, each one looking frightfully fresh. Even the smell in the air was of fresh earth and night wind.

Once I touched the nearest surface it was obvious the walls were only painted to look like a nighttime sky and the headstones were just well-decorated Styrofoam. I nudged one over with my foot, and it flopped backwards without any resistance. No angry dead rose up to avenge the desecration. I knelt and brushed the dirt back from the mound just to be sure no one was buried underneath. All it revealed was a shipping barrel cut in half with nothing under it.

I sat back on my heels and looked around the room, wishing it would tell me something. I needed a clue as to where I was supposed to be searching.

From downstairs came a riotous crashing noise and the sound of a male voice screaming in pain.

I skidded back into the mirror room, not wanting to risk moving forward when I knew going backwards would at least take me somewhere familiar. My shoulder collided into one of the mirrored walls with staggering force and shards of sharp glass rained down on me, speckling my skin with an array of new cuts. Still I moved forward, with more care now but with no less haste.

I reached the main hall and wasted no time with the stairs. I vaulted over the banister, landing at the foot of the stairs with a loud thud, buried instantly by the newly restored fake smoke. When I got to my feet, I was facing the room with the prop coffin in it.

Only now the coffin was open.

"We're glad you could make it," a masculine voice announced from a few feet behind me.

I'd been so preoccupied in hoping to find someone, I hadn't been paying attention for people trying to find me. I turned around slowly and saw Jameson holding Nolan by the neck in a sleeper hold while the boy kicked at the floor, fighting against the wave of unconsciousness threatening to take him over. Nolan was looking at me wide-eyed, but my sight was all on Jameson.

"I came here to *help* you," I said, my voice loaded with the hurt of his betrayal.

Nolan passed out, and Jameson dropped his body to the floor.

"Oh, you will help us, Secret. You have no idea how much you'll help."

I saw the wrought-iron fire poker in his other hand a moment before he swung. And then for the first time in my life I got to find out what it felt like to be bashed in the skull with one.

Chapter Twenty-Eight

"This seems like a silly way to spend your last moments," Brigit said, ever cheerful.

We were lying next to a pool, our skin warmed by the glow of the midday sun while a very handsome young man delivered us mimosas. I'd never had a mimosa before.

"If I make it through this, please make sure I try one of these," I requested.

Brigit laughed, sipping her own drink and adjusting her oversize sunglasses. Her toenails were painted bright pink to match her bikini. I wore black. I looked out at the blue, blue water, enjoying the way sunlight reflecting off it was so glaring in certain places I couldn't look directly at it.

"You'll be fine," she said.

"That's what I told Desmond."

"That boy." Brigit whistled appreciatively. "You hit some sort of beefcake jackpot there."

I nestled back into the chair, enjoying the warmth of the sun on my face. "I don't think anyone has used the phrase *beefcake* outside of a 1978 Harlequin romance novel, Bri."

"Beefcake, beefcake, *beefcake*," she chanted.

We both sipped our drinks leisurely. My dreams had quite the euphoric quality to them lately. Either I was spending time naked in bed with good-looking men, or I got to sunbathe. Of the two, I think I liked this one best. As Brigit pointed out, I got to spend naked time with hot men in real life.

I'd never been able to bask in the sun before.

"Boss?" she said.

"Mmm?" I didn't feel like correcting her, so I just rolled with it.

"Not that I'm complaining or anything, but is there a reason I'm here? I was in the middle of a shower and then, like, *wham*, I'm dreaming. I'm probably pretty pruney by now." She assessed her fingers as if they would reflect what was happening to her body in the real world.

I'd *pulled* her into a dream? How was that possible? Dreamy thoughts ebbed and flowed through my mind, reminding me of something Holden had told me.

Of course! Brigit was my ward, like I was Holden's. I had used my connection with her to reach out for help. My subconscious, as it turns out, is a freaking genius.

"*Brigit.*" I sat bolt upright in my chaise lounger, knocking my mimosa over.

"That's me."

"You need to tell Sig... I... He needs to know where I am."

"Where are you?"

"I'm in Rhinebeck."

She wrinkled her nose. "Weird, why would you go antiquing?"

"Brigit..." I warned.

"What should I tell him?"

"If Desmond did his job, you shouldn't have to tell him anything else."

"Secret, that's sort of a weird message."

"Tell him I have his answers," I lied.

The sun seemed to grow brighter, and the reflection of it on the water became unbearable. I looked away only to find my vision had been whited out by the brilliance of the sun.

"Tell him I tried."

Then the intensity of the light blotted everything else out.

Someone slapped me.

The pain in my head was still real outside the dream, and when I tried to open my eyes, only one of them would comply. Any attempts to open the second resulted in a jackhammer annihilating the left side of my skull. I licked my lips and tasted copper. Blood.

I made to lift my hands to investigate the source of the blood but found they were bound behind my back and neither one of them was holding my gun. My fingers brushed against skin, and a little further touching told me another pair of hands was bound with mine.

Well this just kept getting better.

When I lifted my head, something cracked in my neck, but it was nothing pivotal. In fact, a great release of endorphins followed the pop. Through my one good eye I could see Jameson standing a foot or two away from me.

"Good. I didn't kill you," he said with a nod.

I spit a mouthful of blood onto the floor and let my head loll backwards so I was staring at the ceiling. Spider-web patterns of light exploded across my vision and an achy throbbing sound pulsed in my ears, but I could at least see who was in the chair behind me.

"Nolan," I croaked. "Nolan, are you okay?"

The boy was still out cold, his head flopped to one side like his neck contained no bones. But he was breathing, so for the time being I could assume he was all right. My head rolled to the side of its own volition, and I found myself looking out a large picture window.

In the tree outside, a barn owl glared at me.

I let out a small yip of joy, though to anyone present it probably sounded like pain.

Jameson came over to me and pulled my head upright by my hair, narrowly avoiding my attack when I tried to bite his arm open with my still-exposed fangs. He yanked his arm away, then grabbed my face in one of his large, rough hands. He shoved my upper lip up on both sides and gave a long whistle.

"*Damn*, girl."

I snarled at him but ended up choking back more of my own blood.

Near my chair was an old, tall brass lamp. I'd only have one chance to execute this plan properly, so I had to believe my rudimentary grasp of physics was enough. I swung the weight of my body to one side, jerking my face out of Jameson's hand, and then when he moved to grab at me again I tipped the chairs the opposite way, dragging Nolan's body weight as well as my own to the tipping point.

The chairs tumbled over and the back panel of one broke, but our bonds still held firm. Freedom hadn't been the point, however. The brass lamp wobbled, and I watched it with one eye wide. It teetered violently, and then it too tumbled. Its fall was much more spectacular because it fell into the big window, creating a triumphant crash. The window wasn't destroyed, but a large panel of it was now missing.

The owl blinked at me and I blinked back, but given how screwed up my face was it probably looked like I was winking at it.

Jameson pulled our chairs back up with one tug and glared at me.

"You're supposed to behave," he snapped.

I laughed. "Whoever told you that either never met me or thought you'd be stupid enough to believe it."

He looked flummoxed and repeated, "You're supposed to behave."

I spit more blood out, then touched my fangs with the tip of my tongue to make sure neither was loose. My human teeth I could get caps for. Vampire fangs don't regrow if you lose them, and I wasn't in a position to lose my only built-in weapon. They both felt secure, so at least that wasn't the source of the blood.

"Jameson," I wheezed. "Who told you that?"

"I..." He checked the bonds holding me and Nolan and seemed satisfied they were secure. Behind me Nolan groaned, finally starting to come around.

If Jameson was someone's daytime servant, he lacked any of the sensibilities of the ones I had previously met. Other human servants were whip-smart, devoted and cunning. You had to maintain certain skills in order to survive for centuries without the speed and strength of a vampire. Jameson seemed lost and bumbling. Even during the brief encounter we'd had at Bramley, he had been self-assured and larger than life.

This Jameson was an empty husk of his former self.

A puppet.

"Oh, Jameson, you stupid old fool. You of anyone should have known."

He stared at me blankly. "I don't know what you mean." He still sounded like himself. The Jameson of old was in there somewhere, probably trying to claw his way to the surface. But he had been turned into a Renfield. He was some master vampire's errand boy now.

"They got you."

"No one got me." He walked over to the main doors of the room and yanked one open. "Noriko said you were one of them and she was right. You must be sacrificed for the cause."

I blinked my one eye uselessly. A giant hand of pain squeezed my skull.

"What *cause*?"

But Jameson had vanished through the open door, leaving Nolan and me alone in the room.

"Nolan?"

"Uhn."

"Nolan, wake up. Please."

"Wuhh." At least they were starting to sound like real words now.

"*Wake up*," I screamed, throwing my head backwards and knocking it against his.

"*Ow.*" I felt him shake his head and he groaned, but the sound was more frustrated than pained. He'd probably just realized how far up shit creek we were without paddles. "Secret?" He craned his neck back. "Oh, Christ, they got ya."

"So it would seem."

"I didn't think they could."

"Tell me everything you know," I demanded.

"He doesn't know anything," Noriko announced, stepping through the door. She was followed by Jameson, and two of the vampire ghosts trailed behind them.

Of the two, only one was recognizable as once being human in any capacity. Her skin was still mostly intact, and she had both of her eyes, but they had faded to white. Her hair was patchy and only clumps of it remained, dangling in stringy bunches from her mottled scalp.

The other one was more repellant than the first I'd experienced. Huge chunks of skin were missing all over his body and both of his eyes were gone. His grinning skeletal face was staring at me with his fangs bared and ready. Ready for what, I didn't want to know.

Noriko wore the same black catsuit as she had the last time I'd seen her. She looked like she should be breaking into a bank vault rather than tormenting captives, but if it was her look, who was I to question it?

"You look like a rejected extra from *Mission: Impossible*." Oh, that's right, I was still me.

"You insolent little bitch," she spat. "Don't you know when you're beaten?"

I thought about it for a moment. "No."

Nolan was riveted in terror, staring at the two ghosts. For the time being, neither of them was doing anything threatening. They seemed content to just be creepily corporeal in the background. Their presence was threat enough.

Noriko, carrying the same katana with which she'd attacked me outside of Havana, came to stand in front of me. She raised the sword so it was one hard gulp away from puncturing my neck, and gave me a look that was meant to be a challenge.

"Can I ask you something?" I whispered, careful to not engage the blade.

"What?" was her irritated response.

"Why them?"

"I don't understand."

"Why Jameson? Why Nolan? Why did you go to Bramley and find them?"

"Because sooner or later, even the most foolish vampire hunter will stumble on to a great prize, Secret. They..." she indicated Jameson and Nolan, "...found the first of the council-guarded vampires for us by sheer dumb luck."

She'd said *us*. So that explained her part in this. Noriko was a daytime servant, which seemed quite obvious to me now with her holding a sword to my throat and being followed by an entourage of the undead.

"How old are you?"

She pulled back the sword a bit and contemplated the answer to the question.

"I was born in 1614 in Edo. So, I suppose, I am nearly four hundred." She was briefly delighted by this, as though it never occurred to her to take stock of something so menial as age.

"Who were you in Japan?" I asked. My knuckle-duster ring had slipped loose, and I had nudged it low on my fingers. When I'd punched Sig earlier that week one of the diamonds had shifted, creating a sharp, blade-like point on the surface of the ring. I was trying to cut through my ropes using that point, plus the broken wood from the back of my chair. Nolan was being no help whatsoever.

Noriko's eyes clouded and something approaching rage crossed her face. "I was an *Oiran.* A respected prostitute." Her jaw was tight. I'd asked the wrong question. Why couldn't she have been a sweet tea server or someone's devoted wife? "Enough of this. It's time for your end, McQueen."

But she didn't raise her sword again. Instead she nodded to Jameson, who left the room.

"Noriko?"

"I said *enough.*"

"If you can even still pretend you're human, promise me something."

"I promise you nothing."

I ignored her dismissal. "Nolan has nothing to do with this. Let him live."

Her face sank with regret. "It's too late for that."

"It's not too late. Why is it too late?"

"Because the master is here." She looked over to the door as Jameson reentered, followed by a beautiful, smartly dressed blonde.

My heart stopped and all warmth drained from my face. I would have been less shocked to see my own mother walk in. A lot less, actually.

"Daria?"

Chapter Twenty-Nine

"Daria?" I sputtered again, still unable to connect what I was looking at with the part of my brain that converted seeing to believing. For a minute I thought she was there to help me.

But of course that wasn't the case.

"Hello, Secret." She was pristine, as always. Her hair was pulled back into a smooth chignon, showing her dancer's neck and revealing the delicate features of her face. She wore a simple black dress with a modest neckline. Her lipstick was red, but understated, making her look like the wife of a presidential candidate. She even wore pearls.

This was not the vision of a vampire-killing, diabolical monster I had conjured.

She smoothed her unwrinkled skirt and clasped her hands together in front of her. No part of her seemed shocked by my current condition, and why should it? This had all been her doing.

"No," I protested. "This isn't right."

Daria shrugged, then smiled a little too sweetly for my taste. "This is the way of the world, Miss McQueen." She indicated the vampire ghosts with a perfectly manicured hand. "The strong survive while the weak perish. Simple Darwinism."

"This isn't evolution." I was shocked by how cavalier she was being. "It's murder."

Her hands reclasped. "So be it."

"Why them? Why would you kill the protected ones? They trusted you to keep them safe."

Daria huffed. "What fool trusts a vampire? They were idiots to believe anyone could keep them protected forever."

"What benefit was it to you to kill them? And *what* are they?"

Noriko shot me a warning look and raised her sword, but Daria stilled her with a flick of the wrist. "No, no, Noriko, let her ask. She may as well know what she's dying for. She's been Sig's pawn for long enough. It's time we treated her like an equal for once."

"I'm not Sig's pawn."

"You were the council's pawn, and Sig *is* the council. If you are stupid enough to believe he wasn't using you, then you deserve what's coming to you."

It felt like she'd slapped me.

"I chose my path."

"Foolish girl. Did you choose to let Peyton live? Did you decide who to kill? You come at his beck and call. You are the council's dog. Sig has used you to achieve his ends and he would keep using you for whatever pleases him. You should thank me for releasing you."

"You're just as guilty as he is."

She laughed, clapping her hands together with delight. "You think there is anything approaching equality in the Tribunal? Sig is lord and master, and don't let yourself think any differently."

"So this is all about him?"

Daria sighed, exasperated. "It's about power."

"You *have* power."

"But I am still bound to obey *him*." Her face contorted with anger and became momentarily hideous.

"What did the protected vampires have to do with it? And Holden?"

"Chancery was an easy target. I had another vampire bring forth evidence against him and accuse him of the slayings. Sig was forced to issue the warrant, but assigning it to you wasn't my idea. That was pure Sig. Until right now I'd thought he was being cruel, but now I see it was another controlling move on his part. And a clever one at that. You came quite close to the truth."

I dared not look out the window to see if the owl was still there, but I hoped he had taken wing. Daria had said more than enough.

"And the vampires?" I inclined my head to the less scary of the two.

"Elders. Their power was incredible. I was able to drink from them and take that power into myself. They have begun to fade the more I feed, but they are still bound to me as long as they live."

"They're still *alive*?" I was appalled. No creature should have to live in the state of decay the ghouls were in. They were prisoners in their own bodies.

"A sort of living, I suppose. Somewhere between this life and the next. If they feed, their strength goes to me, so sadly they have begun to show a little wear." She gave a reproachful smirk to the more disfigured of the two. "All for a good cause, though."

The ghost nodded weakly.

Nolan let out a fearful, quivering whimper.

"You're insane," I told her.

"I prefer to think of myself as resourceful."

"You're going to challenge Sig for leadership of the Tribunal, aren't you?"

"And I'm going to win." Her eyes flashed. "The only way to advance is to kill the one ahead of you in a declared fight. Before this he would have destroyed me, but now he won't know what hit him. Sig *will* die."

"Who's the fool now?"

Her features tightened, and Noriko moved to attack again. Once more she was stopped.

"Your dedication to him is admirable, Secret. Like a dog, you would die to protect him. But if your master cared so much about you, then why is he not here to keep it from happening?"

I didn't have a clever comeback for her.

"That's what I thought. Your usefulness is at an end. With you out of the picture, nothing stands in my way."

Outside the window I heard a flap of wings. I was apparently the only one to notice.

"Noriko, I've grown tired of the half-breed and your associates. The time has come."

"The time has come for what?" Nolan finally found the courage to speak.

"For you all to die, of course."

Daria may have called *me* a well-trained dog, but if that wasn't the pot calling the kettle whipped, I didn't know what was. Noriko watched her master leave with the two vampire ghosts, then trained her blade on me with an altogether-too-creepy smirk.

"I'm saving you for last," she promised.

"It's your funeral."

She strode across the room with her footsteps barely touching the floor, and Jameson watched her come with no sign of fear.

"Secret?" Nolan whispered as Noriko pulled the blade back into a traditional fighting stance and squared herself in front of Jameson.

"Close your eyes," I instructed. Both Jameson and Nolan followed my order. "You don't have to do this, Noriko. They trusted you."

"Trust is for fools. You heard what Daria said."

"And Daria is nuts."

The blade held in the air, and Noriko seemed to contemplate my words for a brief pause. I hoped against the odds she might have heard what I was saying. In the lull, Jameson opened his eyes and smiled a peaceful, resigned smile.

"Daria is the future. The past is dead," Noriko announced, then her blade sang though the air. Jameson's head tipped to the side, his eyes still bulging with surprise, and tumbled to the floor with a cracking noise where it hit the hardwood.

"Nolan," I whispered. "Keep your eyes closed. Whatever happens, I need you to believe I will get you out of this alive."

His breath was short and edged with panic.

"I will protect you," I swore.

"You can't even protect yourself." Noriko laughed, rounding on the chair. She took her blade and wiped Jameson's blood on my shirtsleeve. "Everyone claimed you were the greatest warrior of them all. You were a legend."

I forced a smile. "I have a great publicist."

"Tonight your legend dies."

I looked up at her, my one good eye locked on her face. "I've heard that promise before, Noriko, and from beings a lot scarier than a four-hundred-year-old hooker with a toy sword."

Rage contorted her features in an ugly way. Her face wrinkled in on itself, and her eyes darkened dramatically. Her sword stance was less precise this time. She pulled the sword back over her head as if she intended to halve me like a dry log. The blade cut through the air, but I was faster than she was.

"Nolan, pull your hands back. Now!"

He did as he was told and the rope binding us together strained, providing a gap between our wrists. With a hop that made my whole body scream in protest, I shuffled the weight of both our bodies forward a mere two inches.

It was enough.

The blade cut through the ropes, freeing my hands. I pulled my wrists free and looked at my arm. She'd cut me along my right forearm where the blade must have gotten me before I'd pulled all the way forward. Dark blood seeped from the wound, but I could still use my fingers, at least for now.

Then, as deep wounds are wont to do, the pain came as soon as I saw it. But it was no ordinary pain. My skin felt like it was being boiled from within, and the entirety of my arm swam with the burning itch of a thousand fire ants trapped beneath the surface.

Noriko's sword was made of silver.

My eye darted to her, then back to the wound. She'd paused her attack only long enough to smile smugly at my reaction. My bravado had faded, but not my will to live. She swung again, but I rolled off the chair, which was subsequently sliced clean in half. Nolan had gotten off his chair and was struggling with his leg bonds, but for the time being he was not her concern. Her eyes and her sword were all for me.

As I pulled at the ropes around my ankles, the tingling itch spread to my fingers at last, rendering them useless. My own blood was painting my bare legs a grisly black-red. I freed one leg in time to kick myself backwards on the carpet as she slashed to attack me once more.

"For someone who's had four centuries to practice, you're not very good with that thing." I hopped to my feet, kicking the loosened ropes off. I must have made quite the spectacle, with one eye swollen shut and my face and legs smeared with blood. The look on Nolan's face when he saw the front of me for the first time was sobering.

It was probably the same look I'd worn when I met the first vampire ghost outside.

My arm bled onto the floor with a steady dripping sound.

"You will die here tonight," Noriko snarled.

"If I do, it'll be from blood loss due to standing around bored while I wait for you to shut the hell up and attack me already."

She looked astonished. I'm guessing the protected vampires had given her and Daria a lot less trouble than this. Most people, when faced with death, reach the level of acceptance and eventually yield. I got as far as denial and sort of stuck there. It made killing me pretty frustrating.

I gave her a nod, then bolted for the door.

If I believed for even an instant she would turn on Nolan, I wouldn't have run. But I'd seen the hatred in her eyes and the commitment she had to the task at hand. Her sole purpose, for now, was killing me.

In the hall the fog had dissipated, but I still managed to snag my foot on the edge of a rug. My stupid feet were numb from being bound so tight. I stumbled down, catching myself with both hands, and ignoring the screaming agony in my head and forearm, I vaulted myself forward into a somersault and landed in a standing position at the base of the staircase. I looked from the door to the stairs and debated my options for the millisecond I had.

Noriko was through the door and chasing me into the hallway, rage-blinded and screaming in an inhuman, animal wail. I, like every stupid slasher-movie victim, chose the stairs instead of the door and bounded up them two at a time. She was right on my heels.

I was a second ahead of her into the mirrored room, and when she followed me inside she was forced to pause.

Dozens of her stared at dozens of me.

I waved, and the multitude of Secrets followed suit. Her mirror images all looked equally enraged by this turn of events. I didn't speak, because my voice would give away my real location. I used her momentary confusion to track my previous blood trail on the floor, through the maze, to where I'd broken the mirror panel earlier that night.

She followed my reflections, but had apparently never come through this way before. She walked into a mirrored wall at least once, swearing with irritation and smashing the glass to retaliate. I crept back to her, a large shard of mirror in my good hand. She was still too distracted by breaking the mirrors to notice me until my reflections were all right next to hers in the remaining panels.

"Guess you picked the wrong one." And as she turned towards the real me in surprise, I buried the shard of glass deep into her neck. Her body seized, and a gurgling, wet noise escaped her throat. She slumped to the ground with wide, shocked eyes. I crouched next to her, but with the glass in her throat it was hard to check for a pulse, and I'd never been able to feel for one in the wrist. I nudged a piece of glass in front of her mouth and watched for any sign of breath. When none came I scooped up her sword, avoiding the silver blade, and trekked back into the main hall.

"Nolan?" I called out. I was limping and keeping my bloody arm pressed against my belly as I reached the top of the stairs. My head was pounding with the torment of a thousand migraines and it wouldn't dull any time soon. Calliope was in for a treat when I got out of here.

She was an Oracle though; she would have seen it coming.

Too bad I wasn't an Oracle.

Noriko's whole weight slammed into me and we both staggered backwards, struggling to maintain our balance. I had a thing or two to learn about the mortality of daytime servants because I'd have staked even money she'd been dead, but I must have hit something vital. She wasn't speaking in words, just making guttural barks of noise while blood seeped from her neck. The glass was still sticking out the side of her throat.

She tried to throw our combined weight to the stairs, and the only thing I could do was force us in the opposite direction. The struggle was briefly even, a full-body arm wrestle, until I used some untapped reserve of strength and hurled us both into the full-wall picture window opposite the stairs.

In the time I had to reflect on this, while we fell through a shower of glass and wooden window frame, perhaps it wasn't my best plan ever.

Parts of me that were previously uninjured were now a moist tapestry of cuts, and when I got to my feet a glittery stream of small glass slivers tinkled to the ground. Larger fragments were embedded in my palms from pushing myself up.

Noriko was gasping in short, labored breaths, but still she struggled to her feet.

"Just. *Stop*," I pleaded.

"Die," she cursed.

Her sword was on the ground two feet away, and she seemed to notice it at the same time I did. We saw our equal chances of reaching it, and both dove. When we found our footing, she was holding the sword and I was crouched low enough to avoid her first attempt to divorce me from my head. The air above my scalp shrieked.

I got to my feet while her arm limply sagged at her side. If I looked even half as grim as she did right now, it was a wonder we weren't both dead.

In an attempt to make peace I said, "It's your last—"

She lunged for me rather than listen to my bargain, and I was ready for our fight to be over. I turned to my side just as I felt something sting between my ribs. My foot connected with her stomach in a perfectly executed side kick, and she didn't get a chance to regain her balance.

Noriko tumbled backwards down the hill and into the broken wooden fence at the back of the property. The sharp point of the old gate pierced through her chest with fatal precision. She slumped, and the fight went out of her along with her life.

I stood panting, looking at the silver blade stuck six inches into my rib cage, and let out a whine of pain as I drew it out by the hilt. My whole body was aflame with the poisonous torture of the silver. My arm wasn't healing, and the new hole in my side would be just as slow to close.

I was ready to sink to the ground and give up, when I heard Nolan speak.

"Secret?" There was a tremble of fear in my name.

Holding the sword by its benign, silver-free handle, I turned towards his voice.

Daria held Nolan by the neck, his toes brushing the tips of the grass below him, his eyes wide with terror and his face pale from oxygen loss. Daria's gaze trailed to her former servant impaled on the wooden spear. She looked at me, who stood bloody and weak, and then she lowered Nolan enough he could touch the ground and gasp for breath.

"I underestimated you," she told me as she petted Nolan, still standing behind him.

"Uhn," I grunted, gripping the sword tighter. My one eye glared.

"Let us talk, shall we?"

"I'd rather not."

"Then how about I talk and you listen?"

There was no sense in arguing. When a vampire wanted to go on a rant about something, no force on Earth could stop them.

"It seems I am out one human servant."

"Sorry."

Daria waved off the apology. "Irrelevant. I have your man-child."

Nolan's gaze was locked on my face, but I couldn't bring myself to look at him.

"What's your point?" I winced. Every word I spoke caused an explosion of white-hot needles to sear through my bloodstream. For once in my life, my body would have appreciated it if I'd shut the hell up.

"If you abandon your allegiance to Sig and stand by me in my revolution, your power will exceed your wildest expectations."

Things must have been looking bad for her if she was willing to barter with me.

"I thought I was just Sig's loyal dog."

"I think we both know you're more than that." She looked down the hill again. I followed her stare, half-expecting Noriko to have risen from the beyond to attack me again. She hadn't. She was still as dead as I'd left her.

"What does this have to do with Nolan?"

"I'll make him my new servant. That way he needn't die and you can continue to watch over him."

Nolan tried to jerk free of her hold, but she held him steady. He was obviously less than enamored with Daria's perfect plan.

"No." I tried to shake my head, but it hurt too badly.

"No?"

"He goes free or I won't help you."

"He knows too much."

I snorted. "You can kill council elders and absorb their strength. You can frame a warden for an impossible crime. You can threaten the sanctity of the Tribunal. But you can't thrall a kid into forgetting you?" I limped towards her. "Are you really no stronger than a baby vampire?"

She was clearly offended by my accusation.

"You would stand beside me, if I spare his life?"

I looked at Nolan. His eyes were glistening with tears, but still he shook his head to say no. I smiled at him helplessly.

"I will."

Chapter Thirty

Daria released Nolan and laughed with delight.

In the same moment, the owl came to perch on the tree overhead. He announced himself with a mournful *whoo*, but there was only joy inside me at the sight of him. I looked away from Nolan and Daria and right at the bird.

"Your timing is impeccable."

"*Who*," said the owl.

"Are you quite mad?" Daria asked, shifting her gaze from me to the bird. Pretty rich coming from her.

I grabbed Nolan's wrist before Daria had time to react and pulled him behind me, offering what meager protection I could. I would fall dead before she touched him again.

"I'd have to be mad to agree to help you."

"We had a *deal*," she protested.

"I don't bargain with rogues." I raised the sword to stop her advance. My hands were shaking badly and the blade trembled. She laughed again, but this time it was cold and loaded with an unspoken threat.

"You think you can stand against me? You, a boy, and..." she raised her eyes to the tree branches, "...a bird?"

"*Who*," said the owl.

"It's time for you to die, you insufferable little nuisance." Her veneer of politeness was melting away. Now the true monster beneath the surface began to show itself. Her fangs flashed and her eyes became pools of blackness.

The bird took flight again, circling over the house and flapping its wings with flourish before perching on a lower branch than before. Daria attempted to dive for me, and I held the shaky sword in preparation, but the attack never came.

She was frozen in place.

Panic contorted her face as she fought against her own immobilized limbs, trying desperately to move in any direction. She snarled at the futility of her actions, lathering herself into a frenzy.

"Nifty little trick, isn't it?"

"What have you done to me?" she shrieked.

"She hasn't done anything." A voice preceded its owner from the corner of the house. Sig followed his words and came to stand next to the rigid figure of his former right hand. "It was the bird."

Daria's gaze darted to the owl, then back to Sig.

In a spectacular display of shimmering blue light, a show I was no stranger to, the bird dropped from the tree and landed as a man next to Sig. His olive skin glowed softly in the night, glittering with the lingering traces of the magic. He looked at me, a tight smile on his face.

"This, I believe they say, makes us even?" His strange accent made the sentence seem exotic.

I nodded, my head wobbling loosely like a rag doll's.

"I hope your kind will have no further need of my services," he said to Sig. "I helped you only as a favor to the girl's grandmother. We are done now."

"For now," Sig agreed.

The witch narrowed his eyes at Sig's turn of phrase.

"You may release her."

The witch looked at the black depths of Daria's pupils. She gnashed her teeth at him. Unmoved, he straightened the lapels of his suit with casual defiance, as though vampires threatened him regularly.

I wouldn't worry too much about vampires either, if I could turn into a bird at a moment's notice and fly away.

"I have told you what this one..." he indicated Daria, "...has confessed. Now you wish her to be free from her bonds?"

"We deal with traitors our own way." This came from an altogether surprising speaker. Juan Carlos came around the same corner of the house Sig had. With him was Brigit, who looked uncharacteristically grim. "She is our concern now."

"As you wish." The witch spoke the words with the same tone I'd used to invite Noriko to her own funeral. He snapped his fingers, and in a flash of sapphire light and a puff of smoke, he was gone.

"He can teleport?" Brigit asked.

Only I seemed to notice the tiny wasp that emerged from the cloud. It buzzed once around my head before it disappeared into the trees. Sneaky witch.

Once the shock of the magical display had shaken off, Daria became aware the spell had been broken. Her instinctive reaction was to continue her attack against me, which Nolan recognized because he took a step backwards. But Sig had placed a warning hand on Daria's shoulder. All he needed to do was squeeze and she stopped.

"This fight is over, old friend," he said, his voice heavy with a sadness that surprised me.

She looked up at him, her face almost instantly restoring to its former sweetness and beauty.

"Sig, whatever she has claimed, it's a lie. She will protect her beloved warden at any cost. She is disloyal." Her voice was so earnest, her face so committed to the lie, I almost believed it myself. "I would never betray the Tribunal. I have been loyal to you for centuries."

I almost choked on her ingratiating words, but I didn't defend myself.

Sig's hand tightened on her shoulder, and she winced. Juan Carlos had come to stand beside Sig, and I could see him clearly now. The twisted grimace that marred his once-handsome face was now set in a tight frown, and for once it wasn't focused on me.

If anyone here would be willing to believe her lies, it would be him. But his rage was all for her, and she could see that.

"We heard everything you said, Daria. The witch delivered your confession to us."

"He is her puppet," she sputtered. "He did it for her."

"No," Juan Carlos said, grasping Daria by the face and drawing her in close so they were nose to nose and all she could see was his cold eyes. "You have betrayed us."

Her bottom lip quivered. I'd never seen a vampire approach tears. "I didn't betray you."

"To betray the Tribunal is to betray me."

"Don't you understand? He has too much power. I did this to restore balance," she pleaded.

"You did it to seize power," Sig interjected. "You didn't want to divide my power, you wanted it for yourself."

Daria kept her eyes on Juan Carlos, and he pushed her face away in disgust.

"Death is too kind for her," he said to Sig.

Sig had released Daria and was standing with his back to her, looking down at me. Gently, he placed a finger under my chin and raised my face to get a better look at me. Just one touch, and the coiled springs inside me that had been prepared for another fight fell loose. My whole body felt like a sack of broken, disjointed pieces I didn't know how to put back together. I sagged, and he caught me.

"She hasn't got long," he told Juan Carlos. "We need to get her to the Oracle."

Brigit skirted the group and took me from Sig, propping me up effortlessly. The Tribunal leader turned back to Daria.

"You sought to hurt me by attacking that which I hold dearest?" He hauled back as if he might hit her, and she flinched. "It wasn't enough you planned to kill me?"

"Her death would weaken you," she said meekly.

"And your death will weaken us all," Sig replied.

"Show mercy."

"Why? You have shown none."

"I meant to spare her."

"Only when she could not be killed!" Sig bellowed. It was the first time I'd ever heard him raise his voice, and it chilled me to the marrow. I leaned my face into Brigit to shut it out. "You only thought to keep her alive because you realized she might prove some further use to you." He grabbed Daria by the throat and lifted her off the ground.

Even though she didn't need to breathe, she strained against him, kicking futilely at the air and clawing at his hands while his grip began to crush her windpipe. His skin was a patchwork of bloody ribbons when he threw her to the grass.

"You will be confined until a suitable punishment is agreed upon."

Juan Carlos nodded his smug agreement. No one had ever explained confinement to me, but I'd always gathered it was considered a fate worse than death. Daria was apparently among the group who believed this.

"*No*," she screamed. "I won't go."

"You don't get to make those decisions anymore," Juan Carlos taunted. There was something hauntingly sad in his countenance.

"Kill me," she begged, her words directed to Juan Carlos, who turned away.

"No," Sig said, his voice flat and emotionless.

She got to her feet, faltering on the grass in her heels, and continued to look imploringly at Juan Carlos, holding her hands out to him as if begging for something. When he showed her no sympathy, she swung back to me. There was nothing human about her face.

"This is all your fault."

"Okay," I whispered, still leaning against Brigit, blood seeping out of me from the multitude of wounds covering my body.

My acceptance of her accusation enraged her more. With more speed than I would have thought she still possessed, she ripped me free of Brigit's hold. My ward attempted to pull the feral vampire off me, but Daria was of a singular purpose now. She wanted to die and she was going to take me with her.

She tried to latch on to my neck, but I'd come to expect this as the first move for any blood-frenzied vampire. I smashed my elbow across her face, and her neck snapped to the side. She was still pushing on a forward course, and the momentum of my hit caused her to trip on her high heels.

This was why I'd learned to always wear flats to a fight.

Her feet tangled with mine, and she grabbed hold of me, taking me with her as she tumbled down the hill. When we stopped, my head was against Noriko's thigh and the sword was still in my hand. Daria had already found her footing and was standing over me with a victorious leer.

"You want to die?" I asked.

She said nothing and darted in for the killing bite instead. I was anticipating it and was already swinging my arm upward before she dove. The two motions came together with the precision of a well-oiled machine. Her neck fell through the path of the sword, and when her body came down on top of me, her head was watching from a few feet away.

I lay gasping, unable to find the strength to push her dead weight off me.

"Help," I croaked.

It was Nolan of all people who got to me first, pulling the headless corpse off me and lifting me from the ground as if I were weightless. He was joined by the three vampires, and Juan

Carlos checked on Daria's body to ensure she was dead. He seemed satisfied.

"Sorry," I told him.

"Why?"

"You didn't want her dead."

Juan Carlos smiled, and I wished he hadn't. It reminded me of looking at a demented jack-o'-lantern. His joviality was more sinister than his seriousness. "It no longer matters. You've done the job we asked of you as a council, and I believe we can consider your warrant fulfilled."

Sig watched our exchange and tried to take me from Nolan, but the boy refused to hand me over.

"She promised to protect me," Nolan explained. "The least I can do is the same for her now."

Sig looked surprised by the boy's courage and didn't argue. After this, I would have to stop thinking of Nolan as a boy. I sagged in his arms.

"Holden is safe now?" I asked to no one in particular.

"Yes," Sig confirmed.

"Okay," I said, smiling, and then the world slipped into darkness.

Chapter Thirty-One

Three weeks had passed since my trip to Rhinebeck, and August had come to New York City.

The air outside was steamy hot and out for blood. News reports were discussing a wave of brownouts, and people by the dozens were succumbing to heat exhaustion. But in my apartment below street level, with a newly installed air conditioner humming away under its full power, I was satisfied to wait out the heat.

In the weeks following Daria's death, my only contact with the council had been through Brigit. She told me that when she awoke in her shower and remembered her dream, she'd called Sig and relayed my message. While he would have been right to doubt a three-month-old vampire who claimed to have spoken to me in a dream, he had already received word from Christof, the witch. Christof, it seems, had received a fairly insistent phone call from a certain werewolf lieutenant insisting the witch owed restitution to a half-breed by the name of Secret McQueen.

Sig and Juan Carlos picked up Brigit, who refused to tell them where she was going unless she could come with them. The three were met en route by the witch, who relayed to them the confession he'd been able to overhear when I broke the window.

Brigit had driven Nolan and me back to the city in my car, and I hadn't spoken to Sig since. Nor had I heard from Holden since Juan Carlos pardoned him. My sleep had been peacefully blank.

Plus, I had a new roommate to distract me from any concerns I had about the council. A roommate who was currently trying to annoy me to death.

"Where is it?" I demanded, digging through the fridge.

Since Desmond had moved in, my fridge had filled itself with strange things like vegetables and milk. My freezer was packed with frozen steaks and burger patties. My cupboards had spices and peanut butter in them. Plates and cutlery were being used. The kitchen smelled daily of cooking food.

"Where is what?" Desmond's innocent voice replied from the living room. He was teasing me. I could tell by his tone he knew exactly what I was talking about.

"You *know* what."

He appeared in the doorway. "Tell me why you need it, and I'll tell you where it is."

"It's brand new," I whined, shutting the door and opening the freezer.

"Cold," he said, then laughed at his unintentional joke and decided to take it all the way. "*Freezing.*"

"Hilarious." I slammed the door and stomped into the living room.

"Seriously, why do you need it?"

"I just want to know where it is." I knelt on the floor and looked under the couch. Rio's bright eyes reflected back at me.

"*Breow?*" she said.

"No. Not you."

"*Purrrrrrr,*" she said.

I grabbed her by the scruff of the neck and pulled her out. She purred in my arms while I petted her absently and stalked around the apartment. I heard the hall closet open and ran out of the bedroom still clutching the cat.

Desmond was holding my brand new SIG P229. He had the gun in one hand and the cartridge in the other.

"Now you know where it is."

I tried to act nonchalant, which lasted all of two seconds before I placed Rio on the floor and jumped for the gun. He knew it was coming because he held it out of my reach.

"Gimme."

"Shrimp."

We'd been having this same fight for over a week. I thought I was ready to go back to work, and I knew Keaty would be thrilled to have me return. Nolan had begun to work for him in the meantime, and though the boy was a much more suitable student than I had been, I also knew Keaty needed me.

Desmond, on the other hand, loved to point out that my wounds from the silver katana were still healing, and he as Queen's Guard decided it wasn't wise for me to go back to work just yet.

I kept scrambling for the gun until I managed to irritate the healing scar on my ribs.

"Ugh." I stopped fighting for the gun and placed a hand on my side. "Fine."

"Don't make me start hiding it outside the apartment," he threatened.

"Don't make me drain you in your sleep."

He *pfft*'d at me and angled me back to the couch, leaving the gun on the hall table for the time being. I had to admit, once I'd gotten used to having Desmond here, I remembered how pleasant it was to have someone next to me when I woke up every night. It was different than living with Gabriel had been, because with Desmond I could keep blood in the fridge and he wouldn't find it weird.

Though I liked Desmond's presence, I had played up my annoyance with Lucas a little longer than I should have. I told him I would accept a live-in guard, so long as it meant Lucas didn't make any further decisions about my life without discussing them with me. He'd agreed on the condition I had to become a more active part of the pack. We were trying to work things out, but Lucas and I were like gunpowder and a lit match. Sparks flew whenever we were together, and it wasn't always for the good.

With Desmond it was different.

I sat on the loveseat, and he knelt on the floor in front of me, pushing up my dress to look at the scar. I no longer tried to stop him when he did things like this. One, he was only trying to help, and two, I sort of liked it.

His warm hands brushed over the snow-white scar running in a three-inch line below my fifth rib. On my back the scar was only an inch and a half long and almost completely healed. A similar mark trailed ten inches down my forearm. They were all getting better, but with the aching slowness of silver wounds it felt almost like healing at a human pace.

I would never take my speedy recovery skills for granted again.

All the glass cuts were only memories, and my eyes were back to normal again. I had looked like a human punching bag/pincushion the day after the incident, but the smaller wounds healed within a day.

Seemingly satisfied I hadn't ruptured the scar, he bent down and kissed the white mark. A telling shiver thrilled through me. He must have felt it, because his eyebrows rose and a dangerous smile was on his lips. We hadn't had sex since the night of my fight, owing to the precarious manner in which I was healing. I'd been willing, but he didn't want to risk hurting me.

I ran my hand through his hair and gave him my best seductive smirk.

"Are you sure?" He was already starting to second-guess it.

"Desmond." My voice was loaded with heat. "You're not going to kill me."

He rose on his knees, hands seizing my face and pulling me in for a soul-jarring kiss. It was the kind of kiss long-lost lovers share when decades of time have passed since they were last together. He buried his fingers in my hair, and I held him close while his tongue explored my lips, gently at first, and then finding them willing to open for him, he deepened the kiss with a breathless intensity.

His cheeks were rough, having not been shaved in days. I dragged my fingernails against the short hairs, then down his neck, over his back and to the hem of his shirt, which I tugged upwards and off.

He broke away from the kiss to allow for the shirt to be removed, then reclaimed my mouth as he pushed me backwards on the couch. He held my thighs firmly, pushing my legs upward, and his fingers trailed with teasing lightness down the outside of my thighs, before backing up as he raised the skirt of my light cotton sundress.

I was so interested in touching his skin my fingers fumbled stupidly with the fly of his jeans, until I was able to release the snap and lower the zipper. Without hesitation, I slipped my hand inside and cupped his erection within my hot palm. He growled against my lips, lowering his mouth from mine to let his teeth graze my neck. This brought a gasp from me, and he teased my pulse with the flick of his tongue.

I clawed at his back, and he arched his hips against my grasping hand. I released him, which made him bite down harder on my neck. Ignoring his protests, I pushed him backwards off me, and before he could question why, I climbed onto his lap, hiking my dress up so I was nestled against the hard length of him.

I looked down, smiling, and kissed him again while I rocked my hips against his. Reaching one hand in between us, I released him from his underwear. He pushed my panties aside with rushed, deft fingers. Neither of us was interested in wasting time undressing. I raised up on my knees enough that he was positioned below me, then lowered myself onto his shaft with a painfully slow restraint that made his head roll back against the couch and a low moan escape his throat. I went as low as I could, until he was lodged as deep inside as I could take him, then I began to lift up again, but he grasped my hips and held me.

He was looking right at me, and what I saw in his eyes made my heart pound.

He released me so he could brush a strand of hair off my face, and he drew my mouth to his for a kiss that was almost too delicate, given our current position.

"I love you," he whispered against my parted lips.

My pulse quivered, and my heart beat faster than I'd ever felt before. It was what I'd wanted to tell him before I left that night, and what he'd told me not to say. Now my words were coming out of his mouth. I stared at him dumbly, robbed of my ability to speak. Any movement threatened to take me out of the moment by reminding me what we were in the middle of doing.

"I love you too," I said when I was finally able to form words.

He smiled, kissing me softly, his hands brushing over the bare skin of my arms, making me shiver all over. When he held my waist again, the rhythm had changed into something slower and more deliberate than our previous frenetic efforts. We were building towards a perfect finish when the first knock came.

Desmond paused, but I wasn't so willing to stop.

"Ignore it," I begged, my teeth worrying at the sensitive skin of his throat.

He began again, but the second knock came. Followed by a much louder third.

"Fuck," I breathed hotly against his neck. "Hold that thought," I directed before climbing off him and smoothing out my wrinkled dress the best I could.

My hair was in disarray, and even with the blanket pulled over his lap my disheveled boyfriend and I left nothing to the imagination for whoever had come calling. Oh well, I wasn't going to pretend they weren't interrupting.

I yanked the door open in the middle of the fourth knock with an unimpressed, "*What?*"

Holden, hand still raised in the air, stood smirking on the other side of the door. Being a vampire, he knew perfectly well what he'd interrupted. Smug bastard.

"Sorry to bother you," he said, his voice sweet with charm.

"No you're not." But it was difficult to stay mad at him. Seeing him in my doorway, his hair cut and his clothes clean, looking like his old self and no longer a wanted man, made me joyful. Unable to contain myself, I wrapped him in a fierce hug. "I'm glad you're okay."

He hugged me back, then pushed me away. He gave Desmond a polite nod from the doorway. The werewolf waved halfheartedly. "Sorry, chap. I need to borrow Secret. Won't be but a minute."

"Sure?" What else could he say, though? Holden had already pulled me through the door and shut it behind us.

Outside the apartment the wall of heat I'd been hiding from in the air conditioning sucked at me like a hungry ocean, threatening to drown me. Holden walked me up the short staircase to street level where, parked in front of my BMW, was a long, sleek, black stretch limo. The overhead streetlights reflected in each of the glossy windows.

I looked questioningly at Holden.

"What's this?"

He opened the door for me. "Just get in."

I followed his instructions and he climbed in beside me. Sitting opposite us against the driver's window and half-hidden by the low lights inside the cabin were Sig, Juan Carlos and Rebecca the French vampire I'd met at Havana.

I shot a glance at Holden, but he leaned back in the leather seat and laced his fingers behind his head like he was settling in for a good movie. I looked back at the trio of vampires, all of whom were watching me patiently. I didn't have much to say to them, so I watched them right back.

Sig broke the silence. "We want to thank you for the excellent job you did."

"You're welcome," I replied. Something was wrong with this. The Tribunal had never come to thank me in person for anything. Come to think of it, I could count on one hand the number of times I'd been thanked, period.

Silence again. Juan Carlos was looking especially unhappy, his jaw clenched so tight I thought he might break his own teeth. Rebecca was staring at Holden.

"Well." I slapped my hands against my bare legs. "If that's all." I moved to climb over Holden, who stayed put, letting me attempt to clamber over his lap.

"Not quite," Rebecca said.

I sat back down.

"I want to thank you personally," she began. "You see, I may have neglected to mention when we met that Holden is of my line."

I turned from her to Holden. He gave a small nod. "Must have slipped your mind," I mumbled.

"I am grateful to you for saving his life and restoring his reputation."

What she didn't mention but must have known was that I was also responsible for killing one of her other vampire children. A few years earlier I'd been tasked with killing the actor Charlie Conaway, who turned out to be a vampire rogue using the thrall to feed from and kill his young female fans.

No one mentioned this because the whole event was a rather ugly history that was better off not being discussed. I appreciated that Rebecca didn't bring up Charlie.

"It was my pleasure," I said. "Your help was...instrumental."

"There is one more reason for our being here," Sig said, and Juan Carlos groaned. The others ignored him, but I'd definitely heard it.

"You are aware there is now an open seat on the Tribunal since Daria's death," Sig continued. "This, of course, is unacceptable, as a Tribunal of two is no Tribunal at all."

"Right." I didn't see what he was getting at.

"Another must rise to fill the position, and we have been dealing with this matter since the night of Daria's passing. We have now arrived at the natural conclusion, and a third member has been chosen by the elders of the council."

"*Oh.*" They made a house call to introduce me to my newest boss? I looked at Rebecca. "Congratulations. You'll make a great—"

She'd already begun chuckling before my words were formed. Even her laugh sounded highbrow. "*Non, non,* Secret. I am not the one. I am here as a representative of the elders to ensure our decision is properly carried out." She shot Juan Carlos a meaningful look, then smiled back at me. "You see, dear, there has been much discussion among the elders about this situation. If Daria had passed by her own hand or been executed in another fashion, a member of the elder council would be chosen to replace her. In such a case I might very well sit before you as that replacement. However, according to tradition, the only true way for a vampire to become a member of the Tribunal is if they kill the existing member in a declared fight. That night at the park, I understand Daria initiated the fight against you, which qualifies it as a declared fight."

"A declared fight which you won," Sig said.

Once again an unsettling quiet filled the limo. Four pairs of vampire eyes were locked on me, and I was painfully aware of the sound of my own heartbeat.

"So..."

"So…" Rebecca concluded, "…the elder council agreed succession should continue in accordance to tradition. We have made our choice for the new Tribunal member."

"Wait." I gaped at them, unable to believe it even as understanding settled in, and I knew their words could have no other meaning. "You mean *me*?"

About the Author

Sierra Dean is a reformed historian. She was born and raised in the Canadian prairies and is allowed annual exit visas in order to continue her quest of steadily conquering the world one city at a time. Making the best of the cold Canadian winters, Sierra indulges in her less global interests: drinking too much tea and writing urban fantasy.

Ever since she was a young girl she has loved the idea of the supernatural coexisting with the mundane. As an adult, however, the idea evolved from the notion of fairies in flower beds, to imagining that the rugged-looking guy at the garage might secretly be a werewolf. She has used her overactive imagination to create her own version of the world, where vampire, werewolves, fairies, gods and monsters all walk among us, and she'll continue to travel as much as possible until she finds it for real.

Sierra can be reached all over the place, as she's a little addicted to social networking. Find her on:

Facebook: www.facebook.com/sierradeanbooks

Website: www.sierradean.com

E-mail: sierra@sierradean.com

Twitter: @sierradean

SAMHAIN
PUBLISHING

It's all about the story...

Romance

HORROR

Retro
ROMANCE

www.samhainpublishing.com